TAKING THREE

TAKING THREE

Mark R. McCallum

Sense of Wonder Press
JAMES A. ROCK & COMPANY, PUBLISHERS
ROCKVILLE • MARYLAND

Taking Three by Mark R. McCallum

SENSE OF WONDER PRESS
is an imprint of JAMES A. ROCK & CO., PUBLISHERS

Taking Three copyright ©2008 by Mark R. McCallum

Cover Design by Lou Kinard

Special contents of this edition copyright ©2008
by James A. Rock & Co., Publishers

All applicable copyrights and other rights reserved worldwide. No part of this publication may be reproduced, in any form or by any means, for any purpose, except as provided by the U.S. Copyright Law, without the express, written permission of the publisher.

This is a work of fiction. Names, characters, places and incidents either are the product of the author's imagination or are used fictitiously. Any resemblance to actual events, locales, organizations, or persons, living or dead, is entirely coincidental and beyond the intent of either the author or the publisher.

Note: Product names, logos, brands, and other trademarks occurring or referred to within this work are the property of their respective trademark holders.

Address comments and inquiries to:
SENSE OF WONDER PRESS
James A. Rock & Company, Publishers
9710 Traville Gateway Drive, #305
Rockville, MD 20850
E-mail:
jrock@rockpublishing.com   lrock@rockpublishing.com

Internet URL: www.rockpublishing.com

ISBN-13/EAN: 978-1-59663-655-2

Library of Congress Control Number: 2007941778

Printed in the United States of America

First Edition: 2008

To my parents

Bob and Ann

who

let me dream

ACKNOWLEDGEMENTS

Every writer, amid all the encouragement and interest, needs at least one brutally honest voice. That one person who's not afraid to tell you it doesn't work, doesn't make sense or whether it's worth pursuing. For me that person is Tom Hallman. To borrow a line Joe Morgan once uttered about Frank Robinson's managerial style, Tom can step on your shoes and not mess up your shine. After soliciting his editing, I girded my feelings with armor. While his barbs sometimes hurt, they were often on the mark. His help and encouragement were invaluable and worthy of naming Soke's main street in his honor.

But this book didn't rely on just one helpful voice. There were many who offered assistance. Especially Lou Kinard. Her insightful suggestions had a huge impact on the story. She not only reminded me to let the characters speak for themselves but also encouraged me to scare her even more. I hope I succeeded. Helping me find some emotional connections, she never let me forget how much love matters.

South Carolina patrolman James Day helped verify lingo and procedure regarding Merl Burt. I took some liberties with his expertise so any actions Merl took that would not be taken by a police officer are strictly mine and mine alone. Dr. Charles Harper helped guide me—with the little knowledge I provided him on Robbie and his condition—as close as possible to medical accuracy. He in no way resembles Dr. Benton Tyson. I hope that naming Soke's hospital and a Landfalls College dormitory after Dr. Harper atones for Dr. Tyson's depiction.

Michael D. Friedman helped me hammer out some early details of where the story may or may not wander. J. R. Francis laughed at all the right places and kept me honest on modern-day gadgetry. And Sharon Donohue deserves thanks for her parental insights and comments.

And I thank Linda Hansen and all who read the work and didn't just say it was interesting, but offered comment. And to those who asked what the novel was about and expressed interest along the way, I will keep my promise about the autographs.

Finally, I offer thanks when I was so miserable at my former job that the Lord sent me such a disturbing dream that I wrote it down and didn't stop writing until I had the story finished. I never imagined I could sustain a story long enough to create a novel. But like Merl Burt and Robbie, sometimes, you just have to believe.

Chapter 1

On the day Robbie Callahan died, he wanted Pop-Tarts for breakfast. Brown Sugar Cinnamon. Like any 11-year-old, he savored a sweet start to his Saturday. The day meant no school, no church, and, hopefully, no chores. For this day, he harbored big plans.

Tromping into the kitchen, Robbie swung the pantry door open. He scanned the second shelf for breakfast food. He tilted his head down and brushed his lips hard against the sleeve of his oversized Chipper Jones jersey, wiping clean his morning mouth. He jabbed the top of the Pop-Tarts box and slid out a pack. Rather than bother Mom while she vacuumed the den, he scooted the step stool toward the counter. He opened the cupboard, straining to reach a small plate and a glass.

After placing each in front of him, he carefully stretched the top of the pastry pack, trying to open it so perfectly that it tore only at the seam. It was his test of patience and strength. No such luck. His pressure zippered the package. Undeterred, he dumped both treats on the plate, wolfing down one as he poured the milk.

Taking a big gulp, he cleared the way for the second Pop-Tart. Breakfast done, he splashed the plate and glass under the faucet. He left both in the sink. He heard the vacuum go silent as he jerked his jacket out of the hall closet.

His mom heard the hanger bang the back wall and jangle noisily. She debated whether to request a reluctant hug before her young man departed. As she hesitated, Robbie tugged loose the front door and yelled, "Mom! I'm gone!"

"Take care of that new jacket," she blurted. "Remember what I told you about that creek."

"Ok, Mom!" His shouted reply drowned out her "I love you."

He closed the door tightly. Seconds later, the knob rattled.

Mallison Callahan smiled. She knew he always tested if it were locked. Had done so after they read *Little Red Riding Hood*. Ever since, he insisted on securing the door because he didn't want the Big Bad Wolf to get her. He never broke the habit even if he forgot the reason.

Whether he'd admit it now, she knew he remembered. She knew that kid of hers never forgot a thing. She also knew boys will be boys. She marveled at his recall. You could tell a story once and if you repeated it inexactly he'd fill in the pieces you forgot or overlooked. They'd be at the grocery store and he'd know what brand of noodles Grandma requested and on which aisle they were. That time she got one of those new $20 bills? Robbie explained the changes. He knew why Andrew Jackson was on it. Something about the National Bank or Federal Reserve. She couldn't recall which.

He sure didn't get it from me, she thought. *Got to be from Bobby. Bobby.*

Sadness seized her. Six months since her husband's death, her memory continued to taunt her as if it never happened. Musk with a hint of lemon—Bobby's scent—suddenly caressed her nostrils. She thought she felt his hand slide across the small of her back. She leaned into it, but nothing pulled her tightly. Feeling so alone, she wiped a tear away, but—now, wishing she had hugged Robbie—gritted her teeth.

I won't do this today. I won't. Not after last night. I just won't.

Mallison wiped another tear away. She sniffled. Her mind shifted to Winnie Figgs. She recalled their elderly neighbor standing in the April sun, wearing that orange bonnet, clutching her new shears and saying to mind that Death didn't visit her family in threes.

Mallison shivered at the memory. *Why would she say such a thing?*

Before an answer came, Robbie leapt back into Mallison's thoughts, chasing others away. She welcomed the rescue and focused on the little guy still with her. He was so much like his father. She'd noticed it in how he would do things all his own. Nothing outlandish, just different. Like when everybody ordered sweet tea, he'd get water. Or with baseball. If everybody wanted to hit home runs, he'd practice bunting. Or using hockey practice to see how long he could glide on one skate with a single push. When she asked him what he learned from his swimming lessons, he dunked his head underwater and showed how long he could float without air. It made no sense to her.

He could be such a mystery. One time, she observed him through the window. He stood motionless in the backyard as if in a trance. She asked if he were okay. He replied he was just thinking about things, playing. It pleased her that he had such an escape. She wished her imagination could take her away.

Chapter 2

His mind already in high gear, Mallison's son Robbie stood on the front porch.

Today is mine, Robbie thought. *Today, Neil Armstrong. Walking on the moon. Shootout at the OK Corral? Go Lewis and Clark exploring? Nope! Today, I'm on a mission. Today, I storm Landfalls Creek.*

Robbie stepped into the nippy October morning. He zipped up his jacket. He'd be protective of it to keep Mom happy. He filled his lungs and vowed not to breathe until he decided how to spend the morning. *Should I march down the porch stairs as "Hail to the Chief" plays or climb over the railing and parachute into Normandy?*

Robbie often surrendered to his imagination, wandering into the joys of his dad's world—space, sports, World War II, even TV shows they watched together on "Nick at Nite."

Sometimes, when he missed his dad most, he'd search the cable channels for a military program and feel closer to him. Funny that he could find peace watching the world at war. Or hearing "Cheers" patrons greet Norm. Or just by looking at the moon.

The moon. In his head, he heard the radio crackle from Mission Control in Houston.

"You are go for moonwalk."

Robbie turned his back to the stairs. He exhaled.

"Roger, Houston," he said aloud. "I am now outside the LEM."

Robbie stepped backward down the rungs of his imaginary Lunar Module. He took them one at a time, ever so slowly, like a chameleon down a branch. He paused at the bottom. He glanced at the front walk and brown grass.

"Houston, the surface looks very, very fine," he said. "Almost grainy."

"Roger that."

"I'm about to set foot on the moon."

Robbie hopped backwards. He nearly toppled over as he tried to land in slow motion.

"That's one small step for man. One giant leap for mankind," he said.

Robbie moved as if incremental progress conveyed weightlessness. To traverse from the front porch to the side of the house—or in Robbie's imagination, the Sea of Tranquility—he absorbed 15 minutes of mission time. The backyard now beckoned; then, the quest. He knew Buzz Aldrin remained in the lunar module. He wouldn't be out for a while. Time for a bit of fun. Robbie began to bunny hop. He felt so light. He felt so free. Nothing could touch him here. As he neared the woods, he reverted to slow-motion again. He informed Houston that there were rocks here as big as trees.

He stepped into these woods for the last time. T-minus 30 minutes. He checked the imaginary button on his sleeve for his oxygen supply. All systems fine. It was time. Today, he would face his fear.

Robbie Callahan headed for the creek.

Chapter 3

For those that believed the stories, Landfalls Creek conveyed more than water between its banks.

It ferried ruin.

Gurgling into existence deep beneath the Appalachian Mountains, it squeezed through rock and stone with a hiss. When it spewed forth in the foothills below the now abandoned quarry west of Soke, a cold haunting wind accompanied it. From a source never found, the odor of decay emanated.

Unlike most waterways in the region, it was unfed by other streams. It maintained an eastern trek for 13 miles before breaking—for no reason of geography—directly south at the McAbee County line. It flowed 20 more miles before emptying its contents into the Ashworth River. Along the way, it never grew too wide for a cast stone to reach the far bank nor narrow enough for a traveler to cross dry. Its waters either plummeted to unfathomed depths or raced just over the surface of sheared granite.

For centuries, the creek yielded little for those seeking gain. It contained no channel to transport goods or passengers far enough to produce a profit. Where the water could churn a mill, no ground could hold a foundation. The few fish caught offered such a peculiar taste that only the poorest dined on what the locals called "landies."

Where the creek made its second bend, less than a mile from the source pool, Amos Kinard had established a ferry for travelers and trappers in the early 1700s. It seemed folly since horsemen could cross without cost at several spots downstream. Even the passing Cherokee shook their heads. They gave him a name that sounded like "Yo-ne-ga Di-gal-in-vhidv" which roughly translated to "White Donkey." But through luck and guile, Kinard earned enough to move his family back east. Not a soul could name another who prospered from the waters.

Half a mile from Kinard's Ferry where Highway 37 now spans, the stream narrowed and deepened causing the water to swirl and chill. The seldom-used boat launch remained as little more than a respite either for those seeking solace or lost motorists changing direction.

Not much farther downstream, the water widened and slowed into a peaceful, lulling stream. By the mid-1970s, developers seized the area with visions of riches. Houses with big back porches. White verandas. Gazebos dotting the banks. However, Nature thwarted them. Solid ground gave way. Dry land grew wet. It was as if a barrier had formed, pushing them too far from the water to get their price.

Investors relented. Construction shifted to a subdivision between Highway 37 and Kinard's Ferry, a healthy hike from the creek. The Callahans were among the first to move into Creekside Terrace.

Realtor Andy Ross insured they heard no whispers that something sinister swam nearby. *What great schools!* Nor that cold, clammy mists formed at odd times of the day. *You'll love the friendly atmosphere!* Nor that there were places where trees fell rather than let their roots drink, that shrubs swelled into tortured shapes. *Such communion with Nature!* Nor that pets nearing its banks went mad. *No place like it on Earth!*

The Callahans bought into it. They dangled their feet in its waters and felt refreshed. They skinny-dipped and sunbathed. They splashed. They cuddled on its banks, watching the currents and dreaming how wonderful their future would be. They were wrong.

Chapter 4

Alex Simons flicked his lit cigarette butt into Bucky's water bowl. He heard the quick sizzle from the dog's dish. *Nothing but net,* he told himself. It probably would be the highlight of his Saturday.

Alex leaned back against his neighbor's shed. He lit another cigarette. He convinced himself today was a good day to kick this town in the butt, find a stick and poke it right in the eye.

Even before starting high school, Alex developed a keen hatred for his hometown. Soke was a joke, he liked to say. And his opinion of the town matched its opinion of him.

He flashed back more than half his life to his eighth birthday and seethed. In his mind, he saw that old man, Jasper Riddle, standing behind the drug store counter, his then long black hair lassoed in a ponytail by that stupid red string.

"Can I help you, young sir," old man Riddle had asked, dismissing the teenage couple loitering nearby.

Alex had stood mute, mesmerized by the small open Mason Jar nestled by the cash register. He didn't notice the "Danforth Donations" sign taped to the rim with an arrow. He had stared at what was stuffed inside. Never before had he seen so many dollar bills. *Pirates' treasure.*

Noting Alex's interest, Riddle had said, "It's for Becky Danforth's family."

"It's my birthday," Alex said, keeping his eyes on the jar.

"Well, how old are you today?" Riddle asked, putting his hands on hips as if to heighten the moment's importance.

"I'm eight years old."

"Eight? My! You're almost grown. You know, I actually have something every 8-year-old deserves on his birthday."

Alex saw Riddle disappear beneath the counter. One of the teenagers leaned back. The boy glanced at Alex but turned his attention to Riddle. Alex rose on his tiptoes, wondering what he might receive. His eyes widened with anticipation. He heard a clank, a rustle, a clang. Riddle reappeared. He presented Alex a small, sweet treat.

"Here you go," he said with a smile.

Alex grabbed the blue gumball. He looked back at Riddle. "I want a red one."

Riddle pondered the blunt request.

"Ooookay," he decided. When Riddle dropped behind the counter again, Alex popped the blue gumball in his mouth. He was almost to the door when Riddle yelled, "Somebody stop that kid! He stole the donation jar!"

The accusation struck Alex like a backhand from his father. It stung so much he bawled before they grabbed him.

Why would they think such a mean thing?

On my birthday.

Even now as he watched Bucky napping, old man Riddle's words scalded.

I was only 8!

Yep, Alex decided, this town sucked. So did everyone in it. Through the years, he heard the comments, "Never amount to anything."; "A complete waste."; "Nothing but trouble." Since they echoed his dad's words, Alex never tried to refute them. He couldn't ignore the taunts. He simply kept his head down. He kept walking. He kept scheming. He vowed to get even.

One day.

Until that day came, Alex devised small ways to strike back. He devised what he called events. Others labeled it vandalism. Either way, it spurred the town to talk. What a thrill that was. Especially when it made the newspaper. Like when he painted obscenities on the Civil War cannon. Or beheaded those ceramic garden gnomes guarding the thrift shop.

Alex found release in the way he transferred his father's feelings for him to the rest of the world, administering it to the weaker, the smaller, the younger, the unsuspecting. He developed the habit early. As a boy, he'd pulled appendages off Daddy Long Leg spiders and plopped their bodies into water. He graduated to higher life forms. He recalled where kicking the Reed's cat led him. The mere act had thrilled him. Yet, he savored the intrigue of the aftermath, the talk. He had reveled in the family's bafflement that their mewling pet suffered broken ribs. How could it have happened? Alex even spent the better part of that afternoon exploring ways a cat might crack a rib. *Maybe it got blindsided by a kitty linebacker named Tabby McGarfield. Fell out of the sky playing Super Kitty because the catnip wore off. Was—*

Hey! The dog barked. *Feed me! Rub my head! Play with me!*

Alex jumped. He forgot the neighbor's dog had been dozing nearby. Now, Bucky wanted attention. Alex peered into the water bowl. The cigarette butt was gone.

"Got a little nicotine fix, eh, boy?"

Bucky panted, eyes eager. Alex rubbed the brown-and-white Spaniel behind the ears. He looked around for that lime green tennis ball. He walked over and picked it up. Bucky pranced alongside.

For some reason, the dog's bounding gait reminded Alex of those college twerps who invaded the quarry every year. *They act like they owned the place,* he thought. *Every day's a party. Jerks got Daddy's money and no worries. Got girlfriends with killer bodies.* As much as he wanted to, Alex never talked to any of those girls. Never even tried. Instead, he pursued the hope of catching them sunbathing topless. But the once-private quarry had grown too popular. So not only were the college girls out of Alex's reach but a free look at their boobs was too.

It's not right. They shouldn't be here. My turf, not theirs. Alex longed for a way to chase them off. But bullying didn't work too well with college kids. If you hit them, they either hit back, collected their frat buddies and came after you or got their daddies to sue. Alex knew the cops would take their side. He always got accused. Besides, he learned early only to hit what can't hit back, to hurt what won't hurt you and damage what nobody can pin on you. In order to hurt these kids, you had to spoil their fun. You had to ruin their playground.

How to do that? Alex pondered that question for months. The best idea he had come up with was spray-painting "Go Away!" But that required scaling the quarry's cliff. Too much work.

As his mind wandered, Alex chucked the tennis ball toward the house. Bucky raced after it. The dog knew how long his chain was. His exuberance to get the ball before it bounced out of reach proved too strong. It yanked the dog back. He yelped. Bucky padded back and forth. He waited for the elusive prize as it ricocheted off the house and dribbled to a halt out of reach.

Alex got a charge out of teasing the dog like this. It amused him to roll the ball too far and watch the chain choke Bucky. Some nights, Alex would flip dog biscuits out of reach just to tantalize the spaniel. It would paw the dirt. Try to stick its tongue out to reach them. Whimper. Bark at them as if that might make them move. If the neighbors weren't home, Bucky would trot back and forth all afternoon and evening knowing those biscuits were there until someone got exasperated enough to find out what all the barking was about. *Life is full of small pleasures.*

Bucky licked Alex's hand as if coaxing assistance with the ball. Alex popped the dog on the snout.

"You want it, you get it," he said.

The dog shot a wounded look. Alex had seen that look from countless neighborhood kids. It sparked a memory. Not prone to many original thoughts—even his anger was borrowed from his dad—Alex believed the idea now percolating was all his. Bucky wasn't going to like it. Neither were those college jerks. Alex knew how to ruin their playground. He was too pleased with himself, too thrilled that he concocted this on his own, too busy patting himself on the back to realize the thought he considered original came straight from a Hannibal Lecter movie. He had no idea it would lead to his own demise.

Unlike most days when ideas didn't come easy, this Saturday morning flooded Alex with daydreams. His mind rushed past his plan for Bucky. It dwelled on how the town would react.

He knew what everybody would think. It was what he would think. It was what consumed his thoughts these past few months. And had done so since he'd been bored enough to read that stolen newspaper on the day it heralded the anniversary of Bill Talbert's tale. The article claimed to be the full story. Like most news stories, what it dredged up was far from complete. Still, it served its purpose. It hooked a new reader. No longer did Alex waste countless class periods pondering ways to make life just as miserable for others as it was for him. He now harbored bigger plans.

Fascinated by what he previously thought was only rumor, Alex absorbed every word that hinted at what Talbert saw. He yearned for more. Like the reporter, Alex found additional knowledge difficult to acquire. But the story gave him a reason for sticking around this sorry Soke of a town. It gave him a sense of purpose.

Alex discovered this town had scars. He grew eager to inflict more. With Bucky's help, he'd remind the town of its dark secret.

Chapter 5

Nobody knew if Bill Talbert was the first. But it was no secret that he had seen what everybody started calling "Old Coals."

It was Talbert who inadvertently named it, taken straight from his quotation in the newspaper back in the early '70s. To this day, people recited it like a biblical passage, Talbert 3:16—"it threw me a look that chilled my bones. Its eyes looked like old coals that had been stoked."

When Alex read that reprint in the newspaper, he thought it meant the eyes were ashen, burnt out, but Talbert meant they were full of heat and glowing bright, like a scorched coal just dusted of its seared skin. The memory of it so terrified Talbert that the locals joked he gave wide berth to cookouts. He refused to talk about it for years. Even then, you had to get him liquored up first. As the years passed, that ploy became easier and easier. But he'd still shake when the subject arose. And his eyes went vacant as if his soul wanted to hide. Then he'd start telling the story most of the town knew by heart.

It was a crystal clear night in early summer, not a single cloud creeping across a full moon. It was the kind of night that Talbert hoped Katie Brinson was feeling frisky. He planned to romance her with some of Herrington's jumbo fries. He snuck away from his nightshift before the town's burger joint closed and was rewarded as the day's last order with an offer of free fish sandwiches. Even though he didn't care for seafood, Talbert accepted the gift.

He compounded that mistake by taking the shortcut to Katie's—that mile stretch with the big open field next to Marshall's farm, the dirt road that everybody now calls "Old Coal's Alley." Talbert was halfway down it, listening to Looking Glass's greatest hit, when his truck conked out. He quit singing what a fine girl Brandy was. He cursed, not so much at his temperamental truck but that his quest to reach Katie with some hot fries failed. Even if he walked the final half-mile, he figured he'd make better time tinkering with the engine. Either way, the fries would be cold.

He turned the radio up. He opened the white Herrington's bag. He removed a fish sandwich. A soft breeze wafted through the cab. Talbert took a bite. He winced. Already not fond of fish, he hated tartar sauce. He tossed the sandwich on the dashboard and swallowed hard.

Talbert shoved open the door. He got out. He leaned into the truck bed for his toolbox. He popped the hood as Nilsson played on the radio. The singer said to put the lime in the coconut and then you feel better. *What a goofy song,* Talbert thought. He sang along anyway. He adjusted the carburetor. He tightened a pair of tube rings. He knew quite a few songs played, but was unsure how long he'd fiddled. He wrinkled his nose at the aroma of fish sandwiches spoiling the night air.

Suddenly, the memory of the fumble slapped him. God, how it depressed him. Greatest night of his life vanishes with one mistake. If he only had held onto that football, the town's first Class AA title would have been his legacy. Instead, nobody remembered all those yards he gained, all those tackles he made. Just the fumble. Bill Talbert believed it was the worst moment in his life. He was wrong.

In his misery he sang along with the radio. As "Midnight at the Oasis" faded, a prolonged silence followed it. Talbert quit singing about camels. He wondered why the radio went silent. He became aware of what the music had drowned out. In the quiet lull, Talbert heard a bullfrog's croak cut short. He heard the crickets' calls muted. His neck hair prickled.

Something wicked this way comes.

Peering across the field toward Marshall's farm, he saw what he took to be brake lights in the distance. By the time he realized there were no roads there, the gap closed considerably between him and what he now believed were eyes.

Talbert never doubted what he saw—the night was crystal clear and he hadn't been drinking. It was some kind of man-sized lizard.

Running.

On its hind legs.

Fast.

Toward him.

He didn't question the absurdity. He reacted. Dropping his screwdriver, he slammed the hood, knocking the toolbox off the wheel well. He prayed as he scrambled for the truck cab. He slammed the door, almost catching his foot. One hand furiously rolled up the window, the other turned the ignition. Of course, it didn't catch. He barely got the window closed when the creature barreled into the side of the pickup. The truck rocked. Too terrified to look at it, Talbert turned the starter and prayed. No answer.

Any second he expected the window to smash. It didn't. It seemed the creature was sniffing, exploring the glass. Talbert prayed his plugs had one last spark in them. They did. When the engine caught, Talbert turned.

That's when he felt his bones chill. Two coal-like eyes glowed. Talbert floored it.

Too late.

The creature pounced into the truck bed. It jarred the vehicle with its weight. Talbert glanced in the rearview mirror. He saw a pale underbelly and, when the creature ducked to look through the back window, swore, just for a second—it had to be a hallucination—that he saw a man's face. When he looked again, the creature was clambering onto the roof. Talbert swerved across the road. He swerved back, spewing rocks and dust in his wake, trying to shake the creature loose.

To no avail. The creature swatted at the driver's side window. It swatted at the windshield. The door's glass cracked. It didn't shatter. Talbert knew it was only a matter of time. All he could think about was reaching his girlfriend's house, hoping her old man had his shotgun ready. Hope he was ticked off enough to take a shot. Talbert leaned on the horn to herald his arrival.

That's when he saw the claw coming. He ducked in reflex. It spidered the windshield and put a pronounced dent in the roof. When Talbert peered over the dash, he was careening past the Brinson's mailbox. His heart skipped as the radio blared back to life. Trying to regain control, he held tight as his truck bounced through the ditch near the driveway, skidded across the lawn and slammed into the front porch, knocking loose shingles.

Katie and her father tore out of the house. The screen door slapped shut twice. Talbert leapt from his truck. He furiously backpedaled from it. He shouted to get off the porch.

He saw no signs of the creature. Not there. Not on the roof. Not in the yard. Just Katie and her dad in open-jawed outrage at his late-night recklessness, displeased at how loudly Steppenwolf sang through the dashboard speakers.

Talbert barely noticed the music. His heart pounded so fiercely that it muffled his hearing. Through eyes blurred by exhaustion, he failed to register Katie's disappointed stare. Or her father's disapproving glare. It wasn't until the sheriff arrived that Talbert began to believe he wouldn't die that night. But, for the rest of his life, he never felt safe. And he never went long without checking behind him.

The town made fun of Talbert's story when it made the rounds. The police, Katie and her parents were convinced he had been drinking. It was just too strange to be believed. The cracks in his windows were made by the accident. What looked like a paw print in his roof was probably just fallen shingles from Katie's roof. Most believed Talbert made the whole thing up, never bothering to consider why, since it would cost him everything.

Talbert soon took to the bottle. Years later, when he was found in his basement, people assumed he drank himself into a stupor and fell to his death. They hadn't seen the body. They hadn't seen his face. Mostly, they didn't want to believe what Jack Thompson knew. That the man they called Wacky Jacky—like Bill Talbert—realized that Old Coals was no ghost story.

Chapter 6

Back in April before his father died, space exploration rocketed Robbie Callahan into orbit. Dragged to Cape Kennedy by his parents during spring break, he fell in love with the sky. He learned every astronaut's name from Gemini through Apollo and most of the shuttles. Could spot most of the constellations and a few planets. Tracked the space shuttles through his telescope. Collected facts like baseball cards. Could tell you anything. Last man on the moon? Gene Cernan. Commander of Apollo 12? Pete Conrad. Location of the Pinwheel Galaxy? Locate Pegasus first and count stars. First man in space? Yuri Gagarin. So many adults said Alan Shepard. How could they forget the cosmonaut? That was a gimme.

Robbie even understood Gus Grissom's joke of naming his second capsule "The Unsinkable Molly Brown." Knew that Neil Armstrong carried an old comb and a pack of Life Savers in his spacesuit pocket. But he believed the four-day trip to the moon took like 70 gazillion gallons of gas. That's where his imagination had him now—on the moon, not his backyard.

"Houston, moving out of sight of the LEM," he said.

Robbie imitated the static of his helmet mike cutting off. Talking things over with CapCom, his Capsule Communicator, soothed him. Since Robbie pretended it was his Dad, the voice he heard felt protective. It was his way of implementing what his Mother once explained—"If you keep your father here and here," she said pointing to her heart and head, "he will never leave you."

Robbie knew this to be true. Back in kindergarten he let the little brown-haired girl in the red dress into his heart and he never even met her. She was his first love, if that's what love was. Just the sight of her brightened his day. The thought of her made him want to go to school. Sometimes, he combed his hair. Although assigned to different classes, he liked her so much that he often arrived early each morning. Eager to inspect the snake-like procession of classmates filing into their respective rooms, eager to spot the red dress and her. When he didn't, he worried. Was she sick? Did her parents move? It never crossed his mind that she wore other dresses. He only recognized the red one. And on the days she wore it, he performed on the jungle gym. He hoped to put her out in kickball. Despite getting no closer than worshipping her from afar, he never forgot her.

That shy approach altered little as the years passed. In the fourth grade, he developed a similar crush on a girl in homeroom. Again, he never spoke to her face-to-face, but thought about her a lot. She was pretty and could run faster than just about anybody on the playground. He liked her so much that he found out her father's name and looked the number up in the phone book. He practiced calling her for days. He would ask her to go steady even though he didn't know what it meant. They had plenty of time to figure that out. Maybe discuss it while trading baseball cards over tea. He kept waiting for the perfect moment, when his nerve matched his mission conditions. Time? He had a narrow window each day—between school and dinner.

Opportunity? Mom must be busy in the kitchen so as not to interrupt. His status? Brave enough to do it. Twice before, he summoned the nerve. Once, he chickened out as soon as her mother answered; the other, he hung up on the machine. After a week of berating himself, he set his mind. He marched from the bus. He gobbled down his afternoon snack and asked how long Mom would be in the kitchen. Satisfied with her response, he collected his sunglasses and the folded note with Barbara's number from his room. He peeked down the hall. He scooted into his parents' room and closed the door. He dragged the phone after him as he crawled under the master bed. A covert operation required privacy. Without referring to the folded note, Robbie dialed the number from memory. As before, his heart pounded so loudly his ears hurt.

One ring. He grew short of breath.

Two rings. He tried to calm himself. Instead, he stretched and locked his legs, stiffly twitching them nervously.

Third rin—

"Hello?" a lady asked.

"Hello," Robbie said. "Is Barbara there?"

"Yes, she is. Just a minute."

He couldn't believe he'd gotten this far already. He heard Barbara's mother summon her to the phone. *Thank God she didn't ask who was calling!* He was going to do it. This was it. He—

"Hello?"

It was her! Barbara was on the other end of the phone! He'd never spoken to her in class. Here he was calling her like she was his girlfriend. Before you know it, they'd be holding hands.

"Hello?" Barbara asked again.

Robbie panicked. He struggled to breathe. His mind blanked. He blurted, "This is someone in your class who likes you."

Oh God! Kill me now! Robbie wanted to disappear. Instead, he gave himself a cooties shot. A hard one as his mind debated if Randy Johnson recorded more strikeouts than Nolan Ryan. If Cap'n Crunch was a real name. If the "Power Rangers" were on yet.

"Who is this?" Barbara asked.

Robbie sprawled in no-man's land. He didn't know where to run. His plane spiraled earthward in flames. He couldn't find his bearings. His ship turned turtle. He didn't know which end was up. Rather than call a mission abort, Robbie stood and fired again.

"Do you want to go steady?" he asked. His breath spurted.

"Who is this?" Barbara asked again. Her voice grew stern. She remained too curious to hang up.

Robbie felt surrounded. Even a sonic screwdriver couldn't get him out of this. He feared his mom approached.

Alarmed, he hung up in humiliation. He lay among the dust bunnies in a cold sweat. He couldn't believe what he'd done. He wanted to weep. He'd accomplished his mission and failed miserably. He had asked her to go steady but left himself out of the proposition. Or had he? She had to know it was he. *Oh, this was going to be bad.* He knew tomorrow in class, they would all be laughing at him. She'd tell the world. It would be on MTV News. They'd show a graphic of him under the bed with laughing heads bouncing around him, saying "Who is this? Who is this?"

Maybe he could move to Idaho overnight.

The next day, it was all over class. Barbara had a secret admirer. Who it was, she had no clue. Relieved and elated, Robbie felt like he pulled off the greatest caper ever. He never told a soul about the call. He came close at recess. That day, he and Barbara played on the same softball team. He wanted to tell her. He'd wait for just the right moment. Maybe after her first at bat. He'd compliment her to start the conversation. Admit he made the call. Say he loved her. She'd tell him how glad she was that it was he. They'd live happily ever after. Robbie watched her step to the plate. He liked her stance. The pitch came. She swung. Robbie's heart danced. The ball shot into right field. Robbie rejoiced. But after Barbara hit the ball, Fate intervened. She just stood at home plate. She didn't move. Robbie couldn't believe she didn't know to run to first base. She had to be told. The romance died right there. Robbie never thought about her again.

But on this Saturday, in the backyard during this mission, the little girl in the red dress crossed Robbie's mind. He knew she'd be impressed with him after today. So would Dad.

"Houston, are we go or no go?" he asked.

"You are go."

Robbie's make-believe conversations with his dad fueled his courage. He planned to display his courage by marching through the woods to the creek bend, a playground now fraught with fear. When younger, he feared the bend after hearing the older kids whisper about dragons and lunatics and werewolves that hid among the trees. He now knew such things did not exist. At least not around here. Still, his vivid imagination could turn a simple dog bark or crow caw into flying monkeys from Oz if he were scared. His dad taught him how to control that type of fear. But he wasn't sure about the other, wasn't sure about the story he overheard his mom tell last night. What Mom said sounded too real. Whatever scared her so much scared Robbie too.

It was that fear Robbie sought to conquer, sought to face and remove its power. *Like Dad taught me. Do it for Mom.* He needed moral support for such a task. Speaking into his sleeve, he called Houston to learn if entering the woods meant a loss of signal—that Mission Control couldn't hear him, he couldn't hear Mission Control. Best to check. He didn't want to go it alone.

"Houston, please advise on signal strength."

Robbie stepped into the woods. Silence. A chill went through him. He stepped back.

"Houston?"

"Roger that. Hear you loud and clear. No loss of signal expected. You are go for exploration. Godspeed."

If Mission Control felt confident, then they knew best.

Still, Robbie cautiously headed for the creek bend. He knew the path before him would incline slightly before curving to the left. It would snake past a thick copse near the boulder he and his friends liked to climb. Robbie felt it was a great place for an ambush. If he were on his bike, he'd tear past with his head down. Approaching on foot, Robbie halted. He listened. The birds chirped merrily. He spied no Nazis eyeing him, ready to shoot. Instead, the sun sprinkled through the canopy of oaks, elms and pines. The light breeze carried a scent of pine and something unfamiliar. Robbie's eye caught a flash of red. *A cardinal!* He marveled at its vibrant color. He watched it bob and bend its head, surveying the area. It chirruped several times. Robbie felt his neck, crooked at such sharp angle to view the bird, start to ache. As if cued to leave, the bird flashed away. Gone to a better hunting ground. Robbie took a moment, scanning the trees for other birds. He knew they were there. When one took time to search, they flittered everywhere. Otherwise, they blended into the background as Nature intended. In a short time, Robbie spotted Purple Finches, sparrows, Mockingbirds, a few doves and a Blue Jay. He wanted to see another Golden Finch. He couldn't believe how yellow they were—a brilliant bright yellow.

Robbie caught himself. *Time to move along. This isn't a bird-watching tour. I'm on the moon, remember?*

Hearing the creek's gurgle, he didn't barrel down the steep slope toward it. He took his time negotiating the 30 yards to where the plateau provided just enough room to turn a bicycle at a controlled speed. But to a kid, control meant nothing. This hill determined whether you were a man. Robbie had passed that test countless times, charging into the final turn, pretending he was Chuck Yeager in a P-51 Mustang and closing fast on a ME-109. His mind retraced the path from the vantage point of his BMX dirt bike. *Build speed heading into the curve by the boulder. Pedal until near the slope. Bend into the wind and just fly. If you don't cut it just right—a shade to the outside on the final curve and a slice to the inside at the bottom while shifting the pedals so they don't catch—then, "Hello sailor! Welcome to Wet City."*

While the bush by the bank saved many an out-of-control rider, it also dispensed a few scars. It was why Robbie now walked rather than rode. Not long ago, he caught a pedal on the turn and wiped out. Flung off the bike, he watched it windmill into the bush, snapping several spokes. His dad would have fixed it in a hurry. Mom, on the other hand, went into a tizzy.

She saw his ripped jacket, listened to his story and let him have it. She told him he didn't know how to take care of his things. She lectured him about expenses, his having no appreciation for money, the need to be more responsible as the man of the house. Robbie wanted to help, wanted to please his mother. He thought of other times he felt her wrath. *Jeez, didn't she understand that God made mud puddles for splashing. That you had to slide to avoid a tag. That to trap a frog you needed your shirt?*

The bike wreck proved no red-letter day on Master Callahan's calendar. He not only lost a bike and a jacket but—worst of all, he thought—his mom's approval. He couldn't have been more wrong.

His mother had no notion her tirade hit so far from her intended target. If she knew how it wounded her baby, Mallison Callahan would have smothered him with kisses, made it quite clear that she could be no more proud of him than she already was. She'd tell him he was her rock. She still got tears every time she recalled his brave salute at his father's funeral. Marveled at how he had soldiered on without his dad these past months. How he kept joy in his heart and wonder in his gaze.

Through Robbie's example, Mallison had willed herself to be tough. She owed that to Bobby. With her husband gone, she was playing two roles. She had to be strong. So, in private, she ached at every one of Robbie's pains. In private, she wept at any of his tears. She resisted the temptation to be overprotective. Bobby wouldn't want that. Wouldn't want her instilling fear into their son. Yet, she still required Robbie to call when he arrived or left a friend's house. Still waited anxiously for the door to bang open and his irritated voice to announce, "Mom, I'm home."

But hearing how he almost tumbled into the creek overwhelmed her. She lashed out to release her terror. To disguise her fear. To deflect it from the creek. To keep Robbie distanced from what she feared most.

Instead, she pushed him right into its clutches, her own words compelling him.

Chapter 7

When she planned last evening, Mallison Callahan never expected the night would go the way it did. She simply had wanted a distraction on her wedding anniversary. To stare down her sorrow with joy. To revel in what she had rather than wallow in what she lost. She hoped a small party with her son would be a welcome diversion. Robbie's grandmother thought it was a grand idea.

"The heart needs to heal," she had said on the phone. "To retrace happy paths."

Mallison started the process on her way home Friday afternoon, stopping to buy an ice cream cake, one of those watermelon sherbet ones Robbie loved so much. She also ordered a pizza, half with anchovies, wanting to watch her son guzzle them down like his dad did.

Like his dad did. She smiled at the memory. *He's so full of fun.* As she awaited the delivery guy and her son, Mallison drifted toward previous anniversaries. The surprises. The jokes. The passion.

Until ...

Shooing away negative thoughts, Mallison reminded herself to focus on the good. She wondered if this were what it was like for people who lost loved ones at Christmas. Or New Year's. Or for those born on September 11.

Why did it have to happen on our anniversary?!

Mallison walked down the hall and opened the closet door, Reaching up, she pushed the pillow-sized cardboard box to the side.

After several off-balance shoves, it slid far enough out of the way for her to retrieve two photo albums. The doorbell rang. Scooting to the front room, she dropped the albums on the table and snatched the money and coupon off it.

"Callahan?" the teenager said as the door opened. He examined the side of the box. "Pepperoni and anchovies?"

"That's us," Mallison responded.

"Your total's $8.55 with coupon," he said.

She handed him a $10. "Keep the change."

"Thanks," he said, tipping his cap. She accepted the box and closed the door, bumping it with her hip until it latched shut. Entering the kitchen, she glanced at the clock and calculated that Robbie would charge into the house in about 10 minutes. She opened the oven and inserted the pizza box, turning the setting to 150 to keep it warm.

Less than 10 minutes passed before Robbie arrived. He spied the photo albums splayed open on the coffee table. Mom was giggling. He joined her with a hug. He plopped onto the sofa next to her. Laughter abounded as they gawked at each other's past. Robbie saw himself wailing as an infant in his Rugrats wading pool. He saw his dad as an oversized cop crammed knees-to-chest in a battery-powered police car. They both howled at the Halloween photo of Mom dressed as Princess Leia. Were those honey buns on the side of her head? Sparked by the *Star Wars* photo, Robbie stood. He pretended to parry lightsabers with Darth Vader.

"Shssile! Chrzzzackle!" he said, mimicking the sound effects of laser weapons clashing.

Watching him act like Luke Skywalker, Mallison recalled her running battle with Bobby. She wanted her son raised to respect others, be well-mannered, eat right and brush after meals. He wanted to fill their son's head with movie anecdotes and war stories about hopeless situations and impossible odds. She objected, believing such lessons would scare Robbie and make him fearful of life, not inspire him. She saw no reason why it was more important to know that

Patton turned and moved the 3rd Army in 48 hours to relieve Bastogne than it was to say "please" and "thank you." Bobby countered that polite dinner talk wouldn't serve Robbie well in times of trouble.

But knowing about the 1969 Mets would?

It seemed the only thing Bobby taught their son that she welcomed was shaking hands properly, which wasn't easy since Robbie kept extending the wrong hand. Against her wishes, Bobby continued to feed Robbie full of make-believe. Over that issue, they'd said some hurtful things to each other. Recalling those insults, Mallison gave in. She began to weep. When Robbie halted his swordplay, she felt worse. When Robbie apologized for upsetting her, she sobbed and shook.

Robbie hugged her. He felt frightened. She'd grieved in silence for so long he'd never seen her this sad before. She squeezed him tighter, but her tears continued. Robbie began crying. His reaction activated her protective nature. She kissed the top of his head. She told him how much she loved him. How happy she was that he was with her. Told him everything was fine. She just missed his daddy so much on their anniversary.

She wiped his tears and hers. She asked, "Want some pizza?"

Robbie sniffled. "Okay."

"Let me freshen up and we'll both have a big slice."

As she composed herself in the bathroom, a worried Robbie telephoned Grandma. Because of the call, Emily Fletcher arrived quickly. Unsure how to react after Grandma showed up, Robbie retreated to his room. He sifted through his *X-Men* comics, hoping Mom was alright. Even his Hot Wheels didn't distract him. Since something was wrong with Mom, he prayed. He asked God to help her. He asked to be shown what he could do to help. He prayed for Dad to come back because they really needed him now. *In Christ's name, Amen.*

When he opened his eyes, he saw an ant venturing across the floor. Robbie wondered if it escaped from his ant farm. Maybe it was lost. He placed his hand on the floor and induced the insect to crawl onto his finger. He walked over and popped open the top to his farm. He tried to shake the ant off his finger. No luck. He couldn't flick it without mashing it. He tried to blow it off, but just sent sand scattering from below. Finally, he brushed the ant into the farm with his other hand. Robbie reattached the top and watched. The ant started and stopped, its antenna testing. Robbie waited for another ant to approach and welcome the lost ant back. Instead, it attacked. Others quickly joined, their mandibles ripping apart their guest while it continued twitching. Robbie grimaced.

"Ewwwww!"

Averting his eyes from the massacre, Robbie heard Mom and Grandma talking. Mom sounded better. Maybe his prayers helped. Creeping into the hallway, he listened as Mom mentioned Dad. He halted. She talked about how much she missed him and sobbed. Robbie teared up again. He wanted to burst into the kitchen and give her a big hug. Before he moved she described how much she missed Bobby's kisses. Robbie flushed with embarrassment. That was yucky stuff. He backed toward his room, quiet as a spy, when something she said stopped him.

"After that night at the creek, things were never the same," she said.

Mallison's mother had known what her daughter and Bobby told the police about that night. She suspected that Mallison—sworn to secrecy by Bobby—had never told a soul about what actually transpired. Emily didn't know Bobby hadn't revealed the whole story, that each had held something back. It was a subject she accepted as off limits. It was a story Mallison had hoped Robbie never would hear. If she knew he was listening, she never would have begun telling her mother.

Chapter 8

Mallison Callahan's story began more than a decade before. On that late-summer afternoon, she and Bobby prepared for a romantic picnic at Landfalls Creek. He escorted her down the path that wound toward the creek. Rather than follow it at the bottom, they pushed through the overgrowth toward the highway overpass, to the small clearing they often enjoyed. Nature had done well hiding it. The canopy from the trees offered privacy from the road above while allowing a view of the sky. The bushes lining the creek formed a hedgerow, blocking any view from the landing on the other side where folks launched John Boats, fished, turned their cars around or just parked to watch the water meander past.

As Robbie listened to his mom's story from the hallway, he recognized the spot. He'd been there countless times, never knowing it had a history other than his own. He and his buddies spent lots of time there. But it was their hideaway, a place they spied on the older kids, planned secret missions. They even took a blood oath never to reveal their lair. Never bring an outsider here and never, never, never speak when they were spying on someone. So worried of discovery from the boat landing, they tested how loud one could whisper without being heard. Best to stay silent. Being hidden there proved a bonanza for Eddie because they saw his sister let her boyfriend put his hand inside her shirt. Eddie exploited the information. Got him out of so many chores that the others wished they had an older sister on whom they could spy.

A lilt in Mom's voice pulled Robbie back from reminiscing. She sounded almost happy now. He heard her describe how Dad proposed. It never dawned on him that his parents weren't always married. He grinned at the thought of Dad, down on his knee, slipping a ring on Mom's finger. Daydreaming of a fairy tale wedding, Robbie missed the next part of his mom's story. It was not for his ears anyway.

Although Mallison revealed quite a bit, she skipped over memories best kept to herself. Like for the five summers that followed their nuptials, she and Bobby returned to the same spot the same night to celebrate their anniversary. They called it "Passion Under the Stars." It was their little joke on friends who thought they were wasting their anniversary at a theatrical production over in Bedford or down in Cascade. The subterfuge—and memory of that first night—rekindled their desire. Not that revealing their annual outdoor liaison mattered. Emily came quite close to filling in the blanks herself. What proved a revelation was what happened on their fifth anniversary. Some of it Mallison never knew. Some of it Bobby told her later; some, Mallison witnessed.

That night at the creek, Bobby awoke first, his primal instincts alerted by the sudden silence. After a quick scan revealed no immediate threat, he stood. He left Mallison asleep, unaware that her dreams were now troubled. He crept toward the water's edge. He almost cleared his throat but sensed he shouldn't make a sound. Gazing through the bushes toward the landing, he was glad he didn't. At first, he thought his eyes were playing tricks on him. But the streetlight over there wasn't flickering. The moon glowed free from clouds. In a place where no shadow should be cast, a massive shadow lay. It oozed malice. It filled Bobby with such dread that he lost all desire to help the woman he saw standing near the creek. He remained frozen when she tumbled into the water and disappeared. Bobby didn't move even when Mallison stepped alongside him and slipped her warm hand into his. He simply raised a finger to his mouth to signal her silent and kept staring across the creek.

"What are you up to?" Mallison whispered. In the quiet, her words carried across the creek. Eyes hidden by shadow raced toward Bobby's. They clashed. Bobby's mind exploded with dark images. Depressive memories bubbled up. The first struck hard, of a young Bobby sitting bedside, watching his grandfather weep while cancer ate him alive. Twisting the pain, the next vision dangled an image Bobby hoped never to see. It changed him forever. Then the shadow dissipated. With it, the dread abated.

The next thing Bobby knew, Mallison was yanking on his arm, trying to pull him away. He realized he was muttering the word "hopeless" while trying to convince himself that he wouldn't let what he witnessed in those eyes happen. He'd find some way to prevent it. Mallison's fear jerked him into the moment, filled him with panic.

"Did you see it?" he asked.

Mallison nodded.

"Did you look into its eyes?"

Mallison, who had seen what looked like a pair of burning cigarettes surrounded by a cloaked figure, nodded.

"Oh, God, no!" he said. His body sagged. Mallison's grip tightened.

"You're scaring me, Honey," she said, tugging his arm. "I want to go home. Please, take me home."

Neither spoke on the way back to the house. They avoided each other's frightened glances, offering reassurance with loving squeezes as they held hands. But once home, Bobby grilled Mallison until he was convinced all she saw was nothing more than a malevolent shadow on the other side of the creek. That was bad enough because it confirmed he wasn't dreaming. At least she hadn't seen the shadow extend a hand to the woman who seemed to accept it. Hadn't seen the woman plunge into the creek. Most importantly, Mallison hadn't gazed directly into its eyes and seen what he had seen.

At Bobby's insistence, police instituted a search of the creek. Days later, they found a body way downstream. It was Becky Danforth. Nobody knew what she'd been doing out there at that time of night. They believed it to be suicide or an accidental drowning. The autopsy indicated heart attack. But there was no water in her lungs. The town mourned her passing in ignorance.

Although the nightmare ended that night for Becky, it began for Bobby and Mallison. As Bobby slept, Mallison would hold him as he quivered, hear him mumble he had to face his fear alone to overcome it. He'd talk about being marked, about being too young to go. When awake, he refused to discuss it. Mallison didn't realize Bobby had been talking—not about himself—but their son.

While the marriage lasted five more years, she lost Bobby that night. From that day, she'd look into eyes once so bold and see retreat. Part of him was gone. And part of him grew territorial. She feared telling a soul about that night. Especially since he'd made her promise. Looking up at her mother in the kitchen, she realized she'd just broken that vow. Mallison removed her palms from the kitchen table. She watched the sweat prints evaporate.

"I swear that thing is still there," she said. "I can't shake my fear of it."

She inhaled and sighed before saying, "I just wish it would go away and let me be happy again." She mulled that thought, adding, "Let us be happy again."

Listening quietly from the hallway, Robbie now understood why his mom grew so angry when he played near the creek. Why she made him so respectful of its dangers. Why she exacted a promise never to go swimming there without her and then why she never would go. As he listened to her story, he heard the way to win back her love, recognized the way to be the man of the house.

Hearing his mother weep, tears welled. Robbie rushed into the kitchen and engulfed his mom with a huge hug. He promised himself that he'd face that fear for her. He'd go down to the creek. He'd chase it away. He'd make her happy again.

Chapter 9

That night Robbie fell asleep planning what he would do. Although terrified by his mother's tale, he'd ignore his fear to conquer his mother's fear. If that shadow were in the water, that shadow that menaced his mother and father, then he'd face it down.

He awoke this morning thinking the creek wasn't that scary, was it? After all, he never feared it before. He knew to be careful not to fall in, but it was such a great place to play. There were frogs, salamanders, tadpoles and crawdads to catch. Nothing ever tried to catch him. Except maybe Brian Finister. But he'd outsmarted that big bully and landed the first punch. Finister never bothered him again.

Robbie considered his other fears, especially of the ocean. He recalled how much he loved swimming in the sea until his mother read that a shark had been caught nearby. She became so afraid for his safety that he became scared. He stayed out of the water after that, imagining sharp-toothed beasts circling underneath, ready to rise toward the surface and snap him in two. It was years before he'd venture away from the hotel pools.

Like then, her fear became his fear. A dark shadow disappearing into Landfalls Creek became a goblin of hideous proportions in his mind. *Even scarier than a Dementor. Or that slimy Alien.*

However, as with the ocean, his dad taught him that imagination makes things greater than they are. As does fear. One needs to break fear down into smaller portions until it becomes less frightening. Then stand up to it.

"Great men became great men by doing what they didn't want to do when they didn't want to do it," his dad often said.

Dad removed Robbie's fear of sharks through a process of deductive reasoning. He showed Robbie how: Sharks hunt the weak and feeble. Thrashing in the water sounds like a wounded fish. Limit your splashing. Sharks don't see well in murky water and are drawn to blood. Stay out of the water if either applies. Following such guidelines reduces the possibility of attack.

Robbie understood.

His dad said the same reasoning applied to overcoming a fear of the dark. He made Robbie search his closet with the light on. He insisted Robbie touch every object. He found nothing scary. Then, turning out the light and closing the door, he asked Robbie to identify each object by touch. Robbie realized nothing changed from the light to the dark. At least in the closet.

Robbie planned to apply that approach to the thing at Landfalls Creek that Mom feared so much. Break it down into fewer scary bits. If it were really a shadow, then it feared light the most. Robbie would search for it around noon when it would have the least power—shadows are smallest with the sun directly overhead. He'd also carry a flashlight to further weaken it. Best to have an edge. He learned that from his dad's favorite movie, *The Outlaw Josey Wales*. It was the first film Robbie ever watched that had parts where he was told to close his eyes. But he promised Dad he'd never tell Mom. It was their little secret. Which made the movie even more special. They watched it so often that they challenged each other with its dialogue. That grew into a competition between them. One would recite a line and the other had to supply the next one. They might be in traffic and, out of the blue, Dad would quote the Cherokee Lone Watie, "What about the guy on the right?" Robbie, recognizing the line, replied as Josey, "Never paid him no mind. You were there." Then he'd pretend spit. Dad would answer, "I could have missed." They did the same with lines from *Shrek*, *Willy Wonka*, *Star Wars* and countless others. But *Josey Wales* was their favorite.

Back near the creek bed, Robbie thought about Wales. *Always pays to have an edge.* Robbie's edge was no shadows cast. Looking up, he saw the sun shining almost directly overhead. Almost noon. Looking down, he couldn't find his shadow. Robbie had his edge.

Summoning his enemy presented another problem. Since he didn't know how, he decided to apply something Mom once said about Alex Simons, "If he weren't looking for trouble, it would find him." Maybe if Robbie ignored the shadow, it would appear. That's why he was out here, still on the moon. Not stalking anything. *No sir, just me and my spacesuit taking care of experiments.* Robbie started sweating. Slow-motion pretend exacted a lot of effort. He debated whether to take off his new jacket. Might as well ask.

"Houston, permission to remove outer layer."

Robbie knew his request might take a few minutes. Mission control would need to check with the docs in the back room. Doctors! Only thing a doc can do is ground you. Best just to eat an apple a day. Robbie tugged at his sleeve. He was about to ask again. Instead, CapCom replied.

"Permission granted."

Robbie removed his jacket. He let the bush by the creek bank wear it. Pretended it was now a net to trap the solar winds. He'd find out how much radiation this area attracted. He picked up a stick. He poked the ground with it. He pretended to collect core samples. He checked his oxygen supply once more before proceeding further. Safety first. He knew Houston never had an astronaut this well-trained. When he returned to Earth, there would be parades. He'd meet the President. Maybe get on TV.

He felt the wind pick up. He paid it scant attention until it lifted his jacket off the bush.

Chapter 10

For eons, what men now called Old Coals kept watch over these parts.

Back before names meant anything, back before time mattered, this territory belonged to it. It roamed the land before the woods took root. It climbed the hills. It swam the waters. It dwelt in dark places and strode upright in daylight because it knew no fear. It knew not that all feared it.

With no regard nor regret, it stole life—always taking things before their time.

If aware of it, the religious would claim the creature was thrown out of Heaven with Lucifer. Others simply would believe it was the Grim Reaper. In other places, its brethren went by other names in other guises. In Hamlin, the Pied Piper; in Greek mythology, the Minotaur; in urban legend, the Boogie Man. It was none of those things. It was all of those things.

Old Coals heard every name it had been called over the ages. It remembered none. For what did that matter? Labels meant nothing. Nor did time. Decades, even centuries, could pass with it dormant.

But when stirred, it exacted a price.

Unlike some of its kind, it didn't demand full payment up front, never to return. It didn't await end times to cash out. And like many of its ilk, Old Coals arrived on a whim. With an established price. Of three.

What summoned it? None knew. Anger aroused it. Fear fueled it. Despair sated it. It levied its own fines on those victims its interest marked. Before man inhabited this spot, the creature contented itself by overwhelming the life force of birds, squirrels, fish, deer, bear. Whatever could feel could be taken. In that regard, man proved a bonanza. So much anger. So much fear. Such a banquet for torment.

In one thing was it powerless. It could not physically take. It had to receive. Since it could not touch its victim, it relied on suggestion or sense. After all, if something could not be pushed, surely it could be persuaded to jump. This rarely proved troublesome.

Human weaknesses such as despair, jealousy and greed served it well. Any vice mankind could devise, it brought into play, turning them inward—the power of suggestion conquering all. So easy a task with some, such a challenge with others. With no haste in its manner, it could plant a seed of dread and wait for it to strangle hope. When time doesn't matter, patience becomes a weapon.

For in a blink of an eye, Old Coals had watched virgin territory bypassed and invaded. It had witnessed America's move westward and the white man ignoring why the natives left such fertile fields unfettered. Sensing evil, the Cherokee and Etowah had stayed clear.

Maybe Soke's founding fathers sensed it too. Their choice of town name spoke quite close to the situation at hand. Although they chose to honor their guiding light—the Pastor Fincher L. Soke, who perished mysteriously upon their arrival in 1794—they never knew his name held an alternate meaning.

As the centuries passed, few thought beyond the early settlers' reasons for the name. Those curious enough to pick up *Webster's New Collegiate* discovered that "soke" meant "the right to administer justice with the ability to receive fees arising from it, a jurisdiction over a territory or people." It made little sense, unless one believed that something unseen and sinister was collecting those fines.

The townsmen rationalized away the odd sights and ill feelings common to the area. They conjured up ghost stories and fashioned demented tales to tame misbehaving children. They blamed supernatural occurrences on the strange waters that sliced through the town. Most never knew how close to the mark they were.

Not far from that very creek on this Saturday morning, a Purple Finch hopped about the forest floor. It tilted its head to the right to give that eye a full field of vision. It did the same for the other eye, in search of a beetle or a seedling, having long since spent its morning feast of black sunflower seeds from a backyard feeder.

Burning fuel at a furious pace, the finch continued its near constant search for food, its persistence rewarded as a worm wriggled nearby. Delighted by such a prize this late in October, the finch warbled loudly. Pecking the worm into bits, the finch shuffled each morsel down its gullet. With each bite, the finch felt more and more—

Flee!

Spurred by a sudden dread, the finch flashed into flight. It darted into the cover of a thick spruce. Seeing nothing during flight, it still sensed danger. It remained perched near the tree's interior. From there, it investigated the surrounding area for what make it feel like prey.

The woods offered no aural assistance, just a hush. No mating calls. No chatter. Only the breeze filtering through pine needles and leaves. The finch stifled a questioning chirp. It peered down the tree for a cat. No, this was something more sinister. It peered along the branches for a snake, hopping further out the concealed branch.

The little bird took wing, nearly clipping the swooping thing it feared, quickly veering left. It glimpsed dark-and-pale patterned plumage. But it was the red eyes that most terrorized the finch.

A Sharp-Shinned Hawk!

The finch darted up, down, to the side. It sensed the hawk closing in. It dove. It soared. It tried everything to shake such a hideous ending.

Its talons were closing in!

As the finch rolled only to discover nothing in pursuit, its heart burst. It gave a dying squawk and fluttered lifeless to the ground.

Old Coals rose. It had induced the worm to the surface and to its demise. The bird had eaten of the worm and shared its dread. Old Coals then fueled the bird's fear. Yet other sounds called from the woods. The ancient creature would answer. It followed the water toward the quarry.

Toward other prey.

Chapter 11

Although her Saturday shift at the hospital didn't start until 2:45 p.m., Maggie Peterson promised to come in three hours early so Mary Compton could catch her son's soccer game. They had worked out an acceptable shift trade—assuming Maggie arrived in time.

To do that Maggie had to leave now. She didn't need this aggravation. But leaving Montana outside all night wasn't something she liked doing.

"Montana!" she hollered from the back door. Scanning the yard, she called again. "Here, kitty, kitty, kitty!"

She waited. No Montana. She stepped back into the kitchen, reached down and grabbed his orange food dish. She stepped back outside with it.

"Here, kitty, kitty, kitty!"

She shuffled the dish, rattling the dry seafood-flavored Friskies. She knew this enticement always brought the golden-brown Tabby running. Still, no Montana.

Where can that cat be?

"Montana! Here, kitty, kitty, kitty."

She checked her watch. *Five minutes. I've got five minutes you little fur-meister and then you're on your own.* She found it strange that he already wasn't at the back door. He always wanted inside before it rained.

Where is that darned cat?

Maggie checked her watch again. Less than a minute had passed. Impatient, she debated letting Montana fend for himself tonight. But she'd never hear the end of it if her dad found out she didn't wait the full five minutes and something happened to the cat. She could just hear Pops recount what Joe Montana could do with five minutes. Sitting in her dad's lap when she was a child, Maggie witnessed San Francisco's quarterback work miracles in less. She missed those moments, missed time with her parents. Living on the opposite coast, she settled for long distance calls way too often, settled for teasing Pops about his beloved 49ers' fall from grace. How they now were always in the hunt for the first pick in the draft rather than the playoffs. How he'd simply answer with "Five, Honey. Count 'em. Five." Pops didn't need to explain that meant the franchise's Super Bowl victories.

All in the past, Pops. All in the past.

Maggie eyed her watch again. *Got about a minute left.*

"Montana!"

She leaned over and placed his food bowl as close to the house as possible. She hoped it wouldn't fill with rainwater. Or provide a snack for the raccoons.

"Montana!"

She gave the yard one last look. She stepped back inside. She locked the back door and pulled the shade. As she checked her watch one last time, she heard Montana's loud meow. She shook her head and smiled. He had seconds left on the clock.

Chapter 12

Alex Simons strode toward the quarry like he should have an entourage in his wake rather than a curious spaniel. He felt almost regal.

Enthralled.

Energized.

Empowered.

Because what he had planned for this town seemed so sweet, so perfect. And everything appeared to be falling into place.

He had tethered Bucky on the short leash, easily finding the one that spooled like the drag on a fishing line. He wanted that kind of give to accomplish this event. He had also pocketed the tennis ball, just for laughs. *Might just let Bucky chase it one last time.*

Alex cut through the woods. He needed to ensure no one saw him with the dog. That would spoil everything because, most of all, he wanted folks to think Old Coals was back in town. He thought the only cool thing about this town was Old Coals. *Those stories were kick ass, especially how he'd appear out of nowhere and scare the bejeebers out of people.* Alex loved that every strange thing that happened here folks whispered, "Old Coals did it."

Even the abandonment of the quarry hinted of it. The newspaper reported that Ozzie Littleton was working the graveyard shift. Under temporary lighting, he had scooped granite with his crane and struck the spring that feeds Landfalls Creek. When he tried to avoid the fast-rising water, the article speculated that he stumbled in the shadows, both hands bracing his fall. Rather than wipe the grime on his overalls, not thinking, he must have rinsed them in the growing pond and electrocuted himself. By morning, the quarry had grown into a deep dark lake. They never recovered Littleton's body. The tragedy quickly morphed into a ghost story, embellished so that every full moon Littleton rose from the depths to place both his hands on a virgin in order to release his soul. It was complete nonsense, but a few felt Old Coals' presence in the death. Why else would nothing grow in the quarry lake? Why would spring water be so dark? How come no one ever found Ozzie's bones?

The morbid tale made the site a beacon to teenagers. They relished the idea of swimming where skeletons slumbered. But only the truly brave—or drunken pledges during frat initiation—ever stuck a foot in the water after sundown. And they often were lying about it.

Alex hoped his prank would add to the legend, make him a partner of sorts with Old Coals. Make the place creepy in the daytime too. He wished he could meet Old Coals. *Man, they'd be best buddies. Scarin' up all kinds of hell. That would be so awesome.* If he could only have one wish, that would be it.

Ever since he'd read that newspaper article months ago, he'd heard other tales about Old Coals. Made notes of each in his scrapbook. While other shunned teens might retreat to the basement, crank the stereo and channel their anger into lifting weights, smoking weed or gorging on Snickers, Alex plotted in silence, scanning, snipping, pasting, seeking supernatural signs. He'd made Old Coals his hobby. He even tried talking with Wacky Jacky about it, but that nut looked him square in the eye and said, "Send your camel to bed." *What the hell did that mean? Wacky Jacky was supposed to be this town's expert on Old Coals? I don't think so. I know more than him. What a loon.*

Alex believed he knew every reference this town ever recorded about Old Coals. Far from it. He believed those who'd met Old Coals, except for Mr. Wack Job, were all dead. Not so. Instead of digging deeper, he cursed that he didn't get to talk to the dearly departed and discover more. He longed for a way to meet Mr. Bad Ass himself.

That's why Alex thought this event should involve Old Coals. Or at least throw suspicions his way. As they walked, he told Bucky his plan. "I'm gonna take you down to the quarry and tie your long leash to a tree. Yes, I am. Then, I'm going to take my switchblade, slice you up the middle and toss you off the cliff. Those kids are gonna scream."

The dog, thinking the conversation meant food, eyed him in full agreement.

"Does that sound like a winner, fella?" he asked the dog.

"Food!" Bucky barked.

"You know you're right," Alex answered. "That leash would give it away. Old Coals wouldn't use a leash, now would he? What if I fake-throw the tennis ball over the cliff? Let you chase after it? No evidence of foul play there. Think you can survive a 70-foot drop? People will say 'Old Coals scared old Bucky so much he ran right off the cliff.' You like that ending better?"

Bucky panted.

"Yeah, I do too."

Reaching the boat landing, Alex knew crossing could be tricky since there was no telling when someone might be around, especially on a Saturday. But it was the fastest way to the quarry. Debating whether to chance it and run up the entrance ramp or climb the hill to cross Highway 37, Alex grew irritated at the dog's impatient tugs on the leash. Although he was in a hurry, out of meanness, he knotted Bucky's leash to a pine tree, making sure it was secure. *Just settle down, boy. We'll go when I'm good and ready.* Alex sat watching the dog, flipping his switchblade open and closed, listening to the familiar clink.

His mind drifted to those college snobs while he mentally eviscerated Bucky. *This would be so perfect. Those jerks wouldn't want to come near the place.* He could just picture Bucky sailing through the air. Barking to draw attention. And then, those kids would see the leash yank Bucky back into the side of the cliff. Splat! *They'd be so disgusted they'd never come back. No, wait! No leash. They'd be screaming at that dog sailing through the air, smacking into the water.* Alex wondered if hitting the water or drowning would be what killed Bucky.

Bucky barked again. *Play with me! Throw something. I'll bring it to you. Is that a squirrel? Hot out here. I could use some water. Throw it! Throw it! Throw it!*

Bucky suddenly cowered.

Whooow! Weird smell! Weird smell!

The hackles on Bucky's neck rose. He whined. His tail no longer wagged. He spun and backed toward Alex. Bucky wanted to get away. Alex snapped out of his daydream when he heard the dog whine. He watched Bucky's retreat.

"What's the matter, boy?" he said before the memory of his mother telling him he wasn't worth sticking around for deflated his momentary thrill. He failed to notice that Bucky hadn't turned toward his taunting voice. Bucky's head riveted on something unseen.

Alex swapped the memory of his mother with malice, pointing the switchblade at the approaching dog's behind, wondering what the dog would do when it backed into the sharp point. Instead, Bucky, feeling cornered, whirled. Growling with fangs bared, he surprised Alex, snapping at his wrist. Frightened, Alex slashed the dog across the snout. Bucky howled in pain, but charged Alex again. He came up short.

Backpedaling further onto the concrete, Alex stared.

What did I do?

Convinced Bucky could get no closer, Alex watched the dog watch him. Like Bucky was stalking, waiting for an opening. The dog licked the blood dripping off his own nose. Alex knew the leash was securely tied. What Alex didn't know was Bucky's collar wasn't.

Soon, very soon, Alex would be granted his one wish.

Chapter 13

Robbie Callahan's jacket hung off the bush with a sleeve in the water.

This disaster superseded all plans to face his fear. He just got this jacket, this brand-new jacket, the one his mom just told him to be so careful with. It couldn't get any worse than this.

Mom's gonna hate me. If I get it and let it dry, maybe she won't notice.

The sleeve grew heavier as water soaked its way higher, gently tugging the jacket and bending the branches. Whatever Robbie did, he'd better do it fast. He swiped with his arm, snagging it with his pinkie and holding tight as he tightrope-walked the bank to maintain his balance.

Even Simon Cowell would have applauded.

As the wet sleeve slung upwards, a button flew off. Robbie watched it flip in the air. Still safely balanced himself, he tracked its flight as it landed near the bottom of the bank. Water lapped close to it. It was out of arm's reach, but Robbie could get it if the creek didn't beat him to it.

He knew better than to try to tap it closer with a stick. That might knock it into the water. He needed something sticky. Like tape. Or—

Hello! Chewing gum!

Robbie grabbed the branch he earlier employed as a space probe. He plucked the gum from his mouth and mashed it on the end. Carefully, he jabbed the button. He pressed hard. Better make it stick.

Success!

He unstuck the button and popped it in his mouth to clean it off. He acted like he had landed a successful dismount to imaginary applause. He bowed with his back to the creek. As he did, it was as if the town's cyclone sirens wailed their warning in his mind. He heeded it too late.

Robbie's feet slipped out from under him. He banged into the bank and plunged backward into the creek. He inhaled sharply in reaction to the cold water. The chill stunned him. His sudden inhalation lodged the button in his throat. He couldn't cough. He couldn't breathe. He couldn't drown. He floated just below the surface, the creek carrying him swiftly downstream.

Chapter 14

When Bucky's collar snapped, Alex reacted instinctively. He dipped into a defensive stance. As the spaniel leaped at him, Alex rammed the switchblade into the crazed dog's neck and spun. The dog howled, landing on the pavement behind Alex and knocking the blade loose in the process. It clattered loudly.

Not only was Alex now unarmed, but also unsure whether he could reach the blade, the creek or a tree and avoid Bucky's fangs. Alex prepared to deliver his best version of a karate kick for the next rush. *Time it right or it'll be a world of hurt. Dog must have gone rabid all of a sudden.*

Bucky snarled as he looked past Alex. Instead of another charge, the dog suddenly grew timid. He whined and backpedaled again. Alex grew more confused. He inched toward the bloodied switchblade. He kept his eyes on the dog. The dog, panting heavily, focused on the area Alex vacated. Leery of diverting his attention, Alex glanced. He saw nothing.

He quivered when he heard a splash upstream. He turned toward it briefly. The dog didn't. The dog unleashed the most mournful howl and trotted toward the creek. Alex gaped, baffled.

What the hell's going on here? That dog's gone plumb loco.

At the creek's bank, Bucky paused. He looked back at Alex and sprang into the water. *Plumb loco.* Alex raced to the edge. He expected to see Bucky dogpaddling downstream. The way things were going, he wouldn't be a bit surprised to discover the dog jet-skiing. No such luck. The water swirled as if undisturbed. Only the blood wisped away from water's edge proffered evidence of what had transpired.

Bucky's final look flashed in Alex's mind. It seemed so sad, like the dog didn't want to go. Alex felt a tinge of regret, if not for the dog, at least for the wreck of his plan. *Maybe Bucky's trapped underwater.* Alex knelt. He scoured the shallows. Even with the sun at his back for illumination, his vision couldn't penetrate deep enough to examine the creek bed.

Alex never saw Bucky again. No one did.

Chapter 15

Underwater, Robbie Callahan's mind raced. Panic consumed him as the creek conducted him downstream.

Where's my jacket?
Mom's going to kill me.
Dad!

Terror threatened to swallow him whole. He tried to scream but half-gagged because of the button. His head heard the sounds his throat muted. *In space no one can hear you scream.* He heard his heart pound way too fast.

Thuthump, thuthump, thuthump, thuthump, thuthump ...

His clothes weighed him down. He couldn't breach the surface. It was right there. Unable to swallow or breathe, he needed time. He tried to will himself calm. He knew panic consumed oxygen. He remembered that pearl divers slowed their heart rates to delay their need for air. *Remain calm. Devise a plan.* Robbie became consumed with the sound of his heart beating. For a different reason.

Thump, thump, thump, thump, thump, thump ...
Slowing.
Thump ... thump ... thump ... thump ...
So cold. So heavy.

Robbie knocked off his shoes. He refused to release his jacket. He tried to scissor-kick to the surface but was still too heavy, the under current gently tugging him deeper. He began to feel dreamy.

He watched the sun shimmer above him. *Like a kaleidoscope.* It mesmerized him. Shadows from tree branches distorted his view. He marveled at the broken light as the lack of oxygen slowed his blood flow, as the water's chill slowed his need for it. He began to see five-pointed stars. *Like the logos on Team USA's hockey jerseys.* They grew larger as they raced toward him and veered past.

He watched fascinated as they increased in number. Robbie was dying. He felt like he was slowly spinning.

Thump … thump …

Something in his mind asked if he believed in miracles.

YES!

That something hollered there was still time on the clock. Robbie remembered Team USA's Marc Johnson racing up ice past a relaxing Russian defensemen. Seconds left in the period. He swore he heard Dad's voice yelling, *"Don't stop skating until the horn sounds! Keep moving your feet. Good things will happen. Keep moving your feet. Go one more step than you think you can!*

DO!

NOT!

QUIT!"

Focusing on the imaginary rebound he knew would come, Robbie kicked. *Don't look at the clock. Just beat Tretiak.* He saw the puck twang the back of the net. The red light glowed. The buzzer blared. The roar in his ears had to be the crowd. He kicked and raised his arm to celebrate the goal. He felt a vicious tug and drifted off. He believed his teammates were mobbing him in joy.

He passed out.

Chapter 16

Unable to spot Bucky in the creek, Alex Simons' imagination convinced him that the splash he heard upstream snatched the dog. It grabbed whatever else was upstream too. Snatched both right off the bank. He pictured *Jaws* slicing toward him, ready to leap out of the water and gobble another victim. Despite having his switchblade ready, he chuckled at how lame that idea was. *C'mon, a shark in fresh water?* He pocketed the blade and shaded his eyes. He glanced upstream. When he stood, something caught his eye.

Startled, he jumped. *Damn! Is that a body?* Alex couldn't believe it. He slid down the bank. *It is a body. With an arm raised?* Alex grabbed the wrist and used his back leg as a fulcrum. He powerlifted the object half onshore next to himself. Despite the weight, Alex didn't let go. With his other hand, he pulled the back of the baseball jersey high enough for a more secure grab at the back of the jeans. He tugged the body completely out of the water.

It was a kid! A damn kid! Alex pulled himself and the dripping body up onto the pavement. The body was pale and heavy. He dragged it partway into the boat landing's parking area and out of the shade. Alex slapped the kid's cheek.

"Wake up, kid. You all right? Wake up. Say something."

Alex felt heroic. This was the Callahan kid. *I saved the Callahan kid. This town would never say I was good for nothing again. They'd be pleased as punch when I walked by. They'd point and say "That's Alex.*

He saved the little kid. Pulled him right out of the water. Saved his life. Yes, sir, Alex's a hero." It would be in the paper. Front page. I'd probably be on TV too, interviewed by that blonde on the evening news.

But Robbie wasn't answering. Robbie wasn't saying a word. His hand clutched a jacket. His face looked bluish. *Was this kid breathing?* Alex felt for a pulse. *This kid is dead.*

All of Alex's dreams of glory vanished. *Damn it. No parades. No free beers. No pretty girls kissing me. I'll get blamed for this, too. Bad Cop Burt will come knocking. Dad will take it out on me. Damn dead kid.*

It didn't register that Alex was not alone. Not even as discouragement settled on him like fog at dawn. Once again, he recalled his mother's stinging rejection. He punched back tears. He hadn't been attuned to the presence Bucky sensed earlier. He felt no fear when it should have been at its highest. He felt no pity. He was too obsessed that this dead kid just ruined his life. Alex's mind flooded with malevolence. He wanted to make the most of this gift.

A severed head would be way cool.

Alex whipped out his switchblade. Still on his knees, he jerked the limp kid up by the jersey front. It took almost all his strength. As the head lolled back, Alex shoved Robbie and slashed at the throat. As Robbie's body toppled, Alex grabbed the jacket in protective reflex as it slung up from the flailing arm. He saw Robbie's eyes open. He swore they were red, like the Devil in Hell. It terrified him.

Alex ran.

Chapter 17

Robbie revived to searing, sharp pain.

He felt ... everything ... was ... so ... slow.

He hit the ground hard, forcing trapped air to jettison up his throat. The force dislodged the button through the slit in his neck. He gulped fresh air. Some bubbled out the slit.

The pain returned.

Hard.

His lungs seared. His throat burned. It stung like he had swallowed splinters. He couldn't stop trembling, shaking, shivering, twitching. It was as if his body were fighting survival rather than facilitating it.

With his pain sensors overwhelmed, Robbie became numb to the sensations. His brain ignored those neurons' messages. It shifted toward more welcome impulses. He absorbed the warmth of the sun. It felt so good. But he was so tired. He remembered dozing with his cat Gentry. How they curled up next to the window where the sun drenched the floor. How they'd scoot as the sun inched along. *Sun Buddies. Yes sir, bona-fide Sun Buddies.*

Robbie's body, struggling to save him, tried to put him to sleep. As slumber eased forth, pain slapped it away when he curled up. His head throbbed. He tasted what he thought was salty water. Had his eyes been open he might have noticed his blood flowing faster as his body warmed. His teeth chattered. He wondered where his jacket was. Mom would kill him for getting his clothes wet. He tried to see what was missing. *What were those red spots on the ground?* Its significance didn't register. *What a pretty color. Like a cardinal.* The color also reminded him of his first love back in kindergarten. The little girl in the red dress. The one he so wanted to know better, the one he ...

The pain intensified. Robbie hyperventilated, quickly growing light-headed. He knew if he got dizzy, he'd throw up. Just like on the merry-go-round. All over that blue horse he rode. Just like the spinning wheel at the playground when he begged them to stop. He wanted this to stop. He wanted his world to quit spinning.

Mom!

Suddenly, his mind swam with images of his dad's ashen face, almost zombie-like in the white satin coffin. Robbie's heart ached. He missed his dad so much.

Robbie thought he saw a strange hand extend toward him. Rather than reach for it, he passed out again.

He never heard the screech.

Chapter 18

Erin Hollins was at play.

Following her father's collegiate example, she was using her sophomore year at Landfalls College to explore her wilder side, to have a little innocent fun. She'd be true to her boyfriend back home next year. She'd settle down next year. She'd get it out of her system this year.

The semester barely started when she hooked up with a junior from her International Politics class. He seemed so aloof, so sure of himself, so emotionally detached. He wouldn't let love complicate things. Such a challenge attracted her.

In class, she showed her interest by asking to borrow his pen. In the dining hall, she'd catch his eye and smile. In the library, she'd ask his weekend plans and say she had none. He never called. After a couple of weeks of dropping hints he didn't pick up, she made a bold move. Sometimes you have to buy the putty.

"McCumber! Phone!" Cameron Casey yelled from across the room. He eyed his oblivious roommate with irritation because Duncan continued reading—his ears plugged into his iPod—while his cellphone replayed the theme song to the defunct sci-fi TV show "Firefly."

"I'm going to take the sky away from you," Casey muttered as he bounced off his bed, snatched the offending cellphone from the desk and thrust it in front of his roommate.

Duncan popped out his earphones and took the phone.

"Who is it?" he asked.

Cameron shrugged.

Getting nowhere reading Faulkner's *Light in August*, Duncan welcomed the interruption. Before he could check his caller ID, the "Firefly" ringtone strummed again. He answered quickly.

"Hello?" he said.

"Hey, Duncan. This is Erin. Erin Hollins."

"Hey," he said with a tinge of surprise and fear, unsure he heard right and unprepared to talk to the woman on whom he had a budding crush. His mind raced. *Stay cool, man. Don't say something stupid. What do I say? Why's she calling me? Had to be about class. Had to be.*

Suppressing his excitement, he said, "What can I help you with?"

Erin paused. He didn't sound as receptive to her call as she imagined. *Maybe he's gay. This might be tougher than I thought.* She forged ahead. "I was wondering if you'd like to go to the movie Friday night at Randall Auditorium."

Believing she might need more ammunition to close the deal, she injected, "They're showing *Risky Business*."

Never mind that Duncan planned to go to Retro-Flick night with his roommate for a movie he'd seen almost 20 times, he quickly answered, "Sure."

Just take those old records off the shelf.

"Great," Erin said. "Call me later and we'll set up a time. Talk to you then."

"Okay," Duncan said. "Talk to you later."

"Bye," Erin answered.

"Bye." He waited for her to hang up.

Duncan couldn't believe his luck. As he disconnected, he replayed the entire conversation in his head. She'd asked him out. She'd said to call her. They had a date this Friday! Even her goodbye sounded inviting. Picturing Erin as Lana from the Friday movie, Duncan pounced onto the floor. *Are you a good boy, Joel?* Cam eyed him curiously, putting down his *Sports Illustrated* when Duncan jumped back onto his own bed.

Giggles carbonated Duncan's tummy. He felt like his organs grew wings. He never got butterflies like this even back in Little League. This was too good not to share immediately.

"You'll never believe who just asked me out."

"Jessica Biel."

"No."

"Penelope Cruz?"

"Get serious."

"Bea Arthur?"

Duncan laughed. "Erin Hollins."

"Erin? Alright, dude." Cam rolled off his bed and high-fived Duncan. "Rockin."

That was a month ago. Since then, if you asked him, Duncan and Erin had gotten hot and heavy. If you asked her, they were friends with benefits. She established ground rules. No public displays. No overnight stays. She made it clear she intended to marry her boyfriend back home upon graduation. Nothing wrong being friends and having a little fun until then. Just don't fall in love. I'm not your girlfriend. You're not my boyfriend. Consider this an affair or it's over.

That was Erin's game. She could, of course, toy with his emotions. She could draw him out but not in. If anything developed, it was his fault for disobeying the rules. So in his car, she seductively kissed him while he drove. Took pleasure knowing she could make him swerve, got joy at making him linger too long at a stop sign. All the while stopping him just where she desired. Taking him just where she wanted when she wanted. Her own little puppet. His car provided all the privacy she required for a covert romance.

Duncan didn't care at first. Didn't mind the rules. He accepted the cost if it meant spending more time with her, accepted her ultimatums as a challenge. He actually believed he could contain his heart. Convinced himself she'd never be able to get to him. But because he believed love conquered all, he never noticed what was blooming. That writing her poems meant he was losing, not winning. That his heart grew greedier and greedier for her affections. That she came to possess him.

As they saw more of each other, his grades dropped from Dean's List caliber to doing just enough as his focus shifted from Shakespeare and the Ming Dynasty to the fine Miss Hollins.

He welcomed the tradeoff, drifting off to sleep with her in mind, waking to the thought of seeing her again. Hoping she felt the same way. It never dawned on him that he might be the fly and she the spider. It never dawned on her that she could so easily penetrate his detached demeanor. She'd figured he'd be fun to, well, you know, play with and toss away unhurt. How could he not notice how hard and fast he was falling. How could she not? Sometimes those in the whirlwind can't see the chaos.

Duncan swirled in his own maelstrom. He'd violated her first rule: He was in love. He wanted to tell Erin how he felt, but was terrified of her response. It could be bliss or disaster. Ask for a hand in marriage and one is rather sure of the answer. But say I love you? That was the great unknown. That was uncharted waters. He believed she loved him despite her protests. *How could we do those things if it weren't love?* So many mixed signals. She never claimed they were dating, but they spent so many nights together. She grew angry if he gave her a poem. But she'd kiss him until their lips chapped. Love conquered all, right? He prayed for the courage that this would be the day he could say "I love you."

As Duncan drove toward the quarry, anticipating some Saturday make-out time, the radio played a forgotten song. Erin sat next to him. Her shorts accentuated her tanned legs. She shifted closer, her hand playing with the hair above the nape of his neck. She leaned over. She guided her breath as a caress on his neck. She knew he liked it. Time to play siren and dash him upon the rocks. She kissed his neck. He arched to give her more room, determined this time he wouldn't let her take his eyes off the road. He'd win this time.

Except her kisses held such heat. Lost in his rising pleasure, it took a second for the song to register. "... since the return of her stay on the moon, she listens like Spring and talks like June, hey, hey."

"Hey, hey. I love this song," he said, joining the chorus of Train's "Drops of Jupiter." Would he ever find the courage to ask whether "you miss me while you were searching for yourself out there." He had to. If not today, another day, for sure. Another day. Sure.

Erin paid no attention to the lyrics. She didn't like his attention divided. She liked to know his focus was total—on her. If she doubted his devotion, she tested. Like last night at dinner. She encouraged him to order a pitcher of beer with their pizza even though she knew he didn't drink. When he agreed, she changed her mind. It had been enough that he was willing. No sense in corrupting the poor boy. Her self-esteem received its needed boost. She possessed the power. Right now, some rock group's lyrics had him.

Not for long.

"It's pretty," she said. She patted him on the leg. Time for the slam dunk. She eased her hand toward his knee and back, halting at high-thigh. She knew her touch would get his attention briefly. She wanted it full time. Knowing how to maximize the moment, she leaned her shoulder forward and turned. Her half-buttoned shirt gaped. Show some skin, a little black lace and the anticipation of something more always snared his thoughts. She glanced away to prolong the free stare. She noticed he was no longer singing. He was speeding. She smiled slightly.

Singing along with Train sidetracked Duncan's debate. *Should I tell her? Should I not?* He felt the moment of greatness flicker. *I can't.* It won't be today. He sagged slightly as his courage waned. He agreed with J. Alfred Prufrock, *"I should have been a pair of ragged claws scuttling across the floors of silent seas."* It can't be today.

She touched his neck. *God, how her fingers thrill me.* He tried to suppress his desire, convince himself that he could control his emotions while around her. All he wanted to do was share them. *At least hold out as long as possible.* Her mouth on his neck altered his breathing. She blew on her wet kiss. It cooled his neck and warmed him. Drifting into the other lane, Duncan corrected his steering. *Focus on something else. Anything else!* His mind returned to the radio.

He listened to a few lyrics before Erin consumed his thoughts again. Her hand on his leg. Her breasts straining in that black bra. Duncan accelerated down Highway 37. Mesmerized by the thought of what else she might be wearing, of what he wanted to do, of what she'd let him do, he reacted sporadically to the road ahead. Reacted too late when Alex Simons darted into their path.

Chapter 19

Duncan McCumber stomped on the brakes. His weathered Lincoln Navigator dipped promptly but maintained a straight skid in the lane. The SUV didn't hit anybody. It didn't swerve left across the opposite lane, go up and over the railing and into creek below. It didn't veer right, flip over the railing, slam into the hillside and barrel roll into a copse of pines and elms. The anti-lock brakes kept the vehicle's path straight and true.

When it finally stopped more than 100 feet from where the rubber had begun to wed itself to the pavement, Duncan looked at Erin. Her eyes were wide. Her hands remained braced against the dashboard, her legs locked and jammed to the floorboard as if she too were braking. *Was she trembling or furious?*

"You okay?" Duncan asked, his own voice unsteady.

She nodded.

Duncan edged to the roadside. He got out and walked around the front of the SUV. He bent over the railing and puked. The smell of burning rubber filled his nostrils. He retched, vomiting nothing but air. Sweat poured off him. He felt dizzy. His eyes watched the sun dance on the creek below. In the clearing, he noticed a clump. It looked like a pile of clothes. As his eyes focused, he realized it was a body. *Is that a kid? Oh, God, I thought I missed him. I missed him! He ran right out in front me! I tried to stop! Oh, God, no! Please, don't let him be dead."*

Panicking, Duncan suppressed the desire to jump back in the vehicle and drive away fast. *Don't say a word to Erin. Just drive. Race back to campus. Pretend nothing happened. I didn't do anything wrong. It was just an accident. Besides, they have no proof. Proof?* Duncan turned. He looked at the front of his vehicle. Intact. Not a dent. Not a scratch, just more than enough bug splats to qualify as a fighter ace. The skid marks? They went on forever.

Wait a minute? Wasn't the kid running the other way? Could this kid still be alive? Could he—

Erin screamed. Duncan never heard her door open. Now, she stood at the rail, pointing and whimpering, "Call 911. You hit a kid. Oh, God, you hit a kid."

"No, I didn't," Duncan said. "Chill, will ya? I didn't hit anything."

Erin started crying. Duncan ignored her. He yelled down.

"Hey! Are you okay?"

Nothing.

"Can you hear me?"

Nothing.

"Say something!"

Silence.

Maybe he can't speak.

"Move something if you can hear me!"

No response.

Maybe he can't hear. Duncan started to yell again and stopped. *Jeez, that was stupid.*

Duncan started down the hill. He stopped. Remembering his cellphone, he punched 911. He wanted to do the right thing, but wasn't sure what it was. He told the dispatcher to send an ambulance up near the quarry, to the landing. A kid needed help fast. He noticed the signpost and told her Mile Marker 8. He tried to explain what happened, hoping full disclosure now would help the police believe he had nothing to do with this, that he was not concealing anything. He believed the facts would prove him innocent. What if he were wrong? On TV, cops formed fast opinions. He realized too late that being a Good Samaritan might involve serious consequences.

Those skid marks weren't gonna help. And how to convince Erin that he hadn't killed the kid, too. The kid.

Duncan debated whether to continue down the hill and thought better of it. He'd seen enough episodes of "CSI" to know it best not to disturb the crime scene. He stared at the body, pictured the crime scene investigators combing the area for evidence. *Wouldn't mind combing Marg Helgenberger's crime scene. She might be older but she's definitely a MILF. Def-i-nite-ly a MILF.* Duncan felt a flush of shame. *Erin's right there. And that kid might be dead. Dead.*

Duncan looked back at Erin. She was whimpering. Duncan climbed back over the guardrail. He walked back to console her. He wrapped his arm around her and got an elbow for his compassion. He pouted, staring down at the body. She raged. This wasn't how she wanted her day to go. They sat apart and waited silently for the ambulance to arrive. They were not unwatched.

Chapter 20

Making his escape, Alex Simons never saw Duncan McCumber's oncoming Navigator. He didn't care. Never cared if he saw anything again. Demons were after his ass.

He didn't hear the vehicle screech nor Erin Hollins' scream. He only heard that kid's anguished wail. And he kept running from those eyes. Those empty eyes watching only him.

Only those eyes weren't the kid's. And they weren't entirely empty. They were something else. They had stared at him. Tracking him, ensnaring him, possessing him. He saw himself in them, flailing wildly and growing larger and larger before they went dark.

That's when Alex ran, clambered up the hill to the highway, sidled over the guardrail and sprinted across the road. Oblivious to the oncoming car, Alex leapt the other guardrail and half-slid, half-stumbled down the embankment on the far side of the highway. He hit the footpath by the creek and refused to look back.

Good thing. He didn't know that what watched him vanish into the woods would meet him soon enough. It knew exactly where he was headed.

Alex didn't just yet. He needed a moment. Needed time to sort this out, a place to disappear and think. Without realizing where he was headed, Alex angled toward the quarry. He fell into a familiar pace.

As a kid, Alex developed a habit of reciting lyrics to distract his mind when he ran. His current favorite was Tim McGraw, more because he was the son of Phillies' pitcher Tug McGraw than because of the music. That only mattered because Alex's father told him nine ways to Sunday how much he hated the quirky relief pitcher. So listening to McGraw's music became a defiant way to drown out his father's taunts. While running, the memorized lines took Alex's mind off any pain. Focusing on the next line distracted him from how tired he was or how much his body hurt. The ploy automatically kicked in any time he jogged. It became so ingrained that while he debated what to do, where to go and what had happened, his mind recognized his body's activity. It made an ironic choice.

He said I was in my early 40's. With lots of life before me. When a moment came and stopped me on a dime ...

Alex rounded the curve that took him away from the creek and further into the woods.

And I spent most of the next days, looking at the x-rays. Talking bout the options and talking about sweet time ...

Alex's breathing labored. His mind clouded. He needed to stay sharp. As the song played in his head, he also recalled the video: Images flashing of McGraw's life, the shot of Tug McGraw in uniform patting his heart during the 1980 World Series that always made his dad swear. Alex felt a sense of defiance as he started the song's chorus.

I went skydiving. I went Rocky Mountain climbing ...

His lungs labored. His calf muscles tightened.

I went 2.7 seconds ... on a bull ... named Blue Manchu ...

Alex felt light-headed. He couldn't remember the last time he tried to run this far. Never at such a pace.

And I ... loved deeper ... and I ... spoke ... sweeter ...

He began to recite in time with his breathing, his pace.

And I ... gave ... forgive ... ness ... I'd ... been ... de ... nying ...

Alex slowed but didn't stop, still fearful of pursuit.

And ... he ... said ... I hope ... you get ... the chance ... to live ... like ... you ... were ... dying.

Alex started up the hill toward the quarry. Not much farther. He would finish the song in plenty of time. Even though his mind kept skipping, kept repeating one line.

What ... would ... you ... do ... with ... it.
What ... would ... you ... do ... with ... it.
What ... would ... you ... do ... with ... it.

Alex knew the places to hide in this town. Too many close calls in his youth taught him the value of sanctuary. Now, he aimed for the one place he considered his own. He needed time to think. He needed time not to think.

Most of all, he needed to get as far away as possible from whatever that was. He didn't know he headed right for it.

Chapter 21

The 911 call crackled over the cruiser's radio.

"Possible 10-7. Landfalls County service lot 3. Mile Marker 8. 10-52 en route. Please respond."

"10-4," deputy Merl Burt said. "I'm 10-17 to the location."

Merl flicked the siren and sped toward Highway 37 and out of town. He wondered whose body had been found. Would he get there ahead of the paramedics? Was this going to be one of those Saturdays?

Born here more than 50 years ago, Merl Burt belonged to Soke. It was as if subconsciously he adhered to his father's dictum that if you stay in one place long enough, luck knows where to find you. So Merl traveled to other places through books and television. His wanderlust tempted when he departed for the big city after turning 20. He stayed just long enough to believe evil exists. Finding 6-year-old Wendy Sullivan's mangled body convinced him of that. It had to be the worst thing Merl ever encountered. How could another person do such things to a trusting child. He thanked God daily that such evil hadn't followed him home.

Merl—the only people who ever used his last name were those already in trouble—rarely let anyone know his full name was Merlin. Named after the Arthurian wizard from Camelot because his mother loved the story, he consoled himself that she didn't name him Lancelot or Gwain. The childhood teasing was bad enough.

Despite his given name, Merl didn't believe much in hocus-pocus. Although on occasion he wished he could conjure up some magic in his job. Presto! Keep these kids from harm instead of racing the train, driving drunk, smoking pot or playing with a gun.

Instead, Merl settled for kind words and hard work. He watched. He examined. He asked questions. He put pieces together and drew conclusions, mostly correct. He didn't see himself as a plodder like in those detective novels nor did he have quirks like a TV sleuth. Heck, he doubted he could come up with a catchphrase. Besides, not many folks paid you any mind when your main chore was judging talent contests at the fair and catching speeders out on the highway. Or that they believed you were just around to do Sheriff Benny's bidding.

There was a time when Merl believed coming home was the best idea. That was before he learned about the sheriff's attitude. That was before he found Bill Talbert.

Despite what the sheriff told folks, there was no way alcohol killed Talbert. Sure, he was probably drunk, but a drunk doesn't end up that contorted. Or with that look on his face. Talbert died terrified.

It was in finding Talbert that Merl first wondered whether Landfalls County had a big problem, if something else shared this jurisdiction, something he didn't believe existed.

As the turnoff to the boat landing neared, Merl saw the SUV. He noted the tag number, slowed, signaled and hoped he wouldn't find what he expected to find. He parked before the landing's entrance ramp to avoid driving over any possible evidence. He hopped out of the cruiser. He politely asked the two kids to remain where they were. They did. Merl eyed the terrain. He made mental notes as he hurried to reach the body. Even at a distance, he could tell it had been in the water.

He noticed a leash tied to a tree and what looked to be a broken dog collar. He reached the body and, careful not to disturb too much, checked for a pulse. Faint. *Aw, hell. It was the Callahan boy. As if that family hadn't been through enough.* Merl noticed blood seeping from a cut in the throat. Locating no other wounds, Merl gently applied pressure to the slit, making sure he wasn't hampering Robbie's breathing. He covered Robbie's torso with his jacket and awaited the paramedics. He already could hear the siren wailing.

As he knelt, he yelled up at the kids that Robbie Callahan was alive and that they may have saved his life by calling for help. He needed to ask them a few questions after the ambulance arrived. Could they please wait? They agreed.

Hoping his praise and request would keep them still, he continued to examine the scene while remaining next to Robbie. He saw no fresh tire marks. Nobody left here in a hurry. He saw no bicycle tracks, but mud smears showed the body appeared to have been dragged from the creek. Blood drops toward the creek and from the woods—probably made by the switchblade nearby. Small drops. A puddle near the blade. Larger drops heading to the creek. Blood pooling indicated the body fell here after being cut. Apparently, the body—*Man, this was Robbie*—apparently, Robbie was kneeling when he fell.

Merl refused to pursue that line of thought. He refocused on the scene. He had the switchblade. He had a leash and dog collar but no dog. There was a small blood pool and drops further away but not in line where the body seemed to have been dragged. He shifted and looked back down at Robbie.

Where are his shoes? Is that a button? Must have come off his shirt.

Merl looked at Robbie's baseball jersey. It had all its buttons. Merl turned. He examined the slope up to Highway 37 as the siren grew deafening. The clump-filled hill showed tracks. It recently had been climbed. Maybe in a hurry.

The now silent siren still echoed as the ambulance slowed and pulled down the entrance to the boat landing. Jake Banner hopped out and raced to the back, flinging open the bay doors. He scrambled over to the body. As he unhitched his medical kit, he asked, "What have we got?"

"Eleven-year-old. Slit to the throat. Body cold. Pulse faint," Merl said.

He paused before adding, "It's Robbie Callahan."

Jake halted and turned.

"Damn," he said.

As the paramedics stabilized and prepared Robbie for transport, Merl walked over to the dog collar. It was torn. He eyed the switchblade. He'd seen it before. He knew its owner. Merl would collect it and spray-paint its location after talking to the kids from the SUV. Same for the button. He walked over to the creek and confirmed that Robbie had been pulled from it. He discovered no shoes. Just paw prints on the bank. *Probably dog's blood, too.*

Merl ambled back toward the slope. He let his eyes climb the hill, retracing the getaway path he believed he saw. When his eyes reached the top, he was looking at the couple sitting apart.

"Did either of you come down here, earlier?"

"No, sir," the boy said. The girl shook her head.

"Are you sure?"

Same response.

"Either of you make those tracks on the hill?"

Same response. Before Merl became convinced they knew no other answers, the boy added that he had started down the hill over there. He pointed about 10 feet further away.

Merl noted that it had been recently disturbed. He believed him. He heard Jake slam the ambulance doors shut. He turned. Jake saluted. Merl returned the salute with a nod. Edgar Nichols honked as he turned past and sped up the ramp to the highway. He waited until he was well past Merl before activating the siren.

Merl watched them pass. He followed the pavement up to where the two kids waited. After asking both if they were all right and getting their names, he told them that he wanted to talk to them separately and then together. He thanked them in advance for their cooperation.

He chose the girl first since she seemed the most out of sorts. He tried to put her at ease and get her to focus on something simple first before discussing the incident. He needn't have. Almost before he finished asking where they were headed, Erin Hollins' version spilled out like an accusation.

"We were heading to the quarry," she said. "Duncan was driving. He wanted to go up there. I know we weren't supposed to, but it's the middle of the day and he wanted to be alone with me. We're from LC. I wasn't doing anything wrong. We were arguing about a song on the radio. Out of nowhere this kid runs out in front of the car. Duncan slammed on the brakes and the kid kept running. I thought I was going to die. Then I see that kid down there and thought Duncan killed him. I'm not in any trouble am I? I just want to go home. Can I go now?"

"In a minute," Merl said, wondering when she found time to breathe. "You're okay. You're not in any trouble. Just take a seat. I need to talk to your boyfriend first."

"He's not my boyfriend," Erin said.

Merl left it alone. *Woe to him that marries her.* He walked to the front of the SUV. He beckoned Duncan McCumber over. He asked what happened. McCumber told him everything as he remembered it. Merl found him remarkably open. Either he was brilliant at matching the evidence to his tale or he was telling the truth. Merl strolled down the two-lane highway to where the skid marks started. He glanced down the slope. Sure enough, footprints and shoe skids down the side. Whoever climbed up one side of the slope had dodged McCumber's SUV and slid down the other side. Must have been in a heckuva hurry not to check traffic first.

Merl interviewed both kids together, getting them to tell their stories again in hopes it would prod the other with additional details. It was almost a waste until McCumber added the kid running was holding a light-colored jacket.

About that time, Seth Westbrook from the Highway Patrol pulled up. He knew from the radio that Robbie Callahan was being transported to Harper Memorial. He asked if he could deliver the news to the mother. He was such a vulture that Merl quickly said, "I'll do it. Don't worry about it."

Westbrook spotted Erin Hollins. He asked if she wanted an escort back to town. Before anyone could object, she accepted. Westbrook smiled. He winked at Merl and opened the passenger door for her; the only gentlemanly thing he'd do all week and it required breaking protocol.

Mr. McCumber just got lucky, Merl thought. *I'm not sure whether Seth or Miss Hollins bit off more than they can chew.*

Merl popped open the trunk of his cruiser. He anticipated rain soon, so he'd check the other side of the highway in a moment. He wanted to collect as much evidence as he could from the scene first. As he gathered his evidence kit, he watched McCumber drive down the road and circle in the dirt turnaround to avoid making an illegal U-turn. Merl watched him pass back by and nodded before remembering he had news to deliver.

This was the worst part of his job. He knew bad news must be passed in person. It made sense because if you were the one creating a panic situation, you needed to be there to calm the person. But Merl had made a promise. Made a promise that Mallison would know before anybody else. No matter what. He knew he'd get in trouble for not delivering the news personally. He dialed Mallison Callahan's number on his cellphone and hoped he wouldn't get the machine.

Chapter 22

Bleeeeet!!!!

Nobody ever called this time of afternoon anymore. Mallison Callahan remembered when Bobby called her every day. To talk about last night. To talk about tonight. To talk about ... She blushed. Certain conversations were private.

But that was before they were married.

Bleeeeet!!!!

After six months with Bobby gone, his friends didn't call anymore. Nor did hers. At first, they all had. Checking in on her. Asking if she needed things done around the house. Bringing lunch. Bringing dinner. Hauling her trash to the dump. Mowing the lawn. Giving her time to mend. She both appreciated the attention and hated it. It made her feel special. It made her feel weak. Each kindness reminded her of her loss. As she thanked them time and again, she wished they would quit. They soon did, her now unkempt lawn evidence that they considered her back to normal.

Bleeeeet!!!!

Mallison answered.

Bad news.

She sensed it before Merl Burt spoke.

"Mal," he said, still unsure the best way to put an anxious parent at ease without denying them important information. "This is Merl Burt. There's been an accident at the creek."

Creek!

There was no word on Earth or in Heaven that could unhinge Mallison Callahan more. She wailed so loudly that Merl yanked the phone away from his ear. He wished he had never dialed her number.

"My baby! Not my baby! Please God, not my baby," she cried, losing control.

Merl cursed under his breath, argued with himself as he listened for an opening in order to rein in Mallison's panic. *Damn promise. I shouldn't have done this over the phone. But somebody would have called her before I got there and she deserves to hear it first.* He ached at her pain as she continued to babble. *I'm never promising anything again.* He had to regain control of the situation.

"Mal," he said.

"No, no, no ..."

"Mal!"

"Baby, my baby, my baby ..."

"Mal! Shut up!!"

He stunned her into near silence. He could still hear her congested inhalations, her sniffles. He didn't wait for her fear to regain dominion.

"Mal," he said with slow diction. "Robbie's alive, but he's hurt. They've taken him to the hospital for precaution. I'm sending Officer Waters over to take you there. He should be there any minute. Okay?"

She nodded into the phone.

"Are you okay with that?" Merl asked.

"Okay," Mallison answered weakly.

"Good. Would you repeat what I just told you?"

Mallison nodded into the phone again, adding "Robbie's hurt. Andre's coming."

"You going to be all right until he gets there?"

"Yes."

"Good," Merl said. "We'll see you and Robbie in a few minutes."

Still in shock, Mallison reverted to a routine like a zombie. Instead of dropping the receiver, slumping to the floor and bawling, she hung it up. She removed the towel from the refrigerator handle and wiped off the clean kitchen counter. She straightened the doily on the couch back. She retrieved her coat from the hall closet. She'd be ready when Andre arrived. Not once did it dawn on her to snatch her car keys and race to the hospital.

Standing by the door, she nudged the curtain aside. It triggered a memory. She recalled Robbie, years ago, standing here on tiptoes, his face pressed against the glass.

"Whatcha doing, Honey?" she asked.

"I'm trying to see that bird you said Dad plays catch with," he said.

"What?" she said with a snorted laugh. "What makes you think Dad's chasing a bird?"

Unsure herself, she peeked out at the front yard hoping to catch a glimpse of Bobby darting about the lawn. It was empty.

"I didn't say he was chasing a bird," Robbie said. "You said he plays catch. Like he does with me and my ball."

Mallison become more confused. "When did I say Dad played catch with a bird?"

"This morning. Right before Dad left."

Mallison recalled arguing with Bobby in the kitchen. She was miffed he wanted to take out a second mortgage. She had no idea what Robbie might have heard.

"Do you remember what I said?" she asked.

"You said Dad throws cotton to the wren."

It took a second before laughter burst from Mallison. But when she saw the hurt look on Robbie's face, she tried to stop. Still giggling, she gave him a big hug.

"No, Honey, 'wind.' I said, 'He throws caution to the wind.' That's something adults say. It means your dad sometimes does things without thinking about the consequences. He takes chances, sometimes unnecessarily. It's one of the things I love about him. His derring-do."

"Derring-do?" Robbie wrinkled his nose. He grinned.

"Derring-do."

"It means going for it," she said.

A stern rap on the door jarred Mallison from her happier moment. She wiped a tear and pulled the curtain back. Officer Andre Waters stood on the porch. She prepared herself for the worst, the last news she received from Merl Burt reverberating in her head.

Chapter 23

Six months ago on a warm evening in April, Mallison Callahan sat at her kitchen table thinking her biggest regret was giving her mother-in-law a large glass pig for Christmas some 10 years ago. It not only drew open-mouthed disbelief when unwrapped, but offered up a running joke within the family over the next decade. *Get something you didn't like? At least it wasn't a glass pig!* Even Robbie used the line when he saw it drew a laugh.

However, Robbie's grandmother failed to see the humor. She took offense. She made sure her biting comments found flesh. She jousted to wound.

Thank God for Bobby. When Grannie Callahan kicked that Christmas present back across the floor at Mallison, he rode to her rescue.

"I picked it out myself," he lied to his mother. "I thought you'd like it."

Nobody believed him, but she loved her husband all the more for his defense. It helped her weather the good-natured wisecracks with a smile. It helped her resist rising to her mother-in-law's jabs.

That April evening when Bobby didn't come home, Mallison sat at the kitchen table staring at that pig, half filled with her husband's loose change. It reminded her how much God had blessed her. She had a wonderful husband—such a devoted father. She had a son she adored. A nice home. She felt good about their decision not to have another child since money woes confirmed that they couldn't afford all the things they wanted for one child, much less two.

When the power blinked off and back on that night, it stirred Mallison from her Eden. She wondered if the flickering had disturbed the clocks. She decided she'd better check them now before forgetting. She hoped the interruption had been too brief. It wasn't. They all flashed 12:00, 12:00, 12:00. Resetting the bedroom clock, she assumed Bobby would already be back. After all, he said he was on a milk run, his joking reference to an easy military operation. She looked out the window when she heard what sounded like a light tapping. She retreated downstairs and heard it again. She identified it as a tentative rap on the back door window.

Did Bobby forget his key?

She spotted Winnie Figgs through the window. She couldn't imagine what her neighbor wanted at this hour. She flipped on the porch light, opened the door. She spotted concern on Winnie's face.

"Are you okay?" Mallison asked.

"I'm fine. I came to check on you."

"Me. Whatever for?"

"Oh, I'm sorry. I thought they'd told you already."

"Told me what?" Mallison said, her voice rising. "Told me what," she echoed more sternly.

Winnie wanted to retreat but knew she couldn't. She wanted to play the role of consoling friend, not bearer of bad tidings. Mallison's third stern demand pulled it out her.

"Bobby was in an accident. I thought you knew."

Before the words sunk in completely, Mallison heard a car pull into the driveway. *Bobby's home, you old biddy.* Mallison raced to the front door and into the yard. Her breath halted at the sight of the police car. Her heart dropped when she heard the tone of deputy Merl Burt's voice. Her life crumbled when he told her Bobby was dead.

He can't be! He said he'd be right back. He always kept his word.

In the six months since then, Mallison shelved her grief. She poured herself into Robbie. Did all she could to ensure his happiness while, behind closed doors, she battled with losing her first love. She never knew how she'd managed without Bobby. But she'd survived. And Robbie was growing into a dependable young man of the house.

By October, she also erased as many memories as possible of the night Bobby died. She changed the ring tone on her phone to a pulse. She never bought another gallon of milk. She vowed never to speak to Merl Burt again. Not that she felt animosity toward the Soke deputy, but she sensed what emotional catalysts she couldn't control—the phone's ring, Bobby's un-bought milk and Merl's voice spiked pain into her. Until she could inure herself to them, she kept each quarantined. She liked Merl personally. She appreciated that he comforted Bobby in his last moments. She was grateful that he shared Bobby's final message of love, unaware Merl exchanged those words to something more soothing, something that didn't evoke the couple's nightmarish night at Landfalls Creek.

Mallison salved her grief over his death by rationalizing Bobby's decade-long nightmare ended in April while hers continued. She still couldn't shake that fear. Even now it could send tremors down her spine. Even after 10 years, six months and twelve days. In all that time, she never sensed exactly what the creek stole from Bobby. She never grasped that he was teaching their son defensive tactics with all those movies and war stories. Bobby could hide a secret.

She never knew—unlike most who gazed into Old Coals' eyes—that Bobby hadn't foreseen his own death. He perceived a terror greater. He saw his son looking at him and asking, "Why don't you love me?" Saw him sobbing, then lifeless. Saw the funeral, the under-sized casket, an empty bedroom and an inconsolable wife. After that night at the creek, Bobby had dedicated himself to avert that outcome, to do whatever it took to toughen Robbie mentally. To teach his son to be prepared for any circumstance. To be unafraid of what he didn't understand. To know how to apply those lessons under duress. But most of all, to convince him, no matter what, that he was loved beyond measure.

Bobby approached that mission with movies, trusting Robbie's recall would be better with images than words. He courted his wife's wrath in the process. They clashed over his film choices. She preferred a showing of *The Lion King* to *The Fisher King*. She would have gone ballistic if she'd known how often he'd shown a R-rated movie to their son. But Bobby felt the messages in *The Outlaw Josey Wales* were worth the risk. He wanted his son to know that in dire circumstances it's best to have an edge. Even if it's just the sun at your back.

Bobby's edge amounted to a gallon milk jug in the backseat. It wouldn't be enough when the creature came for him. Despite all his preparation, all the lessons he imparted to his son, Bobby Callahan wasn't ready. He even missed the warnings: the Maria Muldaur song that suddenly played on the radio as his headlights flashed across the reflective green and white sign that identified Landfalls Creek; the unexpected mist as he crossed the bridge and the chill that preceded the memory of his grandpa's death. He reacted only when he saw the pale wet image of his drowned son; his throat slit, standing in the roadway. It forced Bobby to swerve into the utility pole. Milk exploded across the windshield. The driver side door flew open, flinging Bobby 20 feet into the embankment that faced northbound traffic. His body broken, Bobby reached to check his throbbing head. His fingers dripped with blood. He couldn't feel his leg. Every breath hurt. Bobby prayed for one last chance to warn his son. Just one. As a pair of headlights approached, he willed himself to hang on long enough. The headlights didn't stop. Nor did the next. Each passing car drove Bobby deeper into despair.

He drifted in and out of consciousness. When he heard footsteps crunch nearby, he feared they weren't human. Until he heard Merl Burt bark at the paramedics to hurry. He pooled his energy as Merl told him to hang in there, that help would be here any minute. That he was going to be okay. Bobby knew differently. Summoning what strength remained, he clutched Merl's arm. Images of his grandpa's tearful face crowded his thoughts. He fought past them and saw Old Coals ooze through the beam from the headlights.

As Merl stared into Bobby's hardening eyes, his own mind yanked out an incongruous memory. Suddenly, Merl couldn't shake the sight of young Wendy Sullivan's mangled body. He almost moaned in grief. He recoiled as if punched when Bobby spoke.

"Robbie's in danger," he said. "Warn him."

Bobby looked past Merl, eyeing the approaching wraith. In despair he silently pleaded Old Coals accept him instead of Robbie. The creature extended a leprous hand. It introduced grief. Bobby wept as images revealed that his death would diminish his son's desire for life, would drown his son in sorrow. Any fight left in Bobby waned as depression mushroomed. Grandpa's tears. Robbie's death. The images overwhelmed him. He surrendered to inevitability. Bobby reached for the outstretched hand as a perplexed Merl asked a final question.

"Warn him about what?"

Bobby heard him not. He only acknowledged the creature.

"Old Coals," he said. "Old Coals."

Chapter 24

Dr. Benton Tyson didn't want to be at the hospital today. He wanted a cigarette. He wanted to board that plane to the tropics. He knew he should have waited to quit smoking. But he'd made a big fuss that he could kick the habit, that he'd start the morning of his trip to the islands. He'd stave off the early cravings of his addiction with heavy doses of caffeine. If that didn't work, he'd raid the stock of nicotine patches and gum. As a doctor, he knew better than to mix the two, but he figured he could handle it.

Before he checked his pager, mentally he'd already reached the beach. Wearing his blue Hawaiian-print shirt. Shoving a lime in the neck of his chilled Corona. Filling his nostrils with the cocoa butter oil baking on all but what the crimson bikini didn't cover on the lovely lady next to him. God, how he loved these singles resorts.

That all vanished as he returned the page and learned he no longer was off for the weekend. Meredith Olson had gone into labor. Dr. Jansen had called in sick. Dr. Brown had been involved in a minor traffic accident. *Damn them.* Still, Olson was his patient. *Damn her too. She wasn't due until next week.*

Dr. Tyson struggled through the birth. It was one of his toughest ever. *This is going to be a great day.* He needed a cigarette. Needed it bad. He'd sneak out for a quick puff. Who'd know he'd only lasted less than six hours? The difficult birth segued to a fishhook in Ernie

Phelps' scalp. That took longer than anticipated because Dr. Tyson fidgeted, jonesing over a nicotine fix. As he bummed a Camel off an orderly—he could almost taste the harsh flavor, feel the soothing chemical rush—the paramedics delivered Robbie Callahan to the ER. Dr. Tyson settled for gulping down another Coke.

The doctor didn't know the Callahans. Had he known that the young patient's father lay cold in the hospital morgue not six months ago, his first impulse would have been to clear space for a family reunion. Had he known what kind of reserves the 11-year-old possessed, he might have altered his diagnosis.

But Dr. Tyson didn't want to know. He didn't view patients as people. They were puzzles to be solved. Challenges to be met. It mattered that his patients got better but he only gleaned satisfaction from the completion of the process. Find the malady. Fix it. Move on. People? People botched things. They didn't take their meds. They never did what you told them. They obstructed and argued. People got in the way of real medicine.

While his approach removed emotion from the job, it hindered his advancement. Tyson's refusal to play office politics hurt too. But not as much as speaking his mind, which he often did at most inappropriate moments. That's how he landed not only at Harper Memorial, but also rather low on the medical depth chart. Dr. Tyson worried little about his career atrophy. He actually liked where he practiced. The small town folks let him be grumpy. They didn't intrude. They respected his free time. He would lose himself in those off hours, fathering mind-boggling crossword puzzles to submit to Sunday's *New York Times*. Throughout his two-story house, dozens of orphaned efforts, abandoned in frustration, awaited his attention.

So what was the patient in front of him? How about an 11-letter word for abnormally cold: H-Y-P-O-T-H-E-R-M-I-C. The kid's breathing held shallow but stable. His throat slit was minor; it was clear and clean and looked like a misguided tracheotomy. His body temperature hovered in the low 90s. His pulse beat weakly. His left hand clutched in a fist. And apparently he was saddled with bad luck after what nurse Maggie Peterson shared of the medically irrelevant family history.

Dr. Tyson continued the quick examination as Merl Burt, without being prompted, recited what facts he knew. He listened, hearing little that helped because it lacked pertinent data. How long was the patient without oxygen? How long was the body in the water? On any type of medication? Merl didn't know.

Dr. Tyson attacked the body chill first. He ordered blankets and a warm saline solution to raise the patient's temperature. He thought less of the throat wound than the cop. Merl harped on it, asking if the cut on the throat caused Robbie's condition.

"No," Dr. Tyson said. "It's an amateur tracheotomy."

"Come again?" Merl said.

"It's a slit, not a hole," Dr. Tyson said. "To open up the air passageway, you poke a hole in the trachea to allow in oxygen. A slit is less effective since it tends to close on itself. It also increases the risk of severing blood vessels. Somebody who didn't know what they were doing did this."

"Why would a drowning victim need his throat cleared?" Merl asked.

Dr. Tyson sighed. He cut his eyes toward Merl.

"The patient didn't drown," he said. "He asphyxiated. Even if he held his breath to prevent drowning, he would have passed out first. If he passed out, he would have started breathing and hydrated his lungs. Something blocked his airway because his lungs are clear. An obstruction caused the asphyxia. That was the threat. Not water."

"The button," Merl said, not realizing he said it out loud.

Dr. Tyson bobbed his head. "A button would do it. It would prevent him from hydrating his lungs. He's also lucky the icy water shocked his system and slowed his heart rate. It reduced the potential damage to his organs from oxygen deprivation. As bad of shape as he's in, it could have been a lot worse."

The button twisted Merl's thinking. Because of Robbie's soaked clothes, his bluish hue and the drag marks from the creek, Merl assumed a near drowning. Because of the wound, he'd assumed assault with a deadly weapon. Was he searching not for a punk but a hero? *Why would someone who just saved a kid run?* Clearly, someone fled the scene. That someone, Merl bet, was Alex Simons.

Mulling over that possibility, Merl missed Mallison Callahan's entrance. Dr. Tyson paid her no mind. He wanted a cigarette. Or at least another Coke.

"Oh, hey Mal," Merl said, caught off guard. He sounded like he had bumped into a friend unexpectedly. He knew it sounded too chipper for the circumstances. Mentally, he braced himself for her to unload on him. Whether he deserved it or not, he told himself to stand there and take both barrels. Even let her reload if she desired.

Focused on Robbie, Mallison whisked past. She almost convulsed, seeing tubes running in and out of her little boy. Merl stepped next to her. When the room burst into a cacophony of beeps, buzzes and shouts, she grabbed Merl's sleeve.

"What's happening?" she asked. Merl didn't know, shaking his head and arching his eyebrows. They watched nurses scurry. They mutely obeyed as an orderly guided them back from Robbie's bedside.

"What's happening?" Mallison asked the nurse with brown hair.

"He's in V-TAC," Maggie Peterson said.

That meant nothing to Mallison. Neither did the EKG numbers that sprang from around 100 to 180. But she could hear. The rhythmic beep every few seconds rushed into the next one until an ear could barely separate them. Before Mallison asked what it meant, the EKG flat-lined. An unbroken tone squealed. In horror, Mallison watched Dr. Tyson pound on Robbie's chest. Watched him administer CPR. Heard the low whine of the defibrillator charging to 200 joules. Saw them apply gel. Pull out paddles. Her hand covered her mouth.

"Clear!"

Petrified, Mallison saw Robbie's body convulse from the electric shock designed to re-start his heart. She trembled. She mouthed a soundless prayer. *Not Robbie. Not Robbie. Not Robbie.*

"Increase to 280," Dr. Tyson said.

He rubbed the paddles again.

"Clear!"

Robbie's body convulsed again. His left hand unclenched and clenched. The process repeated. No change. Seconds raced into minutes.

"You are not going to take both my men!" Mallison screamed. All but Robbie turned toward her. She addressed neither the hospital staff nor God. Her words carried venom. They flung fury. "You cannot have this one too!"

Trapped by her terror over Robbie, Mallison failed to notice no eyes met hers. She didn't register that they ceased working on her son. She didn't hear Dr. Tyson speaking in hushed tones to the nursing staff. Missed his checking the clock and noting the time. Nearly six minutes had passed.

"I'm going to call it," Dr. Tyson said. He glanced up at the clock.

This time, Mallison heard him. She also heard the even tone from the EKG screaming at her.

"Time of death …"

"Robert Wilson Callahan!" Mallison screamed. "You get back here this instant!"

Chapter 25

For Robbie, everything slowed down. His thoughts ... seemed ... to ... drag ... out. He listened to his heart. It thumped quietly. He wondered if he could make it stop altogether. He knew that would rile his mom. Better not. As Shrek would say, he was going the right way for a smack bottom.

Something prodded him. *C'mon! What if?* The beat of his heart thinned as an oppressive force cloaked him. He saw his father's ashen face. He wanted to cry. A gaunt hand offered itself. Robbie's heart fluttered. Two massive orbs suddenly materialized. *Eyes!* Blood-red veins streaked away from pupils, swirling with the reward of dementia. Robbie's heart halted.

He felt himself drifting. Floating. Sailing.

What did Donkey say? Stay away from the light? That was it. Stay away from the light!

Instantly, Robbie's entire world flashed bright as if lightning struck. His body felt like bumblebees covered it. Reeled back to where he started, Robbie drifted again. Floating. Sailing. Serene. Unafraid now.

Pow!

Another bright flash. Bumblebees. Dragged back again.

Drifting. Floating. Sailing. Robbie soared. He looked down. He saw his lifeless body. How peaceful he seemed. Robbie glanced around. He hovered near the ceiling. *Mondo-riffic! This has got to be the coolest thing ever.* Robbie wondered if this was what angels did. He checked if he had wings. He didn't. He checked if he were being held aloft by wires. He wasn't. He wondered why the doctor kept glancing his way. *Can he see me?* Robbie didn't notice the clock on the wall behind him. A desire to depart infused Robbie. But he knew better than to leave his room without making his bed first. Maybe just this once, he could get away with it. He couldn't. His mother yelled. Her voice boiled with anger.

"Robert Wilson Callahan! You get back here this instant!"

Robbie gazed down. He saw Dr. Tyson give his mom a funny look. He saw him signal the man in the green smock. He realized they were going to take his mother away. Robbie ached to feel her arms around him again.

The EKG's even tone broke.

Beep ... beep ... beep.

"Son of a," Dr. Tyson said in shock.

Maggie Peterson smiled.

Way to go, Robbie. Way to go! Somebody up there really likes you.

Mallison rushed to her son's side. She heard the beeps that indicated Robbie's heart was beating again. That he was, indeed, alive. But it wasn't enough.

"Why isn't he waking up?" she asked.

Chapter 26

"Wake up, Robbie!"

The voice sounded far away. Or muted. Almost like being underwater. That thought stirred Robbie. Shook him. Underwater. Bad things happened there. He moaned. He heard faraway voices. One broke through like a sunburst.

"Rise and shine, sleepyhead!"

Robbie spied his dad in the doorway.

"I need you to do me a favor this morning, Sport."

Still feeling dreamlike, Robbie muttered, *"Urgmmhoff."*

"Don't make me get a cold washcloth and cover your face."

Robbie caught the playful tone of Dad's voice. *Is he up to something?*

"Five more minutes," was all Robbie could say before he dozed off again. He barely heard the water running in the bathroom, the splashing of a wrung washcloth. Before his mind could piece together the clues in time, damp cold swamped his face. Robbie bolted upright amid his dad's laughter.

"I told you I'd do it," his dad said, smiling. *"Next time, you'll believe me, won't you?"*

Robbie chuckled.

"Bank on it, Bub," his dad said. *"You ready to do me a favor?"*

Robbie must have nodded because his dad continued.

"Can you be my right-hand man and cut part of the backyard for me?"

Robbie's eyes grew as large as his grin. *Cut the yard? Cut the yard! That was the coolest thing. This was getting called up to the Big Leagues. This was time to thank the Academy. This was the few, the proud, the Marines.*

"Is that a 'yes'?" his dad asked.

Robbie nodded, his mind already in the backyard. His dad grinned. *"Get ready. Get some breakfast. Meet me in the garage."*

Robbie sprang out of bed. He dashed into the bathroom. After a few splashes, he returned. He yanked open his bureau drawer. This mission demanded his green shirt—the one with the snarling T-Rex on it. The one that made him impervious to the backyard dinosaurs. *Kept those Raptors in their place. Kept those Stegos out of your face.* Robbie's head bobbed, keeping time to his song. *Yes sir, keeps the Aliens out in space. Or I'd be gone without a trace.*

Faraway voices again. Robbie strained to listen to them. They were gone. Probably just Dad downstairs.

No T-Rex in the drawer. *Where was that thing?* Robbie peered into the closet. He didn't like going in there. Not that he was afraid, but he'd recently heard of witches and lions in the wardrobe. He wasn't sure if it were a good thing or a bad thing. Best not to take chances. Hanging onto the door frame in case something tried to grab him from within, he scanned the hanging shirts. Nothing there. Debating his next option, he stepped into his jeans and sat to pull on his socks. *Think like a detective. Piece the clues together and draw a conclusion.*

Aha! The shirt had to be in the laundry room with Colonel Mustard and the candlestick! If Miss Scarlet had it, Robbie would be so embarrassed. He had a crush on her but didn't want anybody to know he liked girls, especially that little girl in the red dress from kindergarten. Confident he'd solved the mystery, Robbie slid on the hardwood floor at the top of the stairs. He bounded down them two at a time. He zipped through the kitchen and burst into the laundry, startling Gentry. Robbie laughed. The cat, so frozen she seemed stuffed, stared. Robbie scanned the clothesline. *Yahtzee!* He yanked the shirt. It hugged the hanger as it struggled free, jangling its wire brethren into a frenzied noisy slam dance. Robbie froze. When none fell, Robbie expected Gentry to laugh back. She was long gone. Robbie thrust himself into the stiff t-shirt. The T-Rex sneered at all with the message, "T-ROB Rules." He and his dad bought tandem t-shirts at Six Flags last summer. His dad's displayed a dinosaur from the old movies with the warning, "Don't mess with Bob-zilla."

Robbie opened the door to the garage. He peeked out to make sure his dad wasn't teasing about cutting the grass. Dad crouched over the lawn mower.

"*Eaten anything?*" his dad asked.

Although anxious to start, Robbie chose not to lie. He was bad at it. But he couldn't wait much longer. His dad sensed his conflict.

"*I need time to get the mower ready,*" he said. "*Take me about as long as it takes you to eat a bowl of cereal.*"

Robbie closed the door. *I'm on the clock. Milk. Bowl. Spoon. What to eat? Cap'n Crunch. Cheerios. Corn Pops. Cheez-Its. Aargh, those aren't breakfast food. Stay focused. The Cap'n slows you down with the gunk on the back teeth. Cheerios, there are just so hard to catch when you get to the end of the bowl. Corn Pops are it. Easy to catch. Easy to wolf down.* Minutes later, Robbie charged into the garage, his bowl and spoon clattering in the sink.

"Ready?"

"Yes, sir!"

"*Okay, Sarge, here's the drill. Safety first and foremost. We always protect ourselves. So NEV-VER place yourself in danger. I don't want my favorite person in the whole world getting hurt.*"

His dad tilted the lawnmower up to expose the blade underneath.

"*Get a good look. That can take a toe or foot off faster than you think. I'm not saying that to scare you. I want you to respect this machine. To know it's not a toy. Got that?*"

"*Sir, yes, sir!*" Robbie added a salute for emphasis.

His dad showed him the starter button, where to place the red lever for ignition, where to place it once the engine started. How to stop the mower immediately. He insisted Robbie repeat the routine several times. Robbie relished how powerful the engine revved. So fierce. So thrilling. The blade's danger. The grip's control. It must be like riding a tiger. Could he tame it? Robbie almost missed his dad's next question. He cupped his ear. He released the grip. The engine sputtered silent.

"*What do you do if something feels wrong?*" his dad asked.

"*I release the grip and get you.*"

Dad nodded.

"*If you get tired, release the handle and rest. No reason to rush.*" He drilled that safety trumps all. Doing a good job comes second. Robbie had watched his dad so often that he didn't need this lesson. Yet he welcomed the undivided attention. It felt magical. It seemed like so long since he'd last seen him.

They walked toward the backyard. Robbie tailed his dad. He pushed the idle mower. A flat patch awaited the mower's attention. Robbie knew his dad left it for him. Show time! *Prepare for a buzzcut, numbnuts. Zip, zap. Hair on the floor. Zip, zap. Give me some more. Wait a minute, why not cut in a pattern just like they do at big league ballparks? There was this one game where they cut a pair of socks in the outfield. It was the coolest thing.*

"*Anything wrong,*" his dad asked.

Robbie shook his head. *Go for the haircut.* He rolled the mower to the edge. He primed the pump, locked the lever to start and pushed the button. Growwwwl! Robbie locked the lever to medium. The engine calmed from a roar to a purr. Robbie smiled. He possessed the power now. A new terror had come to Bug City. This mean machine would slice through whole towns like the Grim Reaper. He watched grasshoppers flee in fright. He was the all-powerful. He was the magnificent. His majesty exerted himself through the high grass. Behind him trailed the fresh-mown look of a carpet recently vacuumed. This was a job well done. This was the best grass cutting ever! After a few passes, sweat trickled down his forehead. *Man's work.* Wiping his arm across his forehead offered no relief. His arms were as wet as his face. Robbie released the mower handle. He lifted his shirt to dry his face. He paused, realizing he'd been distracted for too long by his glory. Too busy wiping out bug cities. Robbie had forgotten about the woods. Had forgotten that raptors roamed in there with their sharp talons waiting to rip into flesh. Wasn't that why he was wearing his T-Rob shirt? He knew raptors came at the sound of a lawnmower. It signaled an easy meal. It's what drew them into the neighborhood. *They got Mr. Rilson that way. The raptors got him for sure.* An older boy said their neighbor down the street was cold and stiff when the ambulance arrived. *Sirens must have scared the raptors before they could finish him off.*

Mr. Rilson lay uneaten in the grass.

Right next to the woods.

The woods. Robbie's breathing intensified. He listened hard. He peered intently. He could see nothing out of the ordinary. Just oaks and elms and pines. It wasn't raptors Robbie need fear. What stood among the oaks and elms and pines claimed their feral nature eons ago.

Robbie felt the creepy crawlies. He shivered. He sensed something stared at him.

Chapter 27

The beeps from the EKG now were the sweetest sounds Mallison Callahan ever heard. Better than Beethoven. More soothing than Sarah McLachlan. Those beeps meant she had her son back even if the doctor said he was in a coma. At least, Robbie was alive. And he would awake. Mallison just knew it. She cradled his hand. She couldn't stop smiling as she stared at him. She couldn't stop crying.

"Don't you ever leave me again," she said. She watched his chest rise and fall. "Don't you ever scare me like that again."

She debated whether what Dr. Tyson said were true. That her words were getting through. She thought about what he said, "He's still in critical condition. He's just shown he's a fighter. The next 24 hours will tell us more. Let him hear your voice, hear something familiar, music even. Be positive. Even if he can't communicate, he can hear you."

The doctor also told her all they could do now was wait. Mallison knew how to do that. She'd done it every morning, awaiting her men to come down for breakfast. She'd done it every afternoon, awaiting the comforting sound of the front door to know Robbie was home safe from school. She'd done it every evening for Bobby to do the same from work.

But Bobby no longer came home.

Mallison stopped herself. She wouldn't think that way. *No negativity in this room.* She'd bombard Robbie with so many positive messages, he'd be forced to wake up. *That was reality. Anything else was fiction.*

When he wakes, I'll be right here. But she knew she couldn't just sit waiting, praying. If the past six months taught her anything, it was action. She needed to make progress, to feel like she was accomplishing something. Anything. Waiting, sitting silent, wouldn't improve the situation.

She started talking. She told him how much she loved him. She told him when she first learned she was pregnant—told him a sirloin steak and baked potato dinner helped usher him into the world—that that big meal sent them racing to the hospital. She told him that Dad was so nervous he left a tip on the table but forgot to pay the bill. Mallison recounted that three floors down, Robbie arrived with all ten fingers and all ten toes and a tuft of dark hair. Even back then, she thought, her young man seemed to be entertaining himself. He flashed the silliest grin when the nurses first placed him in her arms.

Thinking how fast he had grown, Mallison continued her one-way conversation. She told Robbie he was the most handsome boy she had ever seen. That he'd make a girl's heart flutter. *Maybe when you have your first child, you won't faint like your father.* She chuckled.

"I'm so lucky to have you," she said. "I thank God everyday for you. You don't know how proud I am when people tell me how well behaved you are. How polite you are. How impressed they are. Though, you know, I don't care for those silly war stories."

She caressed his cheek with the back of her hand.

"The nurses think you are so adorable. They say you're going to be a real heart-breaker."

Mallison felt an onrush of tears. She braced to forestall them. She had to find something to lift her spirits. She couldn't keep doing this alone.

Dang it, Bobby, I need you so much!

A knock on the door startled her.

"Come in," she said.

Her mother already was entering.

"Thought you could use this," she said, hefting a portable CD player into view before setting it on the counter. "They say it's good to play music. Very therapeutic."

"Thanks," Mallison said. She cuddled in the warmth of her mother's hug. It energized her.

"I've got one of the kids at the store tracking down a laptop to play some DVDs too. He said he'd bring it by later."

"That would be great."

Emily patted her grandson on the arm. She leaned over and kissed him on the cheek.

"The Lord is watching over you, Sweetness," she said.

Overwhelmed, Mallison sobbed. Emily rejoiced in the release, but didn't encourage it. She wrapped her arms around her daughter again and offered affirmation.

"There, there," she said. "Everything's going to work out for the best. You know it will. You stay positive. He's got too many people praying for him and too much good to do in this world for the Lord to take him just yet."

She leaned back and waited to make eye contact before speaking again.

"This isn't where his story ends," she said.

Mallison started to speak. Her mother touched a finger to her lips and said, "Nunt-uh."

"Now, I threw some DVDs in my bag for later," Emily said. "I'm not sure what I brought. Let me see. There's *The Princess Bride*, *Apollo 13*, *Shrek*, *The Little Mermaid*, *Willy Wonka* and *It's a Wonderful Life*. Ummmm, *Star Wars* and *The Outlaw Josey Wales*."

"I don't know about that last one, but the rest are perfect," Mallison said. "Did you bring any CDs for now? Or a book?"

"Sorry. Didn't think about a book. There's a CD in there, but I couldn't find any of Robbie's. They all looked like Bobby's old ones."

"They'll do," Mallison said. "He had Robbie listening to them anyway. I still can't get over hearing him sing songs I listened to in high school."

"And you never sang any Dean Martin songs when you were little?"

Mallison laughed. She started singing.

"I really can't stay."

"But Baby, it's cold outside," Emily answered.

"I've got to go away."

"But Baby, it's cold outside."

Amused tears trickled down their cheeks as they continued their duet. They joined hands to add their little tug-and-spin dance to their performance. There were no annoyed objections. When they closed in unison with "Baby, it's cold. Baby, it's cold outside!" nobody had departed in a huff. Laughter echoed off walls more accustomed to groans.

Mallison hugged her mom again.

"Love ya," Emily said.

"I love you too, Mom."

She watched her mother bend and kiss Robbie on the cheek again. Emily winked as she left the room.

Mallison popped open the CD player's door. She eyed the disc and thought maybe Bobby was offering assistance. It housed the CD he gave their son, "Snoopy vs. the Red Baron." She pushed play. It would be the refreshing tonic she needed.

As the recording's narrator shouted gibberish, the music from The Royal Guardsmen took flight. Mallison silently sang along with the lyrics as she watched Robbie. *How he loved this song.* Mallison remembered a dinner party last year. They gabbed in the den when he marched in unannounced. Donned in his Power Rangers pajamas and swim goggles, he had tied a blue towel around his neck as a flying scarf. When the dinner guests turned, Robbie started his solo.

After the turn of the century, in the clear blue skies over Germany.
Came a roar and a thunder men had never heard.
Like the screaming sound of a big war bird ...

Robbie warbled from start to finish before the rapt audience. When done, he bowed deeply to applause and pirouetted. He spanned his arms like aircraft wings and flew back to his room. Thereafter, any time Bobby's friends visited, they always asked how the "Red Baron" was doing. She chuckled at the memory. She sang along with "Snoopy's Christmas" until Dr. Tyson pushed open the door. The blinds on its backside shivered, signaling an entrance.

"Checking to see how everybody's doing," he said, chomping on a piece of gum.

"I guess we're fine," Mallison said. She rose and tapped the pause button.

"Don't do that," Dr. Tyson said. "Got to hear the Baron say 'Merry Christmas, my friend.'"

Mallison noticed that he spoke the line with a German accent. *Did every male own this CD?*

Dr. Tyson flipped through the charts. He chatted idly over the music. She could tell he wasn't listening to her answers. He rubbed Robbie's right hand. He did nothing with the clenched left hand other than note it remained tight. He gripped Robbie's wrist and eyed his watch, tracking the pulse. Mallison wondered if he played a real doctor on TV. He now sounded like he did.

"The tests we've gotten back indicate no brain damage. Everything looks positive. At this point, the rest is up to him. We should know more in the morning. He seems to be on the mend but we're not out of the woods yet. Keep up the good work in here."

"Thank you," Mallison said.

As Dr. Tyson departed, she heard him sing, "Hey, watch out Red Baron. Snoopy is on your tail."

Mallison smiled. She pictured Robbie dashing down the hallway, his scarf flapping behind him. She had no idea the trouble toward which he chose to fly.

Chapter 28

Hearing the rat-a-tat-tat of enemy strafing, Robbie bolted from his barracks and raced toward his Sopwith Camel. He glanced skyward, watching the blood-red triplane zoom back toward German lines.

Robbie shook his fist because he knew that's what Snoopy would have done. As he reached his plane, Robbie felt his scarf flapping in the stiff wind. He surveyed the skies before giving his plane the once-over. As customary, he started at the front and moved clockwise so that when his inspection was complete, he'd be off the left wing and ready to climb into the cockpit. *A-OK!*

He hopped up on the wing and stepped into the cockpit. His mechanic stood below. *It was Dad!*

"You know how much I love you, don't you?" Dad yelled up at him with cupped hands.

Robbie gave a thumbs-up. His dad responded in kind.

"Now, crank the engine and let's bag a bad guy," Robbie shouted.

"That's the spirit!"

Robbie patted the German crosses on his fuselage. He totaled 12, seven more than necessary to be an ace. He knew his nemesis displayed many more, knew because the Royal Guardsman sang about it all the time, "Eighty men died trying to end that spree. Of the Bloody Red Baron of Germany."

Robbie would bring down Baron von Richthofen. He just knew it. His biplane's prop churning, Robbie waved his dad back. He tugged his goggles over his eyes. His dad dragged away the chocks. Robbie eased off the brake. The plane rolled forward.

He steered toward the runway. Knowing too much speed too soon could flip him, he slowly powered the engine. He gathered speed across the field, counteracting the engine torque by keeping the rudder full right. He pulled the flaps up. The plane jumped in the air. Robbie banked slightly, circling the field to gain altitude before racing off to hunt a red dot in the sky.

The sensation of air rushing past felt like the greatest freedom. Even the roar of the engine relaxed him. Robbie believed flying a plane must be the coolest thing. He loved flying dreams. It was like the world was all his. He could go anywhere. He could do anything. He scanned the clear sky in front of him.

Tap, tap, tap.

What was that? Needing no answer, Robbie veered sharply as instinct registered that bullets were striking his fuselage and wing. The Baron was on his six. So close on his tail in fact, Robbie recognized his famed grimace.

Stupid, stupid, stupid. Robbie thought. *Graveyards are filled with pilots not paying attention.*

He pitched his Sopwith Camel into a short, steep dive to build getaway speed. Since he didn't have the drop on his adversary, this battle belonged to the Baron. Robbie's battle was survival. He knew his plane's strength in a dogfight rested in its ability to turn quickly. He knew the Baron's plane could out-climb anything in the sky. But it wasn't as fast as a Camel.

Dipping swiftly out of range, Robbie checked the compass to ensure his heading. He knew the wind blew toward enemy lines so he wanted to make sure he wasn't drifting. He reminded himself that he'd be fighting the wind on the way home too. He checked his fuel gauge and tried to keep the Baron out of the sun. If the Hun were in the sun, Robbie would be victim No. 81.

Again, he scanned the skies. The red plane with the white tail rudder and the bold black German cross had vanished. Constantly altering his course, Robbie angled back to his airfield. He knew flying in a straight line put many a pilot underground. He placed his thumb over the sun to see if the Baron were hiding there.

Bingo!

Phffzztt! Phffzztt! Phffzztt! Three tracers zipped past Robbie's plane. Believing he rolled away from the trailing fire, Robbie now saw the Red Baron zooming straight at him. As the two hurtled closer in an aerial game of chicken, Robbie aimed. He pressed his guns. He watched flowers shoot toward the Baron.

Curses! Foiled again!

The Baron's guns blazed. Robbie assumed they were missing since he was still alive. *"Or was it the bells from the village below" like in the song?* Robbie heard no Christmas bells. *This was it. Would the Baron bank?* If so, Robbie had him dead to rights, provided his bullets weren't still daffodils. The Baron already knew what to do. His cool had killed 80 men. Robbie flew straight on, guns ready. Time running out.

He won't shoot again until the last second. He'll draw me in and fire. Or he'll expect me to run away and he'll be right on my tail. I'm an easy kill either way.

Robbie held one option: Guess right and time it perfectly. Staying alive now meant split-second anticipation. If he broke too late, he'd fly into lethal gunfire. If he broke too soon, he'd fly himself into his foe's perfect pursuit position, be at his mercy. But guess right and live to fight another day. Robbie saw the Baron's plane tilt. He read it as a break to the left. Either follow and hope his guns worked or bank away and head home safely. An instant before the Baron's machine guns burst with bullets, Robbie opted for the safe route. He turned. The Baron banked, too.

In the same direction.

He faked me!

The planes almost collided. As they crisscrossed within feet of each other, Robbie glimpsed his adversary. What looked back wasn't the Bloody Red Baron of Germany. What piloted the blood-colored triplane with the black cross on the tail pointed a finger at Robbie. It beckoned.

Robbie had seen it before. Each time, it extended a hand. Robbie dove his plane for home. He swiveled his head to check for pursuit. None. Robbie took a deep breath and relaxed. He tapped his fuel gauge. He would make it home safely. He wondered about the future. Would his luck hold? He sure hoped so. He had no doubt they would meet again.

But when? Robbie checked the skies repeatedly. No sign of that thing. It now chased after another victim.

Chapter 29

Exhausted by his long run from the creek, Alex Simons stopped in the middle of Toby Keith's "Should Have Been a Cowboy" when he reached his destination. He didn't give a rat's patootie about Marshall Dillon and Miss Kitty right now.

Breathing heavily, Alex scanned the area. Standard procedure. He always made sure no one was about. And those college kids always seemed to be nearby on a Saturday afternoon. Hearing just the wind, Alex fought through thick branches and stepped into a small cave. He crouched and shuffled down the entryway toward the recessed floor, bracing himself with a hand on the granite ceiling.

His lair. Maintaining its secrecy was part reason for his hatred of the college kids. He worried their curiosity of the abandoned quarry's surroundings might prompt exploration. His place was well-hidden, but if they found it, they'd claim it for their own. Alex couldn't abide that violation. This was his sanctuary. This was his church.

Still laboring to catch his breath, Alex realized he held the kid's wet jacket. He had no idea why. Well, maybe he did. He searched the pockets. He discovered a thin black flashlight, a stick of Big Red chewing gum and a wad of trash. Alex tried the flashlight. It worked. He draped the jacket over the cave's largest rock, what Alex considered his rock-hard bean bag chair.

While his body replenished itself with oxygen, Alex tried not to get too light-headed as he sat. Several times he had to walk around to avoid blacking out. He knew to master his emotions, he had to master his body. Once calmed, he could think clearly. He sat down again and eyed the cave opening, listening for what might come. Tried to quiet his breathing.

He unwrapped the stick of chewing gum, surprised that it wasn't soggy. He wadded the wrapper and tossed it behind the rock. He almost yelled "Mail Call!" out of habit.

Long ago, his exploration of this small bean-shaped enclosure revealed a narrow gap that opened into some kind of cavern. The gap, which looked like a mail slot, was wide enough to swallow a soda can, proven innumerable times. Alex tossed trash, cans, pennies, cigarette butts and, sometimes, evidence into the chasm. *Probably leads straight to the gates of Hell.* Alex never could figure out how far down it went. No matter how strong a flashlight he used, he couldn't penetrate its gloom. When he threw pennies and other coins down it, he listened to them clink and clink and clink. Sometimes, he'd never hear them hit. His echoes always would. They seemed to go on forever, almost running away. No matter what he threw, he felt the need to announce it, "Fire in the hole! Incoming!"

Because the chasm drew in air, Alex learned he could toss paper over his shoulder and it would get sucked into Mother Nature's trashcan. The air intake also proved advantageous because Alex could smoke or light a fire without signaling his presence. The smoke funneled into the tunnel instead of billowing out the entrance or fouling the air. The downside was trying to keep a candle lit. The suction from the slit maintained a steady cooling breeze inward that could snuff out a single flame. Alex solved that by a trick he saw on a TV show. He used an upright brick as a shield from the current.

As his body calmed and his mind cleared, Alex didn't focus on what he'd just done. He didn't ponder how Robbie was doing. Instead, he felt an urgent need to glue those gnome heads back on their bodies. On the correct bodies. He knew they remained hidden in his father's shed. Safe. Preserved. *None of them have eyes like that kid.* Alex swore those eyes bored right into him, absorbing him, coming for him. He saw himself in them. He tried not to think about it.

It wasn't my fault.
I thought he was already dead.
I slashed that kid and left him to die.
I'm so sorry.

He'd be denied the chance to apologize. Something far worse than regret loomed.

Chapter 30

Since he would pass it en route from the hospital to the Simons' place, Merl stopped at the police station for a quick coffee. He poured himself a cup and approached Andre Waters.

"Hey, thanks for fetching Mal Callahan for me," he said.

Andre nodded. "She's tore up plenty."

"Rough day," Merl said.

"She went on and on about that creek."

"Suppose so. Quite a bit of history there."

Andre expected Merl to keep talking. He waited for the story. Instead, Merl slurped several sips in succession. Andre waited. He doodled on a notepad. Merl stared out the window. The silence lengthened.

"Ah, the kid gonna make it?" Andre finally asked.

Merl shrugged. "Don't know. Touch and go is my guess. I wouldn't bet against him."

"Don't like his chances," Andre said. "Not being in that creek. Something spooky about that water."

Merl spit out an exasperated sigh.

"Don't believe everything you hear," he said. He ambled across the room. His leather belt creaked as he moved. He placed his cup on top of the gray metal file cabinet and thought better of it. He set it on the table. When he jerked open the middle drawer, the entire cabinet shook. Merl crouched as he walked his fingers down both sides of the drawer to the "L's." He spotted what he sought. He shoved the files to clear room and extracted a folder that hadn't been touched since he put it there years ago. He only remembered its existence because he'd been told to file it back when he was young and curious.

He slapped the file on Andre's desk. He pointed at the creased tab. Andre's chair groaned when he leaned forward. He read the green felt script, "Landfalls Creek—EPA (1974)." When Andre looked up, Merl spun the file and flipped it open to the first page. He pointed to the section that indicated trace levels in the creek tested above government standards. He shuffled pages to the end of the report. He pointed to the handwritten comment at the bottom: "Sample more pure than any previously tested water in the region.—S. Donohue."

Merl waited for Andre to sit back.

"Nothing wrong with that water," Merl said. "Don't go putting much stock in ghost stories. They never solve a crime."

"Can't arrest what you can't handcuff," Andre said, grinning.

Merl pointed his finger like a gun and fired. "Bingo."

"I'm heading over to check on the Simons' place," Merl added. "Keep an ear on the radio, will ya?"

"Expecting trouble?" Andre said.

"Not at all. More worried about that dog."

"Cujo's a darling," Andre said, laughing. "He wouldn't hurt anything but raw meat."

"Comforting," Merl said, spreading his arms. "Come and get it."

Andre waved him off. "I'll stay close."

Merl exited the station and climbed into his cruiser. He turned right onto Hallman Street. He made a quick left on Oak and, two blocks later, a right on Day Drive. He maintained the speed limit the short distance to the Simons' residence. He knew he was being generous calling a torn-up trailer held together by everything but tolerance a residence.

He parked outside the tall chain-link fence. He expected their irritable Rottweiler to be running loose. She was, rolling over a low growl with no bark. Because of the dog, Merl honked. He waited for Eddie Simons to open the trailer door. He expected him to be in boxers and on his way to getting drunk. Right on both counts. Merl hollered from his car window.

"Looking for Alex! He here?"

"Why you want him?"

"I'm just making sure he's all right and to thank him."

"Yeah, right. That stupid kid never did a thankful thing in his life. He could go on and die for all I care. He ain't here. Search the place if you want."

Merl wondered where Eddie kept all his Parent of the Year trophies. He climbed out of his car. The dog attacked the fence, barking madly. Merl almost sat back down, but held his ground.

He watched Eddie stagger through the tall weeds and stop next to a rusted wagon.

"Angel, sit!" Eddie said. The dog obeyed. He lurched a few steps and stroked the dog's head. "Good girl. Who's my baby?" The dog panted, hackles raised, never taking its eyes off the threat it sensed from outside the fence.

"Do you know where Alex might be?" Merl asked.

"Could be in the backyard. Could be in the house. Could be anywhere. Told you he ain't here."

"Mind if I check?"

"Knock yourself out."

"The dog."

"Dog's mine," Eddie said, as if possession were an issue. "She ain't got nothing to do with Alex."

"Chain the dog up, Eddie."

"Dog ain't bothering you. Chaining her is cruel."

Rather than argue the point, Merl reversed tack, one to which Simons was much more accustomed.

"Eddie!" he hollered. "Chain the dog and I won't charge you with assaulting an officer with a deadly weapon."

Simons sneered, inwardly pleased that Angel was considered a deadly weapon. After a few tries, he hooked a chain to the Rottweiler. He glared at Merl as if to say, "You satisfied now?" Merl wasn't. He still wanted to locate Alex.

"Mind if I come in and see if Alex is here?"

"Whatever," Simons said.

Merl accepted the reluctant acquiescence. He kept an eye on the dog, which stood sentinel with the chain taut. Merl looked into Simons' blurry eyes and informed him that Alex might be in trouble. He made it clear that the trouble wasn't with the law. Simons didn't buy it. He repeated he hadn't seen Alex all day.

Merl stepped into the trailer. The stench nearly gagged him. He buried his face in the crook of his arm. He did a quick survey of the interior. He saw no sign that Alex was there. He saw plenty of reasons why Alex wanted to be elsewhere. He checked the back rooms and closets.

"May I check the shed?" Merl asked.

"Already said so," Simons snapped.

Rather than rise to the sarcasm, Merl said, "Thank you, Mr. Simons."

He moved to the back of the yard. He kept his weapon holstered, not expecting trouble. He knew Eddie wouldn't waste energy even to unleash his dog out of spite.

Merl moved toward the shed, a make-shift wooden structure that housed a junkman's dream. The front was covered with hubcaps and rusted license plates from states that Simons had never seen. He even had two chrome fenders hanging unevenly. Merl thought they looked like a pair of sneering lips.

"Alex, you in there?" Merl called out. Silence. "Robbie's fine. He's at the hospital. The doctors say they think you saved his life." He left the reason he was here dangling, hoping to prompt a response. None came.

Merl unhooked the safety lock on the door. He flipped the steel latch to the side. Pushing the door open, he peeked through the crack. Nobody behind it. He glanced inside, exposing himself only as a small target. He scanned the room. There wasn't much space to hide. He doubted Alex was in there, but he'd been trained to doubt.

After completing a mental checklist, Merl stepped inside. Instantly moving away from the door, he re-evaluated the scene. His quick inventory revealed the horizontal freezer as the lone hiding place. He glanced behind it. No space and no Alex. He observed the doorway. Neither Eddie nor the Rottweiller cared enough to watch.

Merl knew he had to open the freezer. He heard it humming. He realized it was sealed. The worst possible place to hide. He hoped Alex was smarter than that.

Alex was.

When Merl lifted the lid, he almost laughed. There among the frozen venison were eight ceramic gnome heads. All were wrapped in clear plastic bags as if to prevent them from spoiling.

While the freezer's contents solved one mystery, it presented another. *What is Alex going to do with those heads?* Merl would ask when he found him.

But if Alex weren't here, then where? Merl got a bad feeling. He knew one secluded spot to check for him. It would be his next stop. He only hoped he got there in time.

Chapter 31

Alex Simons hid in the only spot he felt safe.

He felt invisible here. Like he had disappeared through a trap door in the forest floor. Giving the slip to those hunters last summer confirmed it. After spotting him pinching some smokes out of their pickup, they had searched the area for almost an hour. From his lair, Alex listened to their feet crunching the pine straw. He snickered at their threats and curses. Only he knew how close they were to snaring a holed rabbit.

This place had always offered haven for Alex. Now, as a chill shivered through him, he began to doubt his security. He feared tree branches pointed to where he hid, that the squirrels chattered his location to something dreaded before they fled. In the quiet, Alex imagined peril approached. He just knew it was no woodland creature. He riveted on the cave opening. Waiting for a shadow to pass. Watching for a hand or claw to draw back a branch. Wondering who, or what, would step inside.

Seconds passed. Minutes. Felt like hours. Something neared. He sensed it. He feared it. Alex stared, afraid what might happen if he blinked. He was sure the instant he shut his eyes something horrible would grab him. If it didn't, he feared opening them and seeing what came for him.

Breathing in a hush, Alex tried to disappear within himself. Make himself so small and immobile that not even a snake would pay him any mind. *Just move on. Nothing there.* Whatever stalked him would pass by like those hunters, never knowing he was here.

Despite the faint breeze from the cool depths of the cave, sweat dripped off Alex's nose. It plopped on the cave floor. It sounded like an explosion. He almost wet himself.

He thought the air went still. Rather than notice the faint odor that intruded, Alex, instead, pictured the day his mother left. Pictured her packing her belongings, sizing him up with a hard stare and deciding she would rather do without him. He shoved that memory aside with annoyance. He focused on the plan, the one to ruin the quarry for those college kids. Even that depressed him. It had gone so awry. He'd wasted that opportunity, failed to create that great spectacle of Bucky diving off the cliff.

Hell. Dad was right. I'd screw up a one-car funeral.

The air shifted.

Alex immediately noticed a slight breeze no longer brushed his face. It now caressed his neck, conveying heat. It pulsated as if—*as if it were breathing!* Alex's heart hammered harder and harder. His brain translated the pounding into eight gnome heads banging against a freezer door. They wanted freedom. They wanted revenge.

A wadded gum wrapper rolled past like sagebrush. Cigarette butts sprinkled onto the floor.

What the ... ?

Coins plopped into the dust. Alex's eyes bulged.

Expecting to see Old Coals when he turned, he anticipated a menacing shadow with red eyes. Or a lizard-like creature with the face of a man.

Instead, a headless gnome presented him an empty Mason Jar.

Alex screamed and ran. He burst from the cave. Branches swatted him in the face, scratched him, drew blood. Oblivious to his direction, he fled fast. His feet propelled him in the wrong direction. He never realized his wish had been granted and more. He'd met Old Coals. He'd ruined the quarry for those college snots. Best of all, he'd become part of the town's legend. None of that seemed so important as he watched the smooth surface of the quarry lake. He didn't realize the irony that he traded places with Bucky in his aborted plan. In seconds, he'd learn if impact or drowning would be the cause of death. Alex had run right off the cliff.

Chapter 32

The very nature of law enforcement often dictates that an officer arrives at the scene too late. The crime's been committed. The accident's occurred. The tragedy's transpired. To prevent any of those ranks a top priority with any cop. It was for Merl. As he pulled up to the locked quarry entrance gate, it fueled his thinking.

He parked and locked the cruiser. His bad feeling grew. Rather than ignore it, he popped the trunk and removed an evidence kit. He slammed the trunk. He glanced at the rusted and rent "No Trespassing" sign. He knew it dissuaded few. Same for the chained gate. Like others, he bent over and stepped through the steel rungs and onto the gravel road.

Merl followed one of the ruts carved from when traffic kept this location busy. He paused at the fork. If he went down to the left, it would take him to water level. That was the direction the college kids headed, the direction they'd take to do a little swimming, sunbathing or beer drinking. Unless someone complained, Merl let them be. When sent here, he tried to convince the kids to clean up after themselves and be careful. Otherwise, the owner would make sure they never got to use the place. He knew the kids gave lip service to his suggestion. Rules didn't apply to them. Still, he hoped they wouldn't be too obnoxious about staking claim to the place.

Merl walked briskly up the hill. He recalled this place as a kid. Sneaking up here late at night. Inching to where the quarry wall fell away from the forest. Almost blinded by the sudden bright light that froze him. Realizing, seconds later, he hadn't been caught. He'd seen the moon reflecting off the glass-smooth quarry lake 70 feet below. That flash, he believed, saved his life. It stopped him in his tracks a step shy of a header over the side, a one-way ticket to a crushed skull and snapped neck. On that thought alone, Merl detoured toward the small cave nearby he knew as Hell Hole. He approached with caution.

"Alex, you in there?" he hollered.

No response. He noted snapped branches, like something had charged out.

"It's Merl Burt. You saved Robbie Callahan. I'm worried you're hurt. You okay?"

Silence. He moved closer.

"Alex? Just checking if you are all right."

Merl pulled back a branch. He shined his flashlight into the opening. Nobody home. He ignored the brownish glints in the dust. He noticed the jacket. Merl duck-walked into the hollow. He caught a whiff of cinnamon. He touched the jacket. Damp. It appeared speckled with blood. The jacket must be Robbie's; it was too small for Alex. *Why would he bring it here?*

Unsure if this were a crime scene, Merl erred on the side of caution. He unsealed his kit. He tugged on a latex glove. He dropped the jacket into a brown paper grocery bag so that the blood would dry. He knew slipping it into plastic trapped condensation, rendering the blood too damp to process. That didn't matter with the other evidence. He pulled out a plastic bag. He dropped the fresh gum wrapper in it. He put cigarette butts in another. He shined his light on the ground. It seemed to be littered with ...

Pennies?

Merl reached down and picked one up. It was a Wheat Penny. He checked the date: 1917. He examined another. *Was that an Indian head?* He hadn't seen one of those since he was a kid. Even then it was rare. *There's another.* Merl picked both up. He glanced at the date. Both were 1866. He picked up another Wheat penny. 1917.

That's odd.

He spied a strange coin. It depicted a ship on one side and Lady Liberty on the other. He read it. *Wow!* Liberty and Commerce 1794. One cent for NY.

What is going on here?

Merl found a Lincoln penny. He checked its date: 1974. Another showed 1980. As the dates rattled in his mind, a sense of dread circled. Merl didn't yet know why, but felt ill at ease. He felt worse when he checked the shiniest pennies. They displayed the current year. Merl swallowed hard. *Was something here?* He swept his flashlight around the cave. Spooked, Merl pocketed as many coins as he could find. He'd compare the dates later. He sensed the pattern meant something. That concerned him.

His worry intensified as he headed for the quarry's edge. Unsure if he might slip in the pine straw, he side-stepped toward the precipice, keeping an eye behind him as he crept to view the stagnant lake below. He noticed footprints kicked up the ground cover all the way to the edge. He identified no signs of a struggle. No signs of anyone … stopping. Merl peered down toward the quarry water. He'd bet every penny he had that what he saw floating below was the body of Alex Simons.

Not sure whether Alex were still alive, Merl called in a request for an ambulance as he raced around to water level. His pockets jangled heavily with the curious evidence of pennies. Because of the weight, he removed his jacket and pitched it toward the flat sunbather's rock. It hit there but slid off into the water. Merl didn't take time to watch it descend into the depths. Instead, he heard the splash of his jacket, the copper pinging of pennies bouncing off rock and the ploop of their escape. With more pressing issues, he waded over to the body. He rolled it over. He looked twice to make sure it was Alex. It was.

Merl had seen that expression before.

On Bill Talbert.

In 1980.

This couldn't be happening. Not again.

Back on dry land, Merl radioed that he had located Alex Simons. He asked to cancel the ambulance, to summon the coroner. He hoped it wouldn't take long. Of all days, he didn't want to be here when the sun set. Of all the things he didn't want to face, only one man could help. Merl had to find him.

Chapter 33

No doubt, the Old Coals legend registered with Merl Burt. He heard most of the stories. He witnessed the lives that deteriorated, unaware or unreceptive to the true cause. He knew others believed. He dealt with the consequences. None offered a conversion experience. If for no other reason than somebody had to remain rational in this town, Merl refused to accept the creature existed. A formal introduction and handshake couldn't shake his faith.

This is a fool's errand, he thought as he turned into the paved, white-striped lot of Becky's Place. He had his choice of spaces. Only Dollar Beer or Ladies Night caused this patch of asphalt to fill. Right now, only Mitch's red pickup occupied a spot. *Satellite dish must be out again or somebody would be here watching college football.* Just beyond the truck, Merl recognized the emerald green bicycle. He had guessed right. Despite the light mist, he parked opposite the building and reached under the seat to retrieve his windbreaker. Working it over his head, he realized it had been more than a week since he dropped in on Jack Thompson.

Few did. Not long after his accident, Jack Thompson became the town's invisible man. Resigned to odd jobs because of his diminished capacity, Jack faded into the background. At first, folks treated him kindly, like they do a small child. That quickly matured into evasion which soon downgraded to being noticed not at all. None of those options suited a man who could do Sunday's *New York Times* crossword in under an hour when his head was clear. When it wasn't, he might think one thing and say another. That unsettled people. Frustrated, Jack turned to books. Merl always admired that he hadn't settled for the bottle.

Although the church tried to turn Jack to something else, Merl simply befriended him. Most times, they met for nothing more than a chat. They'd done it weekly for years. This time, Merl had a purpose. He knew the idiotic subject he wanted to dismiss was one Jack had difficulty discussing. With others, the topic came up more often than Jack liked. He understood why. Folks were curious. Folks were cruel. And folks round these parts believed that Jack Thompson had met Old Coals. They also assumed his mind snapped that night. Never mind that the accident that scrambled Jack's brain happened years before. Like most legendary tales, storytellers fudged on the facts. Ignore the truth—Old Coals was why Wacky Jacky was "messed in the head."

They thought Jack proved it every time the subject arose. It had to be the reason he couldn't talk about Old Coals directly, or for any length of time, before it summoned the child-like side of his personality. That unnerving conversion earned him the nickname he hated so much. What cemented his despised alias was that Jack sometimes spoke in non-sequiturs. His responses made perfect sense in his own mind. However, they registered with few others. It was like being outside of an inside joke. Everybody's laughing but you. Strangers might ask for directions to the highway. He'd smile and say, "The Muslims would have beaten the Christians in the Crusades if they had not worried over which direction they should pray." Nonsense unless you knew Jack. His words were clues that led you to the answer. They didn't understand he was saying, "toward Mecca." Which was east of here.

To know Jack took patience, something few possessed or were willing to invest in someone they labeled a knucklehead. Merl invested. Jack loved his company, rarely receiving more than a sentence or two of conversation from anyone else. Merl enjoyed the challenge of deciphering Jack's words. It appealed to the detective in him. In time, he deduced how Jack's mind worked. Able to fill in the blanks, Merl felt like a parent translating a child's gibberish into comprehensible sentences. He was further rewarded with access to the encyclopedic knowledge of Soke's history stored in Jack's head. Jack even offered insight on how to interpret Wacky Jacky—that when he sang or offered a quotation, it carried meaning. But when those clues came, Merl still struggled to decode them. For him, understanding Wacky Jacky was untangling a crumpled spider web. Merl could never be sure which strand went where.

Merl opened his car door. He flipped his collar to keep the mist off his neck. He tugged his hat tight on his head and strode across the parking lot. He expected to find Jack either munching on the free bar pretzels or meditating in one of the few places he was welcome. Merl shoved the black door open. He heard the squeak and wondered why nobody ever offered it a squirt of oil. He assumed that the bartender probably wanted to know the door had opened or closed. Before Merl's eyes adjusted to the dark, he heard Jack blurt his name.

Merl removed his hat and headed toward the booth. Jack seemed in good spirits. He nursed a soda.

"Whatcha got there, Jack?" Merl asked.

"RC Cola. Want ... one?"

Merl leaned back and pondered his choices. "Yeah."

"Hey, Mitch. Set ... my friend ... up here ... with ... the same."

In conversation, Jack was an acquired taste. Every word he uttered seemed like a cliff-hanger. His voice and that halting pattern either enticed the listener to hang on for the next word or to drop away, impatient. He sounded like a stutterer without the stutter.

"How you been lately?" Merl asked. He figured Jack already knew about Robbie and Alex since he seemed to know everything in town before anybody else. That was the upside of being invisible. Jack proved it. He ignored the pleasantry. He pounced to the point.

"That Simons kid ... talked to me a while back," he said. "Asked about ... our favorite villain. ... Found him ... Maybe."

Merl cringed. This was not what he wanted to hear. The last thing he wanted was an uncertain cause to a certain case. He hated the hysteria this produced. Old Coals took my cat. Old Coals killed my cow. Old Coals rolled my yard.

"What did you tell him?" he asked Jack.

"Told him to ... 'Send your camel to bed.'"

Merl laughed in a short forced burst like a boxing combination. He instantly recognized the line from "Midnight at the Oasis." It was the last song Bill Talbert heard before he met Old Coals. Merl knew the line was Jack's way of warning people off. They both knew kids taunted Talbert with it just to watch him react. Anytime that song played, he needed sedation.

"Simons didn't ... get the point. ... Flipped me off," Jack said. "Think he was ... going where he shouldn't. ... Where no one should ... unprepared."

Merl thought about how much Alex's expression reminded him of the look on Bill Talbert's face. How much this situation was shaping up like the previous two.

"What happened ... to your regular ... jacket?" Jack asked, noticing the windbreaker.

"It drowned," Merl said blankly. Before Merl pulled his mind back into the present, Jack pushed into the past.

"You know ... Bobby Callahan ... talked ... to me ... about it ... too," he said.

Merl nodded. He knew Bobby and Jack held sputtered conversations about Old Coals. He thought it was as useful as fantasy football, but didn't object. Bobby had been one of the few that made Jack feel like he had purpose. To Bobby, he wasn't just old Wacky Jacky sweeping up. He was Jack—strategist and spy. From what Jack told him, it was like Bobby was planning an attack, mining as much as he could about an enemy. Merl felt a chill, recalling Bobby's request to warn his son. The reference made him uncomfortable. Twice before, he ignored Jack's insight, dismissed his expertise. He considered it too far-fetched either to accept or pursue. But in hindsight, everything fit so neatly. Besides, Merl respected intuition. Being here felt right. All of it made him ask the question.

"Situation with Robbie and Alex," he said.

"And Bobby," Jack injected.

"Bobby?"

"Bobby."

"That car accident happened months ago," Merl said. "Back in April." Hoping he wouldn't get the answer he expected, he asked anyway.

"What does Bobby have to do with Robbie and Alex?"

"Payment."

"Pavement?" Merl asked.

"Pay-ment," Jack said, accenting the first syllable.

"Payment," Merl repeated. "Payment for what?"

"He's the first," Jack said. He continued his answer with a children's song.

"Some ... where in ... the ancient, ... mystic trin ... trinity."

"You get ... three as ... a magic number."

"The past ... and the present ... and the future."

Merl actually recognized the verse from the '70s "Schoolhouse Rock" tune. He cursed that Wacky Jacky appeared so quickly. Then, he caught himself. Wacky Jacky didn't talk with a pause.

"Pay attention ... to three," Jack said. Wacky Jacky burst into his own song.

"Ring around the Rosy ..."

Chapter 34

A silly song from childhood cycled through Jack Thompson's head.

"Pocket full of posies ..."

He still had things to discuss with Merl Burt. But that song blared so loudly it nearly drowned his thoughts. He couldn't think here.

"Ashes, ashes ..."

Jack expected his ears to explode when this happened. Often, he fled. Ran as fast as he could to place as much distance between himself and that annoying racket.

"We all fall down ..."

Why is he singing that stupid song? The words boomed. They thundered.

"Ring around the rosy ..."

Jack could take it no longer. He wanted to stay. Instead, he retreated. He pictured the narrow path and sprinted down it. In his mind, the trees blurred. His feet burned at the friction of his pace. Wacky Jacky's words muffled. When Jack reached his spot, they could no longer be heard. That's why he liked it here. The spot brought him peace from the noises in his head. He patted the rough bark of the gnarled cypress. He ran his hand down the awful split caused by a lightning strike. He admired that the tree had been too stubborn to succumb. He marveled that it seemed to draw strength from the creek rather that lose it. Jack perched on a thick exposed root and doused his feet in the cool gurgling waters. He closed his eyes. He took a deep breath. His mind cleared. He sorted his thoughts in silence. He reviewed his conversation with Merl and planned his next one. He felt confident Merl understood the reference to three, understood it meant Old Coals had returned. That it wouldn't depart until all was paid in full. Whether or not Merl accepted it was up for debate. Jack knew he sought rational explanations, not supernatural ones. He could only hope Merl would take that leap of faith this time. He hadn't in 1980. Nor 1995. *Maybe third time's the charm. Got to get him to cross that line.*

Although Jack had much to tell on the subject, he knew Merl was a hard sell. Always had been. Through the years neither brought it up much; Jack because of his difficulty addressing the matter, Merl because he recognized how uncomfortable it made Jack feel. But mainly, because Merl didn't believe in the Hook Man either. *Little bit at a time and he'll get there.*

Jack wished just once he could hold a debate with his buddy, free of Wacky Jacky's interference. A point/counterpoint on the existence of a creature he knew had returned. Talking around the subject hadn't worked. It took too long and required so much mental energy. Besides, Merl didn't always get it right.

An uninterrupted conversation. With that, Jack knew he could convince Merl. But discussing Old Coals directly triggered such stress that it always brought Wacky Jacky running. The Pavlovian response often shifted control of his personality so swiftly that it prevented Jack from articulating what he wanted, needed to say. Over the years, he stumbled upon one way to suppress his alter ego: Anger.

That emotion trumped stress briefly enough to delay Wacky Jacky. Jack discovered that phenomenon while arguing with Becky Danforth that her depression wasn't fatal. That she could best her dread. He had grown so incensed by her defeatist attitude that he didn't realize how long he talked about Old Coals before Wacky Jacky arrived. Over the years, Jack understood it wasn't a switch that always worked. When it did, he felt such a surge of accomplishment.

Chapter 35

As Jack Thompson splashed in the waters of his mental paradise, Wacky Jacky remained at the table in Becky's Place. He hummed and doodled.

Mitch Danforth, Becky's younger brother, came over to check on him. Mitch owned the place. After Becky passed, he renamed it in her honor. Even though Wacky Jacky scared some of the customers and never paid, Mitch ensured he was always welcome. He knew nobody else in town would have done what Jack did for Becky. He also knew Jack had shown the same type of courage before.

The first time came on a summer afternoon when Jack was 15. He, Jimmy Hoskins and Jimmy's younger sister Denise were playing in the hayloft. It was one of the few places weeks of heavy rain hadn't soaked. One second the kids had been laughing and squealing; the next they were stock still in scared silence. Jimmy stood inches from a cottonmouth coiled to strike. Jack acted. He distracted the snake. He knocked Jimmy aside and kicked the reptile out into the yard. Unfortunately, Jack stumbled backwards, pitching himself out of the loft and onto the barn floor. Although the soft, damp ground cushioned his fall, his head banged against the stall. Doctors said Jack suffered a mild concussion. They offered no explanation for the trauma that ruptured enough blood vessels in his brain to cause neural disruptions. An act of heroism brought Wacky Jacky into the world and saddled Jack's.

In the time before Jack interceded for Becky, they became friends. She would take him to the drive-in over in Bedford. She'd accompany him to the quarry to talk, or to listen to the cows moo at dusk. She liked Jack because she didn't feel on guard around him. He'd listen. Aside from being so polite, she noticed he wasn't bad looking either. Still, she kept the relationship platonic. Jack understood.

He never pushed the issue. He knew better than to act on his feelings and jeopardize the nicest relationship he'd ever had. Besides, she deserved someone whole.

The night Becky encountered Old Coals, she was—for what Wacky Jacky did—ungrateful and grateful. Robbed of her happiness by her brief look into the creature's eyes, she battled depression until disappearing into Landfalls Creek. Some days, she cursed Jack for letting her live. Other days, she thanked him. Those days far outweighed all else for Jack. He never felt prouder of anything in his life. However, what Wacky Jacky did for Becky came not from a sense of gallantry. Nor courage. It was curiosity. He walked right out into the field and placed himself between the two. Such a brazen act should have obliterated his mind. Staring Old Coals down had proved a damning precursor to everyone else's demise. Could it have been Wacky Jacky didn't accept what he was seeing? Didn't comprehend its intent? Intrigued, Wacky Jacky stared into those depressive orbs. He foresaw his own death, but didn't perceive it as himself. He probed for more, fascinated by what he saw.

Wacky Jacky discovered things nobody else knew.

Chapter 36

Before Wacky Jacky spotted Old Coals, dread crept over Jack Thompson. He felt as if his dog had just dashed out into the street. He winced at the remembered sound of screeching tires; the sickening thump that killed Ringo. Sniffling at the memory, he slammed the trunk of Becky Danforth's car. He had offered to carry her telescope, but she, so protective of it, insisted on toting it to the car herself, insisted on securing it in the back seat with the seat belts. Jack turned, expecting to see her lugging the cumbersome astronomy gear.

What he saw infused him with fear. Becky stood immobile. Her telescope sprawled awkwardly at her feet like a broken giraffe. He gaped at the murky figure towering over her. It held her gaze as if drawing forth her soul. Jack didn't move. Terror robbed him of motion. Becky's anguished gasps carved through him. He so wanted to help. He so wanted to flee. His muscles refused to respond either way. His stressed mind reacted protectively. Jack receded. Wacky Jacky emerged. The alter ego beheld the creature. Not sensing Becky's hopelessness, he assumed her stare denoted curiosity. He swiftly covered the distance from the car, impatient to discover what she found so fascinating about this creature. In his haste, he bumped Becky aside. It saved her life. He peered up into a red and wild wonderland.

What held malice and dread for others held wonder and excitement for Wacky Jacky. He saw smoke, swirls and foam. He saw actors in some Hieronymus Bosch-like production. He saw someone who looked familiar choking. He didn't recognize Jack Thompson. Maybe it was the beard. Wacky paid no attention to the death scene. Instead, with his mind, he crossed into this strange place. A sticky membrane clung to him and vanished. Whether he passed through it or absorbed it mattered not to him. He was probing, searching, hunting. Where he now wandered filled him with want. He possessed an overpowering need to take something, anything. All kinds of smells inundated his nostrils. He could discern few. However, one faint odor stuck with him forever. He identified it as the scent of Old Coals. That might prove useful, but it wasn't what Wacky sought.

What did this creature want?

He brushed aside what looked like cobwebs. He watched shiny, gold-tinted beetles swarm off the exposed branches. They scurried up his arm and over his body. *Maybe I should take these back.* They crawled over his clothes. They climbed under his clothes. He watched transfixed as his body looked like a rhinestone dream come alive; the insects' hum enthralled him. A second of silence preceded the pain. As if cued, the beetles bit as one. Hard and deep. Wacky Jacky refused to scream. He refused to acknowledge the pain. He didn't believe beetles bit. He turned his attention elsewhere.

What did this creature want?

Ignorant of his skin becoming leprous, he strolled into a fog. He waved his hand in front of him. It disappeared. He poked his other arm forward, too. He retracted nubs. Wacky stopped and wondered why his legs were still there. His torso banged to the ground. Wacky cackled at what he considered a practical joke.

"Good one," he said. "Got me on that one."

Eager to volley jokes, he couldn't remember the riddle of the Sphinx. Or the one about legs on a stool. He couldn't recall any he liked. The only one that came to mind he dredged from a childhood book. He used it.

"What's big, red and eats rocks?"

He waited. Nothing answered. He shrugged.

"A big, red rock-eater!" he bellowed.

Even though he heard no laughter, Wacky grinned as an image materialized from the billowing mists. As it came into focus, Wacky recognized a barn. *I've been there!* He was playing with some kids. *There's Jimmy and Denise!* A snake. A fall. Laughter. The image morphed. Confused, Wacky thought he was looking into a mirror. He was whole again. He reached out an arm to touch it. The image didn't reciprocate. Wacky squinted. He read the nametag on the man's shirt, "Jack Thompson." *Hey, I know him!* Wacky danced in celebration. He clapped as the man received an award. Cheered as he watched him taking temperatures. Delivering babies. Consoling patients. Saving lives.

Jack Thompson would have wept at what might have been. Wacky enjoyed the movie. He applauded as the mist formed again. He waited for it to thicken. He inhaled deeply. He blew at the air in front of him. The mist cleared. Rather than filling the void just created, the mist dissipated. Wacky found himself amidst tortured souls, riches beyond compare and trinkets of value to no one. He approached them.

Fused mangled bodies reached out with open palms. Their arms of rent muscle and exposed bone held their shape under rotted cloth. They pawed him. Skulls with orb-less sockets turned as he passed. Mouths barren of teeth begged for hope, but their tongue-less caverns produced no sound.

Wacky didn't stop.

Gold glowed. Silver shone. Diamonds sparkled. Rubies flared. Emeralds glistened. Sapphires winked. Crowns summoned him. Ornamental eggs beckoned. Art spoke. Power thrust. Glory harkened.

Wacky didn't stop.

A piece of red string lay twisted. Pennies rested in a scattered stack. A globe. An empty Mason Jar. Cigarettes. Unpaired socks. Bailing wire. A section of garden hose. Eight short headless statues. Fishing poles. Empty soda cans. An unworn baby shoe. Wacky stopped. He spun. His eyes glanced over all that he witnessed here. He gazed back at where he'd been. He saw what the creature wanted.

Somewhere in ancient, mystic trinity. You get three as a magic number.

When Jack came to, he retained no memory of what happened. Becky lay beside him, breathing steadily, not a mark on her. Speckled over Jack's body were ugly red welts.

Damn ants.

Chapter 37

Robbie knew he was dreaming. But he still felt fearful. Like a gazelle at a watering hole.

Every time he tried to confront his fear, it changed. He knew, in dreams, not to run from them. Dad taught him that dreams try to tell you what your mind might be avoiding when awake. That dreams sometimes speak in symbols, so things aren't what they seem. What scares you might represent something else. That nightmares often showed us what was bothering us. It was the mind's way of saying "face this and let's move on." Robbie knew this, but his mind never proffered a chance to bypass his initial panic.

He couldn't control this dream. He couldn't turn into the skid.

Robbie found himself at school. He stood in an empty hallway. He wasn't wearing any pants. He saw the clock about to strike the hour ending classes. In less than a minute, the hallway would be congested with classmates. He raced for his locker. He couldn't find it. He'd be so embarrassed if the little girl in the red dress saw him. He had seconds left. No way could he reach the Boy's Room and hide in a stall.

DRRRIIINNGGG!!!!!!

Robbie shoved at the janitor's door. It gave. He plunged into the ocean. Spitting out saltwater and gasping for breath, Robbie breached the surface. He saw a fin splitting the sea, circling. From the shape of the dorsal fin, Robbie identified the Great White Shark. Judging from the dorsal to the tail fin, a gigantic Great White. Robbie turned with it. He marveled at its size. He wanted to reach out and touch it, but feared its sandpaper skin would shred his fingertips and draw blood. He knew blood in the water meant death. His fingers now bled profusely. He twisted with the toothy carnivore. He believed as long as he saw the fin, he was safe since the shark would descend into the depths before mounting an attack. As if on cue, the fin disappeared. Robbie inhaled deeply. He ducked underwater. He searched for the shark. *There it is!* He watched it rise slowly. With a flick of the tail, it came at him like a locomotive.

Horrified, Robbie closed his eyes. Before he screamed, a hand clamped on his mouth. It forced him silent.

Bewildered, he spun and saw a ragged P.O.W. limping away. Robbie heard hounds baying nearby. He saw he, too, wore ragged clothes. They were being pursued. *By whom?* Robbie chased after the prisoner who had disappeared into haze. Hearing guttural voices, Robbie didn't understand the language. They must be the enemy. He scouted for a stick with which to defend himself. He discovered he wore matching six-shooters.

Suddenly, he straddled a horse. He looked to his left. Butch Cassidy asked, *"You didn't see a guy in a white straw hat, did you?"*

Robbie shook his head.

"Good! For a moment there, I thought we were in trouble."

Both turned as a Tyrannosaurus Rex crashed through the bushes. It unleashed an ear-shattering screech at them. Robbie spurred his horse only to find it needed quarters to move. He looked up at the T-Rex. It looked back down at him. It tilted its head. It sized him up. It roared again. Terrified, Robbie darted underneath the massive body and dove into the shrubbery.

He tumbled onto a chessboard with life-sized pieces. Rising and dusting himself off, he froze when a Knight slammed a sword to block his passage. Robbie surveyed the pieces on the board. Not many black pieces remained. He watched a white Bishop slide six spaces away and grew curious. When a black Knight blocked the

Bishop's path, Robbie understood his dilemma. He was black. He was the King. He saw the white Queen move to cover the Black Knight. Checkmate loomed. Death would arrive in two moves. Robbie wondered what would happen if he just fell down. While he pondered if a stalemate would free him, the white Queen morphed into a playing card. She screamed, *"Off with his head!"*

Robbie ducked and saw Oompa Loompas fleeing in fear. He knew what scared Willy Wonka's dwarf-like assistants most. He just couldn't see what was chasing them. Robbie had never seen what they were, but believed they must be pretty terrible if they ate Oompa Loompas for breakfast without a second thought. He decided what was coming probably wasn't a Wangdoole, Hornswoggler or Snozzwanger. It had to be a dreaded Vermicious Knid. He didn't know what to do with a Vermicious Knid. There was nothing he could recall from Willy Wonka that told him how to deal with a Vermicious Knid. He grew ever fearful of what approached. He trembled. Maybe he should yell he wasn't an Oompa Loompa.

"I'm not an Oompa Loompa," Robbie blurted. It didn't seem to matter.

When it extended its hand, Robbie decided, maybe, this was a stranger introducing himself like they did at his father's funeral. Robbie wanted to be courteous. He'd make sure his handshake was firm, like his dad taught him. Not one of those dead-fish shakes. He'd be polite. His mom would want that.

Robbie's mind tried once more to get a message through. Robbie paused.

Didn't the Vermicious Knids spell something? It was ... It was ...
S-C-R-A-M.

The only word they knew. Willy Wonka told everybody that!

Robbie decided it was the best advice he ever heard. As he withdrew his hand, Robbie felt so alone. It felt like the dogfight. Robbie realized he was being stalked. He winced. He didn't know how much more of this he could handle.

More was coming.

Chapter 38

Mallison worried that the strained look on Robbie's face signaled bad news.

Dr. Tyson disagreed. By now, he was disagreeing with everybody. Only he hadn't noticed how much more irritable he'd gotten despite chewing tab after tab of nicotine gum. Even after putting on one of the patches, he would have refuted the sun setting.

"He's dreaming," Dr. Tyson said. "Sign of healthy brain activity."

He glanced down at Robbie. He read a wince as a hint of a smile.

"I haven't seen a smile like that since he's been here. Like he was up to something."

Like he just sneaked out for a cigarette.

Tyson wished he could join him.

Mallison chased another scenario. *Is he on his fire engine holding that purple crayon?*

That purple crayon. One of Mallison's favorite memories. She recalled preparing dinner. Hearing his hard plastic wheels scuffling across the floorboards as Robbie pedaled his fire truck down the hallway. His bell clanging as the vehicle jolted back and forth. She thought she heard him singing. It sounded like "Little Red Corvette." *Where in the world did he hear that? Probably MTV.* She thought how cute it might be to dress him up for Halloween in a purple suit like the artist formerly known as Prince. She waited for him to drive past. He didn't.

Instead of taking his usual route, Robbie stayed in the hallway. He rode up and back. Up and back. Mallison didn't worry about him. As long as she heard the wheels grating, heard the jostled bell clanging and his concert performance, she knew all was fine. Now, if he got quiet. Quiet meant trouble, but she couldn't resist. She peeked around the corner. She gasped. Robbie clutched a purple crayon as he rode. On both sides of the hall, he had traced his passage. He made each wall look like a depiction of wavy seas. Mallison wanted to tan his hide. When he saw her, he stood up with a huge grin. He spread his arms to welcome her to his masterpiece.

"I painted this for you!" he said.

"Thank you," was all she could think to say. She knew that wouldn't work as well when Dad got home.

She leaned over her boy in the hospital bed. Robbie's breathing sounded so normal. She watched the rhythm of his chest. He looked peaceful. She recalled nights not so distant, nights when things grew harried around the house. Those times, she'd sneak into his room. She'd feel such serenity watching her baby sleep. His innocent slumber put her cares in perspective. This was her reason for being. She'd whisper in his ear how much she loved him. She loved him so much that she wanted to make sure he knew it.

Even in his dreams.

She couldn't begin to describe the connection she felt to him. It was what made Robbie more special to her than anything in the world. That something so special about the first-born that those without children can't fathom. That special bond no other child, no matter how much he is loved, can attain between a mother and her first.

Mallison ran her hand down his blanket-covered frame. *The hospital sheets look so alien. No Snoopy atop his doghouse. No scattered NHL logos on pucks. No fighter planes.* She watched Robbie breathe. In. Out. The whoosh from his oxygen mask so constant she no longer heard it.

What's my baby dreaming?

Mallison choked down a surge of tears. All day, she won this battle. Bobby would have been so proud of how strong she'd been. Her mother would have been so proud of how positive she'd stayed. She gritted her teeth to keep from crying. When the feeling ebbed, she whispered in Robbie's ear—"I love you so much."

She thought his face flashed concern. She wondered if Dad just got home and saw the purple-crayoned hallway. Was it something else? Her worry mounted.

Dr. Tyson countered her thought.

"He's battling," he said. "His vitals look good. Like I said, the rest is up to him. I'm encouraged enough to prescribe some rest for you."

"Rest?" she mumbled.

"Rest," Tyson answered.

Mallison feared where her mind went when she closed her eyes. She'd fought her exhaustion all afternoon. She couldn't nap now. Robbie needed her. Yet, her eyelids grew heavy.

Chapter 39

Robbie's mind registered the word, "rest." It mulled its meaning. It drew a conclusion.

Rest? Rest in peace?

Robbie lay in darkness. Softness surrounded him. He tried to sit up and banged his head. He tested the space with his arms and legs. He had little room to move. If he were claustrophobic, he'd be in trouble. *At least I'm not underwater.* Robbie pushed at the roof. It wouldn't budge. He banged at the side. It was hard underneath the cushion. He heard something bang back. It shook the container. He listened. The container shook again. It sounded like something dropping on top of it. He pressed his hands against the roof. He felt the vibrations from each successive hit. Robbie held his breath.

No way.

He ran his hand over his chest to confirm what he wore. His Sunday suit. His tie. He only wore this to church and ...

Funerals!

Suddenly, Robbie stood in the church, parked between row after row of dark wooden pews with white trim. Matching brass chandeliers dangled from above. The fluted pulpit in the corner towered as if to meet one of them. The place seemed so huge. This was where grandfather went to be with Jesus. Robbie heard the mournful music emanate from the huge pipe organ. He imagined that's how hippos sounded when they spoke underwater.

Robbie edged into one of the pews. He hopped up on the red velvet-cushioned seat. He leaned forward. He selected a hymnal and flipped through the pages. When he stopped, it lay open to "Onward Christian Soldiers." He set the hymnal down. He pulled out the guest register. He methodically wrote out his full name in block letters. He did the same with his address. Just like he practiced with his mother when he was younger. He looked at the boxes at the end of the line that asked if he wanted to be contacted. Robbie checked "Yes." He returned the register to the slot on the back of the pew in front of him. He inserted the pencil in its holder.

That done, Robbie glanced around. He saw people crying. Almost all were dressed in black. Robbie slid out of the pew. He walked down the aisle. He hunted for his parents. He couldn't find them. He felt like everybody was watching him, talking about him. Pointing at him. Even the figures in the stained glass windows seemed to follow him. The place seemed so cramped. Robbie wanted to run. He couldn't. It seemed the faster he wanted to move, the more sluggish he became. He turned to face the congregation. He backed up. The people sitting in the pews just stared. He saw Mrs. Felton with a kerchief over her mouth. She looked so sad. Robbie had never seen her without a smile. There was Mrs. Cassidy. She always smelled like lemons. And Mr. Richards. He always shook with cold sweaty hands. Robbie didn't understand why everybody was so sad.

He banged into the casket.

His grandfather stood next to him. He rested a hand on Robbie's shoulder. He shook his head. Robbie turned. The casket was much too small for his grandfather. *How come it was closed?* He remembered seeing how peaceful grandfather looked in there. He looked like he was asleep. His head on that white satin pillow. He wanted to wake him. Robbie cracked open the coffin lid. It creaked as it flipped up. Robbie stared down into his own face.

Am I dead?

Chapter 40

Merl stepped into the rain outside Becky's Place. He cursed. Not only was he trying to get that inane Posy tune out of his head but also reconcile handling the current situation without resorting to voodoo spells. He didn't know which was worse—a useless nursery rhyme on extended loop or chasing a ghost. And Saturday's always got worse.

He felt certain Jack believed Old Coals was back. He knew if Jack believed it, then the town wouldn't be far behind. This was so much worse than crazies cavorting at the full moon. Worse than the opportunists striking when a storm knocked out the power. How Merl dreaded those nights. Checking every store in the dark. When the power returned, doing it again after all the alarms sounded. He had to be everywhere at once.

Climbing into his cruiser and closing the door, Merl braced himself mentally for the anticipated flood. He resigned himself to encounter people who didn't want to face reality. The frightened old ladies who couldn't find their cats. Angry residents with battered mailboxes. Farmers missing livestock. Grieving relatives. All their solutions would crescendo with Old Coals. Not Nature. Not pranksters. Not life itself. Old Coals.

Merl coasted to the street side of the parking lot. He braked. He flicked on his blinker. He listened to it while waiting for the lone car to pass.

Click-coo. Click-coo. Click-coo.

A beat-up maroon Mustang slowed. Merl heard the bass in The Knack's "My Sharona" pulsing through rolled-up windows. Recognizing the tune, he drifted. It carried him back to when he first met Jack Thompson. It was 1979. Merl spotted him wandering down by the two-lane highway. He strolled near the billboard that once proclaimed "Jesus is the answer." Someone later climbed up and spray-painted "What was the question?" A few days later, someone added "Who was Felipe and Matty Alou's brother?" Despite how hard the Soke First Baptist ladies besieged him, Merl didn't hunt hard for the culprit. Instead, he bit his lip to keep from chuckling about it. He often wondered if Jack had done it, but never had any proof. Although it was his brand of humor, Jack neither confirmed nor denied it. He did admit that he wished he'd thought of it first.

Click-coo. Click-coo. Click-coo.

The blinker's rhythm brought Merl back into the present. He checked the rear view mirror. He scanned the empty street. Rather than make a left and head back to the station, Merl decided he'd rather have a good cup of coffee. He exited to the right, followed by a fast left on Herrington Way.

HepCat's Hive stood on the corner. Merl eyed the black and yellow sign—a cheetah with wraparound sunglasses, thick whiskers and beret chased by an irritated swarm of bees.

What is it with these people? Do they think we don't understand the concept of 24-hour stores?

Merl parked by the door. He wanted to be seen. No surprises. A quick in and out. Just some black java, three creams and two sugars. Since he preferred his coffee brewed from a pot, he loved that this store hadn't upgraded to a dispenser that spewed caffeinated liquid into a preset cup.

Before he exited his cruiser, he scoped the store through the glass. He noted the animated manner of the young man at the counter. When the teenager turned, he seemed in a hurry, agitated. Merl popped the strap on his holster. As he exited the cruiser, he sheathed his night stick.

When he entered the store, instantly he sensed tension. He nodded at Rachael Nash behind the counter. Her eyes expressed concern. Her smile looked like someone glued it in place improperly.

"Afternoon, Rachael," he said.

"Afternoon, Officer Burt," she said.

Merl assessed the young man. Hands jammed into the pockets of his tan jacket. In his early 20s. About 5-11, 175. Athletic build. Black hair. Clean shaven. Thin nose. Black flannel shirt. Blue jeans. Grass-stained white Nikes, the right shoe marked with some strange symbol on the swoosh.

"Evening, sir," Merl said.

"Yeah," the suspect said. "Evening." He avoided eye contact. He kept his head lowered. He was nervous. Rather than beeline for the coffee, Merl looped the store. He acted as if he sought a snack. Or a comb. Or motor oil. He wanted to eavesdrop but neither had spoken other than to acknowledge him since he entered. Merl bided his time. As he patrolled each aisle, he either kept the corner of his eye on the suspect's pockets or trained them on the mirror in the corner. The young man fidgeted. He shifted his weight to his other foot. He seemed to be debating. His hands strained against the jacket's fabric, stretching it.

Merl was running out of store to explore. He felt the suspect couldn't wait for him to leave.

"Coffee ready?" he asked Rachael.

"Yes, sir."

The young man glanced up at Rachael. He turned to survey the parking lot.

Merl shook loose a large styrofoam cup and pulled the pot off the heated template. He glanced over at Rachael. She raised her eyebrows and offered an embarrassed smile. Merl paused. He glanced back at the suspect. He seemed to be sweating.

Something was up.

Merl poured his coffee. He dumped about three creams worth into it. Tore two sugars and emptied the contents while he stared at the jacket pockets. He saw no outline of a weapon, just clenched fists thrust forward. The jacket hung evenly. He listened to the buzz of the overhead fluorescent bulbs. Rachael seemed anxious. So did the young man. He stood there waiting. Looking at Rachael. Looking at the counter. Back at Rachael. Waiting for his courage to stick.

Don't do it, kid.

Merl decided to make the first move. He reached for a red straw to stir his drink. He intentionally missed. He knocked the container over. It banged off the shelf and spun wildly. Red straws arrowed out and splattered on the floor like strewn spaghetti. Rachael gasped. The young man whirled. His hands whipped of his jacket.

Merl, with eyes trained on those pockets, sighed with relief. Both hands were empty.

"Sorry, about that," Merl said. "Getting clumsy in my old age."

"I'll get that," the kid said. He quickly slid to a knee and began gathering the straws.

"I appreciate that," Merl said. He watched how fast the kid cleared the floor.

"Got any more straws, Rachael?"

"Stirs are in the tan box right behind you."

"I'll take care of it," the kid said, almost racing over from the trash bin. He grabbed the box. He popped open a corner and shook the red stirs loose into the replaced container. He looked at Merl and nodded. He breezed past Rachael and said, "Later."

Merl set his coffee down on the counter. He reached for his wallet.

"Thanks for saving me there," Rachael said. "He was trying to ask me out."

See what happens when you start to believe in ghosts?

Merl chuckled.

"Really," he said. "So that's how it's done."

She laughed and rang up the sale. He handed her a $5. She counted out the change and dumped it into his hand. He placed the dollars on the counter.

"Keep it," he said.

"You sure?"

He nodded.

"Thanks!"

"You're welcome."

Something made him pocket the change. It nagged at him. He walked outside and placed his cup of coffee on the car roof. He fished out the coins. He examined the date on each. The three pennies almost jumped out of his palm—1974. 1980. 2004. Those were the same dates from the cave. He ran through those dates in his head—1794, 1866, 1917, 1974, 1980 and now.

Were they connected? Because of Jack, his mind sprang toward the absurd—Old Coals linked each to the other. *Don't go there.* He elected to salve his skepticism with empirical evidence. He'd start simple. No sense whistling in the dark. He'd deduce if three deaths fell in those years. He turned the ignition. He shifted into reverse. Before he turned to check behind him, he noticed Rachael waving excitedly through the glass. He saluted her. He reached up out the window to rescue his coffee. Properly caffeinated, he headed toward the station house.

Chapter 41

Had Merl Burt been a reporter, he would have started his search at *The Soke Citizen* archive. He'd zoom through microfilm until his eyes wavered. Or flip through stacks of yellowed tear-sheets. Like the station, the newspaper hadn't made much of a move to the online world yet. Even so, *The Citizen's* archive could only chase him back to 1955 when that security guard's dropped Marlboro ignited the fire that consumed him and the newspaper's past.

Better to start in your own backyard. Or basement. Merl opened the Records room door whose browned paper "Morgue" sign curled despite repeated scotch-taping. He flipped the light switch. The stairs down to the station's case archive always looked like a bad movie set, complete with fluorescent lighting that flickered and sizzled. Merl left the door open. He clomped down the wooden steps.

The musty room contained a table and six rows of metal-framed shelving, mostly cobwebbed. The shelves were stationed two-by-two with an aisle through the middle like an erector-set's version of a library. Merl examined the nearest box. The typed card read 1923-30. He was quite familiar with the filing system here. One dumped the box in the first open space and went back upstairs. He scanned the half-filled shelves. It amazed him how so much time occupied so little space. He found 1970-1978 with little trouble. He blew on the top of the cardboard box. Dust billowed. Merl sneezed.

If for nothing more than to sate his curiosity, Merl decided to explore what dates he could. He started with 1974. Maybe it was familiarity. He already knew what he would find, but didn't want to rely on memory. Besides, a review either confirmed the truth or opened a new lead.

Merl lugged the 1970-1978 box over to the table. He removed the top. He extracted the thin 1974 file. He missed the case during his sojourn to New York, but Merl was quite familiar with the death of deputy Marvin Reynolds.

Unlike the Big Apple, Soke wasn't exactly a hotbed of crime and corruption, so Marvin's passing was big news. It stayed a hot topic for years because almost all believed the news was edited.

Merl re-read the report. It indicated Marvin was found in his cruiser just off the interstate. Dead. Gunshot wound to the head. The report said he died struggling with an unknown assailant after a traffic stop. The report didn't say what many believed: Marvin shot himself. They had reason. Office gossip remarked that Marvin, a veteran cop, began drinking off-duty not long before he died. About that time, he shifted from gregarious to withdrawn. Nobody said anything. Nobody pried. Very few looked any deeper after he died.

The sheriff suppressed the suicide angle. He forged other facts completely. He let it be known that Marvin wrestled with a suspect. The gun discharged. The bullet passed through the mouth and into the brain. That version raised questions. If it had been a traffic stop gone bad, how come Marvin failed to radio that he had pulled someone over? If it were a suicide, how come the gun was found in his left hand? Marvin was right-handed.

Even Merl doubted the sheriff's written report. He had reason, once catching a hint from Marvin that he might kill himself. In town on a weekend trip, Merl bumped into his former high school teammate at Ray Ray's. While reminiscing after a few beers, Marvin confided that some things were just too much to take. Told him that Jack Thompson had met Old Coals. Although Marvin never made the same claim, he had said, "Don't ever meet that sorry old bastard.

Be the death of ya." Merl didn't make much of it. Until Marvin died. With 20/20 hindsight, Merl pondered how he missed the signs. Everybody had. Although nobody suspected that Marvin and Old Coals met, he all but told them with his actions: his sudden interest in Bill Talbert, his new-found concern for Wacky Jacky, his despondent disposition.

Merl thumbed through the rest of the 1974 file. No more deaths reported. Or more accurately, no more bodies found. Merl suspected the Fitzs belonged in this folder too.

Jack's absolute faith that Old Coals delivered death in threes alerted him to the possibility. He and Jack had been discussing that morbid old wives' tale when Merl countered that only Marvin died of questionable means in 1974. Jack shook his head and said, "Out of sight … out of mind." Once Merl deduced what Jack meant, he investigated. He discovered that the Fitzs planned to move to New York that year. They never arrived. No one, outside of Ruth Felton, ever asked about them. They just disappeared. Merl jammed the lid back on the box and slid it aside. He retrieved the 1979-1989 box. He hesitated, not wanting to open it. He finally pulled the 1980 file. He re-read his report on Bill Talbert. He read about Raymond Battle's 9-year-old son—shot while playing with a pistol. He read about Jim Manfred, 37, dead of a heart attack, jogging near Landfalls Creek.

Two for two.

Merl knew any more dates coinciding with three deaths couldn't be confirmed from this room. At least not the dates he remembered. *Were they the only ones to check? I didn't examine every coin.* They now rested at the bottom of the quarry. Merl wondered if Ozzie Littleton's ghost had spent them all in one place. *Ozzie? Nah.* Merl quickly dismissed him as a factor in this equation. That was just a strange, but obvious, accident.

For the dates of mysterious death in Soke, Merl sought each storage box's master sheet. He anticipated a lengthy perusal. He grabbed 1923-30, starting his chronological search for any trio of deaths. He was grateful this station house included a catalog for each year. It consisted of 12 pages, one for each month, with spaces for each day. Merl flipped through each. If not blank, each was conspicuously sparse. In many of the files, it was the only paperwork. For a while, Merl feared that they weren't being filled out. He was wrong.

Although it took the better part of the afternoon, Merl found his effort mildly rewarded.

In 1938, during the town's tuberculosis scare, three brothers died in a house fire. In 1995, Becky Danforth and the two high school kids who OD'd. This year, he counted Alex Simons, Bobby Callahan and Robbie.

Robbie's not dead!

Merl mouthed a silent apology. He reached for the rotary phone. It still worked. He dialed Ruth Felton over at the library. If anybody knew strange facts about this town, it was she. Ruth was older than dirt when Merl was a kid. She had to be in Methuselah's age bracket by now.

Before the call connected, Merl hung up. He concluded a change of scenery would be better. Stretch his legs a bit. He'd opt for the short stroll to the library.

Chapter 42

Ambling down Hallman Street to the library, Merl debated whether Ruth Felton was the nicest person he'd ever met. When he was a Cub Scout, she gave him a gold star for carrying some books. After he moved to New York, she had gotten his address and mailed him a post card to wish him well. He'd seen her quietly raise funds to help those in need, including Jack. Seen how she ensured new families in town felt welcome. Seen her keep the maternity ward decorated. He concluded if she ever ran for Mayor, she'd get elected in a landslide. Ruth already had his vote, bought when he was 10 with a single gold star.

Merl removed his hat when entering the library. Even if he weren't in her presence yet, he showed respect for her place of work. He saw Linda Williams working the checkout counter.

"Hey, Linda," he said just above a whisper as he approached.

"Hey, Merl." She winked at him.

Merl smiled back.

"You catch those college kids yet?" Linda asked.

"Excuse me?"

"The ones who ran over Robbie Callahan."

Merl shook his head.

"Nobody ran over Robbie Callahan."

Rather than elaborate, he asked, "Is Mrs. Felton in?"

"Ruth's in her office. Go on back." Linda lifted the countertop.

"Thank you," Merl said. He nudged the half-door under it and stepped past. As he knocked, he poked his head into Ruth Felton's office. She sat behind her desk.

"Mrs. Felton, do you have a minute?"

"I always have time for you, Merl Burt," she said. "How are you this afternoon?"

"I'm fine. You?"

"I'd be much better if you'd call me Ruth. You know better than to call me Mrs. Felton."

"Yes, Ma'am. Old habit."

"Ma'am?"

"Sorry. Ruth."

"Now, to what do I owe the pleasure of your company?"

"You mind if I close the door?"

Ruth nodded. Merl shut it before sitting down in the chair facing her.

"What's on your mind, young man?" she asked with a curious smile.

"I was wondering if you could help me with some dates in Soke history."

"I'll try. What do you need to know?" She watched him pull out a small pad and pen. It made her think of her days as an English teacher.

"Well, Jack and I were talking about death. You know, how it always visits in threes."

Ruth wasn't a bit surprised by the topic.

"He's right. When the eternal footman grabs your coat and snickers, he always makes room for a trio."

"Dickinson?" Merl said, trying to score points by recognizing her literary allusion.

"T.S. Eliot. But it's nice to know the words of great poets still merit notice."

Merl found the correction unexpected. Anybody who ever visited the library knew Ruth worshipped Emily Dickinson. She displayed a portrait of the poet over the poem "In a Library" near the building's entrance. Several other framed prints referenced books.

"What are the dates," Ruth asked.

"1794."

"Well, as everybody knows, our town's founder, the Reverend Fincher L. Soke, disappeared. So did the first two who searched for him."

"How about 1866?"

"Hold on a second."

Merl waited as she picked up the phone and said, "Thursday."

"My apologies," she said. "Linda wanted to know when to change the bulletin boards. Now, you said, '1866', right?"

"Yes, Ma'am."

"That was a rather noteworthy year around here. Some folks still haven't forgiven the Bender family for what their ancestors did. Less stubborn folk would have long since left. Not the Benders."

Merl nodded. He couldn't believe the incident hadn't jumped out at him. Although her elaboration was unnecessary, he didn't dream of cutting her off.

"Colluding with the Yankees doesn't sit well in these parts," she said. "It was quick as a wink when they found out what Jim, Jay and John Bender did and when they strung 'em up."

Merl looked back down at his notepad.

"How about 1917?"

Ruth hesitated. Merl thought he heard her catch her breath. It looked as though she were trying to retain her composure. He wondered why.

"Check with the hospital," she said. She had trouble getting the words "crib deaths" out.

Merl didn't know if he should continue. Ruth answered that question for him.

"Any other years?" she asked.

Merl stalled, buying time by flipping to a blank page in his notepad. Since he was out of specific dates, he hoped Ruth might fill in the silence with other recollections.

She didn't.

"Can you recall any years where Soke had three deaths," he said. "Or ... anything ... out of the ordinary."

Ruth sat back. She tilted her head. She rocked slightly in her chair, keeping an eye on Merl.

"My, 'when sorrows come, they come not single spies, but in battalions,'" she said.

Ruth closed her eyes momentarily. Merl could almost see her flipping through the years.

"Back in the late '30s we didn't lose anybody during the TB scare," she said, "but all three Finley boys died in a house fire. That was 1938 or '39. No, it was '38. Funny how I remember that. But it's because of Lou Gehrig. He quit playing in 1939. When his streak ended. The summer before, the Finleys played golf with him. All three hit the ball further than he did. They were so excited. They just knew if they could hit a golf ball further than that mighty Yankee, they were a cinch to make the big leagues. But nobody knew he was sick. Such a sad story all the way around."

Ruth sighed. Merl waited. He didn't know if she were finished or fast forwarding through her memory.

"In 1955 Benjamin Phelps died in the newspaper fire, but that's only one," she said. "Never did believe he smoked."

After a pause, she added. "In 1974, Marvin Reynolds. Possibly the Fitzs. They just disappeared. In 1980, Bill, little Ritchie Battle, poor thing, and Mr. Manfred. In 1995, Becky, Reggie and Melinda, bless their souls. Does any of that help?"

"I'm not ... entirely sure," Merl said, scribbling quickly. "But 'where knowledge is insufficient,'" he added, "'all decisions are hazardous.'"

"J.R.R. Tolkien," Ruth answered.

"Is that where that's from?"

Ruth smiled. She nodded.

"Thanks for the help, Ruth."

"You're most welcome," she said.

As Merl stood, he said, "I'd like to keep this between us, if that's all right?"

"It is."

"I appreciate that. I owe you one, Ruth."

"Merl Burt, remind me who wrote this stanza and we're even, 'Because I could not stop for Death. He kindly stopped for me. The carriage held but just ourselves. And Immortality.'"

"Eliot?" Merl said.

"Dickinson." Ruth chuckled. "You have a good afternoon, Mr. Merl Burt."

"You too, Ruth."

He stopped at the door. Ruth arched an eyebrow, anticipating a final query.

"Do you believe in any of this supernatural mumbo-jumbo," he asked.

"That's something you need to decide for yourself, Merl Burt. Nobody else can."

Merl frowned.

"Thanks, again."

She volleyed a parting thought at him.

"Have you ever asked yourself why churches in the country refuse to use Landfalls Creek to baptize their members?"

Chapter 43

Merl's head pounded as he made his way back to the station. Either Ruth hadn't helped much or helped too much. He reached into his pocket. He ripped open a packet of migraine medicine. Although the package instructed to take the pills with a glass of water, he swallowed both dry.

En route to his desk, he slurped down some water from the hallway fountain. He plopped down in his chair, burying his face in his hands. He wanted his head clear now. He knew he needed to corral the facts galloping back and forth in his brain. He needed to do it before they stampeded his skull.

He scanned his desk for a large notepad.

"Whoops," he blurted. He almost forgot. He tapped his Casey Stengel bobblehead, thinking it brought good luck. Any time a Hall of Fame manager agreed with you, it was a good thing. Long since memorized, he still read the embossed quotation from the base of "the old Perfessor," "I always heard it couldn't be done, but sometimes it don't always work." Such simple wisdom from a ceramic collectible.

Merl flicked through the folders stacked on his desk. He shoved them aside. He lifted the outdated desk calendar with its boxed days tic-tac-toed by coffee rings. No writing pad. He opened his lower drawer. Mr. Potato Head glared back with one eye. The toy had both hands raised as if surrendering. Merl reached past, dumping it as he lifted out a legal pad. He ripped off the first sheet in favor of a blank one. He drew a line down the middle. On one side he wrote "Sightings." On the other, "Deaths." Under each, he listed the dates. He left three lines between them all. He referred to his earlier notes. He filled up the "Deaths" side with what he believed were facts. For 1917, he wrote "hospital" with a question mark. He followed Robbie Callahan's name with one, too.

Five confirms, two probables—if you count the Benders—and two possibles.

On the "Sightings" side, he matched the Soke founders to 1794. Ben Phelps the security guard to 1955. Question mark. Bill Talbert, Marvin Reynolds, Becky Danforth and Jack Thompson to 1974. Bobby Callahan and the two kids to 1995. Alex Simons and Robbie to this year. Question mark. He left 1866, 1917, 1938 and 1955 blank because—except for Ruth's comment about the security guard not smoking—he recalled nothing that hinted at supernatural involvement.

Or did the Benders see something that turned them traitor? Did the babies in the hospital receive a visitor from the Netherworld? Did the Finleys? Did Gehrig?

Merl shook his head and aimed closer to reality. He studied the sheet.

Two confirms and two possibles.

The names didn't line up. *Good thing or a bad thing? Are the deaths random?* Merl sought a connection, a bridge from one side to the next. *If the sightings didn't match the year of death, then what?* He recalled how Marvin Reynolds behaved. How Becky Danforth battled depression. How Bill Talbert never strayed far from the bottle. Is that it? If they met Old Coals, do victims act strangely until they die? Do they get depressed? That doesn't narrow the category any.

Merl wanted to laugh off this exercise. *If meeting Old Coals brings on depression, does it follow that to avert the next death, I check who's stocked up on Prozac?* Merl wished a way existed to confirm who'd seen Old Coals over the years. But that was like getting someone to admit they'd seen a UFO. Nobody wanted the ridicule. Those that did just wanted the attention. Merl couldn't just hold a town meeting and ask for a show of hands. He couldn't request a list of every citizen who suffered from depression.

Why not just go online?

Merl bet he could surf over to OldCoals.com and learn everything he needed to know. Joking about the idea, he tapped the computer with the Internet connection. He thought, *Why not? Everything else has a website.* He typed in the URL. He figured, at best, he'd get a site that satisfied his charcoaling needs.

As he waited for the page to load, he read the title field. He knew it was a red herring. He was still a bit surprised. He bet Big Foot and Nessie had more websites than you could name. *Didn't all myths and weirdness populate the world wild web?* He knew the perfect webmaster. Thinking of Jack, Merl took another stab, typing in Old Coals on Google. Seconds later, the search engine delivered references to "raking over old coals." Merl clicked on a link and felt a chill as he read that the phrase meant to bring up something unpleasant from the past that others don't want to talk about.

Merl stared at the screen. He had some new questions. He checked his watch. He'd bet Jack probably hadn't moved. He'd take the gamble. He wanted to know if three pennies were the payment Jack meant.

Chapter 44

The door's squeak signaled Merl's return to Becky's Tavern. This time, he didn't even notice it. Larry Jackson cornered him near the jukebox.

"Hey, Merl," he said. "Catch that loon with the machete yet?"

"What?"

"The one that done chopped off that boy's head."

Merl coughed out a laugh at how far rumor had run from truth. The news of Alex Simons and Robbie Callahan obviously spread through town in various guises. The townsfolk digested certain facts and cooked up their own version of events. It was as if they bastardized Churchill's wartime adage that truth is so precious it should always be attended by a bodyguard of lies. This day in Soke, truth traveled well-hidden. It made Merl wish some people would just shut up.

"Well?" Larry persisted.

"Nobody's lost their head," Merl said. "'Cept maybe for you."

Before Larry uttered another word, Mitch Danforth interrupted. Merl welcomed the intrusion.

"Merl," Mitch said. "What can I get ya?"

"Nothing," Merl said, flipping his hand to emphasize it. "Was hoping Jack was still here. Didn't see his bike out front."

"Yeah, he bolted not too long ago."

"Say where he was headed?"

"Think the library. Said he had some reading to do or something."

"Well, that would be the place."

"Thanks," Merl said. "You got late shift tonight?"

"All this week," Mitch said.

"Call if you can't handle 'em."

"Always do."

Merl drove the short distance to the library. When he entered, Jack sat near the front, a newspaper sprawled on the table in front of him. He seemed to be engrossed.

"Merl Burt," Ruth Felton said softly from behind the counter. "Back so soon?"

"Evening, Mrs. Fel—" Merl stopped himself. "Evening, Ruth. Looking for Jack."

Ruth swiveled her hand and pointed. Merl smiled and nodded. Jack continued staring at the newspaper.

"What's got your attention?" Merl said. He slid a chair out and dropped into it. Jack spun *The Citizen*'s living section so Merl could read it. He waved at what passed for human interest in these parts—Rabbit Cone's quest to collect a million Mountain Dew cans. The picture showed Rabbit grinning under his grimy Jim Beam cap. He stood in front of a mountain built from over 100,000 green and yellow soda cans.

"And they call ... me ... Wacky."

Merl laughed a little too loudly. He drew stern looks from Ruth and the few checking out the latest book arrivals. Merl cringed in apology.

"You think he ... drank all those?" Jack asked.

"It might explain why they call him Rabbit," Merl said.

Jack chuckled. Ruth cleared her throat. She placed a finger over her lips.

"How old you think she is?" Merl asked.

"102," Jack blurted.

"Be serious."

"I am," Jack said, unsuccessfully fighting a grin.

"She still looks like she's in her 60s. She looked that way when we were kids."

"Yeah ... but you ... should see her ... portrait ... in the attic."

"When have you ever been in her attic?"

"Forget it. ... It was ... a joke. ... If I have ... to explain it, ... it's not ... funny."

"I just saw him," Merl said.

"Who?" Jack asked.

"Rabbit."

"Yup ... was in here ... making ... copies."

They let the topic fade. Sitting across from each other at cross purposes, each groped for the right words. Merl wanted to discuss dates and pennies. Jack wanted to present warnings and ammo. He sensed Merl needed protection. Wanted to instruct him not to lose hope. That despair killed. Merl seized the silence first, angling his approach to get what he wanted directly.

"You ever collected coins?" he asked. "Found some while looking for Alex."

"What kind of ... coins?" Jack asked.

"Pennies, mostly. And this really old silver coin—Liberty and Commerce from New York."

Merl described the variations—the Wheats, the Indian heads, the Lincoln heads. How he lost them with his jacket. The dates he mentioned in random order, to stall an immediate connection.

Jack nodded.

"Those dates ... Payment. ... It will take ... three. ... Just ... like ... before."

"You keep talking payment," Merl said. "Like you can just pay—" He stopped himself, mid-sentence. He almost brought Old Coals directly into the conversation. The last thing he wanted to do was re-summon Wacky Jacky.

"Pay me ... now ... or pay ... me later," Jack said. He sensed Wacky Jacky stirring. He decided to block his approach. Lock doors.

Close windows. Turn off lights. He thought about lightning bugs as the conversation lapped against dangerous banks. He had to hurry.

Merl digested the comment. He wondered if it meant dates don't have to match up. If it mattered what year you met Old Coals and when you died? *Is that what Jack just confirmed?*

"So, you might get the bill one year? And not have to pay until another year?"

"If three ... have paid," Jack said. He grew restless. Merl saw him fidget. *Not a good sign.*

"What happens while you're waiting for the bill to arrive," Merl asked.

Jack heard a doorbell ring in his head.

"Mormons," he said.

Snorting a laugh, Merl wasn't sure he heard right.

"Did you say, 'Mormons?'"

Jack nodded. For Merl, this ceased to be a conversation and become a jigsaw puzzle with words. He had seen this piece before. Merl remembered the religious anecdote because it tickled him. Those three young men dressed in their Sunday suits standing on Jack's porch, unaware that Jack believed they were salesmen. That he wasn't listening to a single word. Merl repeated the exchange out loud.

"They said, 'We want to bring some happiness into your life.' And you said, 'No, thanks. I don't want any.'"

Jack smiled broadly that Merl remembered the lines. Merl chuckled.

"Some paint themselves ... into a corner and ... think the paint ... will never ... dry," Jack said.

"You mean the victims, right?"

"'Despair ... is for ... those ... who ... know the end ... without doubt.'"

Merl stared blankly at Jack for a moment. He didn't recognize the line from Tolkien. Not that knowing the source mattered.

"Is that a yes or no?" Merl said. The question came too late. Humming in a staccato manner, Wacky Jacky furiously began doodling on the newspaper. He looked at Merl. He said, "Do you know what the word 'mead' means? You might think it has something to do with a meadow but it doesn't, aside from the fact that it is in the word meadow. Most people think it is a meadow but it is not. Mead is the substance of drink."

Merl frowned. He rose to leave. He almost patted his friend on the shoulder when he halted. Wacky Jacky wasn't doodling. Merl realized why the dates sounded so familiar. He discovered the connection. Looking down, he read the childhood rhyme Wacky Jacky had written. It contained a line Merl's grandfather never taught him.

> *In 1794, I returned to take three more.*
> *In 18 and 66, I made them swing like sticks.*
> *In 19 and 17, I came back and was unseen.*
> *In 19 and 38, I did not show up too late.*
> *In 19 and 55, I made them all burn alive.*
> *In 1974, I found I had more in store.*
> *When I take another three.*
> *That won't be the last for me.*

Merl silently mouthed the final two lines again. *When I take another three, that won't be the last for me.*

Merl shivered as a chill coursed through him. He had to remind himself to breathe as he stood and stared at the rhyme in front of him. With his sleeve, he wiped the sweat beading on his brow. He ignored the sing-song lyrics Wacky Jacky uttered in a subdued tone. Merl was too absorbed in the printed rhyme.

He pulled out his small notepad. He compared his facts with the nursery rhyme. He didn't like how they seemed to match up—Pastor Soke and two others in 1794; the Benders hanged in 1866. Even 1917's lack of information fit—"Came unseen."

He reminded himself to call the hospital about crib deaths that year. Nobody questioned crib deaths as being out of the ordinary. It could be completely overlooked.

Too late in 1938? That was the house fire, but anything would fit there. Who else burned in 1955?

Merl pondered the eerie wisdom of this rhyme. It reminded him that "Ring Around the Rosy" wasn't just an innocent ditty either. It detailed something sinister. It described the stages of bubonic plague. He realized it was the song on Wacky Jacky's lips for the second time today.

Ring around the rosy: Blood spots formed a red ring about the neck before turning black.

Pocket full of posies: Flowers were kept in the pocket to staunch the stench.

Ashes, ashes: They burned the bodies, the bedding and clothes.

We all fall down: We die.

Merl wondered who in Soke would fall down next.

Chapter 45

Robbie refused to accept he was dead. He didn't care what he saw in that coffin.

Can't fool me. Got to be a joke. Or some kind of mind trick. Yeah, that's it. A mind trick. Like Darth Vader pulled on Dagobah with Luke. Putting his face inside that dark helmet. Won't work with me. I'm not dead.

Robbie checked his surroundings.

Hey!

He now lay in his bed. Relaxing, Robbie inhaled deeply, catching the familiar whiff of jelly beans he had once melted to the floor with his chemistry set. However, the odor didn't linger, chased off by a more foul scent. It took a moment before Robbie realized he wasn't the only one who noticed. His poster of Ilya Kovalchuk over his headboard no longer looked for a loose puck. His poster of Chipper Jones next to the yellow seafarer lamp no longer looked for an incoming pitch. Both athletes stared elsewhere. Before turning, Robbie knew where their eyes trained: the open closet door. The door Robbie always kept closed at night. Kept it closed so when it opened, the creak it produced alerted him that the monsters had arrived.

Robbie quickly scanned the room. No monsters. He leaned over and glanced under the bed. No monsters.

Maybe they are still in the closet!

Robbie steadied himself as he slid from under the covers. His heart pounded. He flinched as a bead of cold sweat dripped from his armpit. *Shut the door!* Robbie halted. *Shut the door now! Work up the courage. Act. Sleep secure.*

Robbie had done it dozens of times before. The beasts lurking in the dark never once nabbed him. Because he'd been careful.

As he summoned his courage, Robbie scouted a path through his toys. If he'd put them away like his mother asked, he wouldn't have to worry about tip-toeing through a minefield of noisemaking obstacles, each guaranteed to alert a snoozing goblin. Robbie trained his eyes on the door. He stepped over his G.I. Joe and around his Millennium Falcon. He made no sound, breathing so lightly he wouldn't fog a mirror. He took another step. And another. He lost his balance slightly and swayed. He planted a hand on the floor to steady himself. He just missed waking his battery-operated Robot Man.

That was a close one. Robbie stared into the closet.

Nothing stirred. Still undetected, Robbie glanced down at the robot. It stared blankly back at him, that silly grin frozen. Robbie lifted his arm. His pajama sleeve snagged the robot's arm. The toy clanged. It whirred. It lights flashed. Robbie's heart jumped. He whirled toward the closet door.

Nothing stirred. Darkness stared back.

Robbie squealed as Robot Man clambered up his forearm. It shredded the pajama sleeve. Robbie whipped his arm out, trying to sling the metal toy across the room. It gripped harder, tearing bits of flannel. Focusing on the robot, Robbie overlooked the other toys encircling him. He banged the robot on the floor, scattering plastic army men and battering a tank. The harder he smashed the robot, the tighter it gripped. Its claw pierced Robbie's skin. He saw blood streak down his arm, dripping to the floor. He shuddered to see his teddy bear licking the drops. It grinned savagely. Plastic army men launched an assault on his leg. Robbie recalled his dad's lessons.

Break down your fear.

He corralled his galloping panic in order to tame his fear. He assessed the robot as the greatest danger. He keyed on it. Knowing he couldn't defeat it with might, he opted for the alternative. He flipped open the hatch in the back. He popped out the batteries. The robot released its grip. It clunked rigidly to the floor.

Robbie ripped off the Army Rangers scaling his leg. He threw them against the wall, disregarding their anguished cries. He grabbed a shoe to swat the rest of the battalion before something predatory pounced onto his back. He heard the snarl and guessed his replica saber-tooth tiger had joined the attack. It sank its long fangs into his upper back. The pain sucked Robbie's breath away. He stumbled, flailing vainly to reach the pre-historic plastic beast as it bore deep into his muscle. Robbie backpedaled and slammed hard into the wall, hoping to mash the creature. It worked. Too well. The creature now hung limply, its fangs embedded so deeply they impaled a lung.

Robbie grew dizzy. He watched the room shrink. He thought he saw his teddy bear lumber toward him. Barely conscious of doing it, Robbie grabbed the tennis racquet near his hand. He served the bear through the bedroom window before his vision fogged. He felt himself slipping away. He took a deep breath.

Don't give up. Remember what started all this. The closet door!

Robbie no longer stood in his room. He was camped excitedly in a John Boat with Grandpa, their lantern fighting back against a moonless night in the Okefenokee Swamp. Crickets chirped incessantly. Bullfrogs volleyed baritone croaks. An owl screeched. Robbie and Grandpa gently dipped their paddles into the inky water. They navigated toward that special eddy where the biggest fish rose on a night like this. Trying to shake off some disgusting green slime, Robbie banged his paddle against the boat. The noise reverberated across the swamp, through the shallows and into the depths where things best not disturbed suddenly stirred. Silence answered the call. Grandpa raised a hand to still Robbie. He doused the light. Blackness charged forth so ferociously that Robbie struggled to breathe. The mute swamp paused as if awaiting the okay to attack the quiet again. Crickets tested first. Frogs followed. They chorused into a symphony as water lapped against the boat.

Robbie still could see nothing while his other senses heightened. His imagination did too. A cypress creaked as if walking toward them. A splash echoed in the distance.

Spanish moss gave the wind its whisper. The breeze mixed decay with the putrid scent of greenbrier. Spiders dangled silently from branches as if inspecting what floated past. Water moccasins zigzagged closer, chasing after wake. A rumble rolled from the depths. Something brushed Robbie's face. Grandpa grunted. The boat rocked viciously to the left. A huge splash.

"Grandpa!" Robbie shouted. No answer returned, only the word racing into the distance.

After the ripples that fanned out met exposed roots and died, silence regained control of the night. In the black, Robbie trembled. He waited for whatever snatched Grandpa to return for him. He flinched as it breached the surface. It spit, sputtered and coughed. Its laughter cut through the night. Its hand patted the aft side. It secured a grip. The boat tipped at the weight as it swung a leg over the side.

It's climbing aboard!

Water sloshed off the creature as it stood before Robbie in the dark. It shook itself. Robbie sat mute. He held his breath. He listened to water—or slime—drop from the creature. He stared into the inky blackness.

Drip, drip, drip ...

Robbie resigned himself to his fate.

Drip, drip, drip ...

It cleared its throat.

Drip, drip, drip.

"Robbie?" it said.

Chapter 46

"*Robbie?*" Dad said. His voice immediately calmed all fears, like Grandpa's voice had when he climbed back into the John Boat.

"Yes, sir?"

"*You need to remember some things.*"

"*Okay,*" Robbie said.

"*You know those movies and stories we kept watching over and over again? Like* Star Wars, Lord of the Rings, Apollo 13, Miracle, *the 1969 Mets? Those war stories—The Battle of Britain, Bastogne, the Battle of Leyte Gulf?*"

Robbie nodded, unsure of what his dad wanted. He wondered if they were going to play the movie game. Maybe they were going to watch a new one.

"*Do you know what all those had in common?*"

Robbie shook his head.

"*Think.*"

Robbie thought. His mind chased after lightsabers, orcs, spaceships, pucks, baseballs. After Spitfires, tanks and battleships. Alien creatures and men in uniform. He saw explosions and missiles and rockets and stars. He pictured dogfights, sea battles and swordplay. He saw death and danger. Danger everywhere. He wondered if that were the answer, if danger was the answer. Before he spoke, he reviewed his choices. *There was no danger for the Mets or the hockey team. Nobody thought they would win anyway.* That's when the tumblers began to click into place. *Nobody thought anybody would win.*

"Nobody would win," Robbie blurted.

Dad shook his head.

"I mean, nobody thought they would win," Robbie said.

"You're on the right track," Dad said. *"Turn it around."*

"They would win ... They won when nobody thought they would," Robbie said.

"Very good," his dad answered. Robbie beamed.

"Every one of those stories involved somebody doing the impossible. They succeeded against incredible odds. Like David versus Goliath. They never said 'can't' because ... "

"Can't never could," Robbie injected.

"That's right. They decided they could. They didn't quit. They didn't listen to others who said it can't be done. They did what they had to do. Remember what Josey Wales told those in the house if the Comanche arrived?"

"To keep an eye on the roof?" Robbie said. He wondered why Dad didn't recite a line of dialogue from the movie.

His dad smiled.

"That's not the line I meant. It was, 'Now remember, things look bad and it looks like you're not gonna make it ... '"

Robbie finished the line.

"'Then you gotta get mean. I mean plumb, mad-dog mean. 'Cause if you lose your head and you give up then you neither live nor win. That's just the way it is.'"

"Do you understand what that means?" his dad said.

That wasn't the next line. Robbie realized it was a question and not the game.

"Yes, sir," he answered. *"It means 'don't give up.'"*

"You need to take those words to heart right now, Bub. No matter how bad things may get, they will get better. You never thought Frodo and Sam would make it, but they did. Because they kept going. Gene Kranz with Mission Control refused to accept the impossibility of saving Apollo 13. He said failure is not an option. Those astronauts returned safely. Because he kept going.

"There's no telling what the future holds. You must be prepared for anything. Remind yourself of these stories. Use them. Embrace them. May your desire to know the story's end outweigh your sorrow."

Robbie puzzled over his dad's advice.

"And most importantly, Robbie," his dad said.

"Yes, sir?"

"Never ever forget how much I love you. No matter what you see, no matter what someone says, know that your mother and I will always love you. Nothing can change that. And I will never say otherwise. You got that? I will never say otherwise."

"What's gonna happen?" Robbie said.

His dad silenced him with a stern smile.

"You're going to make me so proud. You're going to do something that can't be done. Think about those stories. Remember what they mean. Use them to remind yourself that the impossible IS possible. Know that doing the impossible makes you mighty. Now what was that scripture I taught you?"

"'Tho' I walk through the valley of the shadow of death, I shall fear no evil for Thou art with me,'" Robbie said.

"Again."

"'Tho' I walk through the valley of the shadow of death, I shall fear no evil for Thou art with me,'" Robbie said.

"Again."

"'Tho' I walk through the valley of the shadow of death, I shall fear no evil for Thou art with me,'" Robbie said.

"Again."

Robbie continued repeating the 23rd Psalm, understanding its message. He didn't understand its relevance. He didn't know why his dad suddenly reminded him of all those heroic episodes. Still repeating scripture, Robbie drifted off. He pictured coach Herb Brooks pushing his 1980 Olympic hockey team beyond themselves in *Miracle*. He heard the whistle.

Again.

Chapter 47

"'... for Thou art with me.'"

In slumber, Robbie's mind absorbed each of the lessons his dad tried to re-enforce. Even if Robbie didn't grasp his dad's import, his memory did. It cut right to the chase.

It reminded him of the Battle of Britain. Of Winston Churchill honoring the RAF with the line "Never in the field of human conflict was so much owed by so many to so few."

It recalled the 101st Airborne surrounded and outnumbered in the snow during the Battle of the Bulge at Bastogne. Of the American commander Anthony McAuliffe offered the chance to surrender and replying, "Nuts."

It remembered a small Navy force known as Taffy 3 outgunned, overmatched and facing certain annihilation attacking the entire Japanese fleet during the Battle of Leyte Gulf. Of seeing the superior fleet in retreat, a sailor exclaiming, "Damn it, they're getting away!"

Robbie floated to a scene where David faced the giant Goliath and slew him. The scene morphed. Robbie saw himself throwing rocks at that bully Brian Finister.

He found himself in the castle from the movie *The Princess Bride*. He wielded a fencing foil. Instinctively, he recited his favorite line, *"My name is Inigo Montoya. You killed my father. Prepare to die."* He swished his weapon through the air. Before he could turn and run his épée through the six-fingered man, it became a lightsaber. Robbie whirled to find Darth Vader breathing noisily with his saber unsheathed. The Evil Lord spoke, *"I find your lack of faith disturbing."*

Robbie quivered. His mind deployed re-enforcement. It swiftly settled into the routine his dad taught him. *Break down your fear and overcome it.* Robbie tried in his own fashion. *If I have a lightsaber, I'm a Jedi Knight. I can wield this power. Recall Yoda's lessons, "Beware anger, fear, aggression. The dark side are they. Once you start down the dark path, forever will it dominate your destiny."* Robbie remembered a Jedi draws his power for defense, never attack. That there was no try, only do or do not. He calmed himself. He waited to parry Vader's strike. When it did not come, he peeked. He recognized Lord Aragorn in the village of Bree.

"Are you frightened?"

Robbie nodded.

"Not nearly frightened enough. I know what hunts you."

Robbie felt something cool touch his forehead. He felt like he was burning up. His mind raced. It was like watching the Tolkien trilogy on fast forward. There was the white-bearded Saruman telling him *"against the power of Mordor there is no victory."* Robbie saw the armies marching. The wastelands. The Nazguls screeching overhead. He ducked. He reminded himself that Frodo and Sam made it. He saw Sam sitting in Gondor, telling Frodo this present darkness could not be the end without doubt.

"Folk in those stories had lots of chances of turning back, only they didn't. They kept going, because they were holding on to something."

Robbie didn't need to ask what that was. He knew, but his dream let Sam continue. *"That there's some good in the world. And it's worth fighting for."*

Galadriel then appeared. She looked so much like his mother. She smiled and leaned close. She said, *"Even the smallest person can change the course of the future."*

Robbie stood on the wall of the White City of Gondor. He eyed the gathering storm. He believed he was ready for anything.

He wasn't.

They were only movie scenes. What came for him was real.

Chapter 48

Hurrying back to its nest, the wasp lost its orientation; its internal mechanism for guiding it to and from its hunting grounds and home gone haywire. The insect circled, trying to locate its bearings. Suddenly, it no longer mattered. The wasp sensed peril. It fled.

The creature known as Old Coals didn't notice. Over eons, its want rose and fell. It either lingered or hurried, driven by some primordial need to acquire, to possess. It cared not if it were sated by life or soul. Only that its need was fed, was satisfied.

Old Coals waited, motionless. It did not know that when it lingered too long in one place that the air there would always carry a chill, the ground would be as if salted, nothing ever growing there again. To the pines the creature passed under, branches snapped and dangled as if yanked from below. On the pine where Old Coals paused, the bark peeled back. The wood blistered and then split vertically, giving birth to an ugly knot. It would mature into a deformed hump below a wound that never healed.

As Old Coals stood, woodland creatures trembled. Some brought offerings. Old Coals cared not. As with any of the deadly sins, acquisition only delayed the desire for more. Want anyways returned. The creature's want grew. The desire for a third festered, siphoning strength as it intensified.

Old Coals felt that compulsion rise. Time grew short. Its want increased. It was time to choose.

On this Saturday evening in October, Old Coals stirred again.

Chapter 49

Merl inserted the key in his cruiser's ignition. His thoughts stopped him from turning it. He felt like he was reviewing for an exam. He believed Jack verified this much for him: That it didn't matter when you saw Old Coals. If you did, despair followed. Then, death. Merl saw little other way to interpret Jack's three clues: 1. Not wanting any happiness; 2. Painting one's self into a corner and thinking the paint won't dry and; 3. That despair is only for those who know the end without doubt. Seemed rather cut and dried.

But why can't they break free of it?

Merl recalled Jack found little success changing Becky's outlook. He assumed Bill Talbert's drinking was an attempt to escape. Same went for Melinda James and Reggie Morgan and crack. Maybe the Fitzs tried to run. Did Alex? Marvin resigned himself to it. Bobby Callahan? Bobby Callahan attacked it.

Look where it got him.

Merl rolled the quotations over.

Don't want any happiness.

Painting one's self in corner and thinking the paint will never dry.

Despair for those who know the end without doubt.

From Marvin to the two teenagers, from Bill Talbert to Becky Danforth, each seemed resigned to his or her fate.

Merl ground down the quotations into categories.

Depression, resignation, surrender.

He repeated them to himself.

Depression, resignation, surrender.

He thought if he were depressed, he wouldn't resign himself to it. He damn well wouldn't surrender.

Best just not to look in the first place.

Not to look in the first place. Merl shook his head that he even thought that. If a cop knew what were coming, there wouldn't be any crime. It wasn't like he could put an artist's rendering of Old Coals all over town with the warning "Don't look him in the eye." Besides, this town already knew better.

Jack's explanation rattled in Merl's mind. *No, not an explanation. More like an admonition. A warning.*

Depression.
Resignation.
Surrender.
Death.

The voice of NFL Films boomed in Merl's mind. He heard John Facenda's baritone describing a historic moment, *"Outlined against a blue, gray October sky the Four Horsemen rode again. In dramatic lore they are known as famine, pestilence, destruction and death. These are only aliases."*

The Four Horsemen of the Sokalypse: Depression, Resignation, Surrender and Death. The town's four horsemen.

Four …
Three …
Two …
One …

"Down to one," Merl said to himself.

Death comes in threes. Bobby is the first. Alex is the second. One remains.

Merl assumed it was Robbie. His gut told him it was Robbie.

What if his gut were wrong? What if it were someone else? Rather than guard every border, he decided to narrow the focus. Eliminate the knowns until there's only one choice left. Leave no doubts. *Key on who may have seen Old Coals.*

Chapter 50

As Merl cycled through potential victims other than Robbie, the college kids in the Navigator jumped to mind. He didn't think they were at risk. But why wait until it was too late? He was paid to serve and protect, not sit around and object. He'd cross them off the list before returning to the hospital. See how Robbie was faring. He wondered if his Casey Stengel bobblehead agreed it was a good idea.

Merl turned left. He hurried down Hallman to the highway. He sped south toward the campus. He knew it wouldn't be easy to locate a college kid on a Saturday night. He had to try. Maybe they saw something strange. If nothing else, he'd learn how they were.

Since it was after hours and the offices were closed, he checked in with campus security. He requested Duncan McCumber's address. He got it: Harper Hall, Room 203. Merl told Security it was a favor for a friend. He could find it on his own. The security guard nodded. He slid across a campus map, circling the dormitory with an arrow showing the quickest route there. It was a short L-shaped line. Merl thanked him. He headed toward the dorm. Along the way, he marveled how a complete stranger could traverse a small campus and be noticed by everybody and noted by none.

Guess in certain environments, the outside world rarely intrudes.

Merl entered Harper Hall. He climbed the stairs to the second floor. Instinctively, he smelled for illegal smoke. He detected none. He found McCumber's room at the end of the hall. Merl knocked.

Cameron Casey yelled it was open. Merl opened the door. He stuck in his head.

"Is Duncan McCumber around?"

Casey didn't look up, answering without realizing that only a non-student would ask for someone by their full name.

"Library," he said.

The information surprised Merl. He expected Mr. McCumber to be out at the frat houses. Or in town at the movies. Or drinking at Mason's. But the library? On a Saturday?

Each to his own.

The campus library. A missed opportunity. It never dawned on Merl to check the college library for information on Old Coals. He had checked public works, police records, the public library and even the internet. He smiled to himself. *Guess in certain environments, the insulated world rarely intrudes.*

Entering the library, Merl asked the young lady behind counter if she had seen Duncan McCumber.

"You going to arrest him?" she asked.

"No, just doing a favor for a friend."

She looked disappointed. He didn't know if it were because she wanted to see the action or she didn't like the kid. Since he had enough mysteries to solve, he didn't pursue it.

"Do you know where he might be? I was told he was here."

She suggested the study room toward the back of the library. Merl found him there. He entered what looked like a lounge room, only quieter. Duncan and two other students looked up. None spoke but Duncan.

"Didn't expect to see you again," he said. Merl heard trepidation in his voice. The other students cast annoyed looks, more at the breach of library etiquette than anything else.

"How's the kid doing?" Duncan asked, his voice hesitant.

"He's hanging in there," Merl said, adding what he hoped was a comforting smile. He rightly deduced that Duncan feared arrest. He tried to dispel such anxiousness.

"What you did this afternoon was very commendable," Merl said. He slid out a chair and sat across from Duncan. "Some people would have just driven off."

Duncan blushed.

"Just common courtesy," Duncan said. "Doing what's right."

"Courtesy isn't so common any more," Merl said. He paused, electing to shelve his lecture topic for more immediate concerns. "I need some help with my investigation."

"Sure. What can I help you with?"

"I need you to recall if you saw anything strange. Anything out of the ordinary."

Duncan leaned back. He scrunched his lips. Merl tried another tack. "Did you sense anything … creepy?"

Duncan's expression changed.

"Yeah," he said with enthusiasm. "There was this great big hawk. Just perched in a tree. Looked like it was, you know, watching us. Thought it was a vulture at first, you know, waiting on the body, maybe waiting for us to leave. But it never moved. It just sat there. It was kinda got creepy, you know. Even from a distance, you could see its eyes. Kinda glowed. Red eyes. Weird. What bird has red eyes?"

Merl leaned forward.

"Are you sure about that?" he asked.

"Oh, yeah. We both said how weird it was. How we'd never seen a bird with red eyes. Erin joked it was the crow from *The Stand*. You know, the walking dude. Stephen King."

Merl speculated how far from the truth she was. He debated how the kid would respond if he asked about the girl, considering how he last saw them. He was thankful when Duncan volunteered the information.

"Erin's out with that cop friend of yours."

"He's not a friend," Merl said. "I'd say you're probably much better off."

Merl didn't want to ask his next question, it seemed so un-police-like. But he needed to know if the kid were depressed. He felt silly inquiring.

"You doing okay. Not feeling any ill effects?"

Duncan scrunched his lips again. He cut a glance at one of the students in the room before responding.

"Naw. Doing fine." He leaned against the table and lowered his voice. "Actually, feel a lot better. Dating Erin is like walking on eggshells. Always had to be careful not to upset her, you know. Didn't realize how much energy that takes. I feel like a huge weight is lifted."

Merl smiled. That wasn't the question he asked but the answer would do.

"I didn't learn that until I was much older than you," Merl said. He patted the table and added, "Thanks. Appreciate your help."

"No problem," Duncan said.

Before leaving the table, Merl slid a business card toward Duncan. He told him to call if he thought of anything else. Merl deduced the kid was in denial. The pain of heartbreak would hit later. Hit hard.

Be strong, young man. Be strong.

Because he was here, Merl seized the moment. He stopped at a computer terminal. He typed "Soke" and tapped Enter to search the library database. It returned one entry of note: *Off-Kilter: Roswell, Fiction, Soke and other Strange Town Tales* by Francis Friedman, 1988. Merl recalled that the author wasn't from around here. That most thought the book to be hogwash. He never bothered to read it. Merl scribbled down the catalog number. It was not on the shelf. He double-checked his scratch sheet. No matching number. He hunted the surrounding shelves to see if it had been misplaced. No such luck. He returned to the front desk. He asked the young lady behind the counter if the book were checked out and by whom. He told her the title and handed over his crumbled note. She called the book up on the computer.

"Whoa," she said. "It's been checked out for a while."

"By whom?"

"Bobby Callahan."

"How long has it been checked out? Six months?"

"More like six years."

"Six years?"

She nodded. "Six years."

"Might as well mark that as lost," Merl said, shaking his head.

"Already is. Can't believe it's still in the system."

"Is there a fine?"

She told him there was. Obviously, it was unpaid.

"What happens if it remains unpaid?" Merl asked, fishing for his wallet.

"Mr. Bobby Callahan can't check out another book or park on campus until all fines are settled," she said.

Merl shoved his wallet back in his pocket. Bobby wouldn't have a problem with those penalties.

Obviously Bobby didn't find the right answers in that book. He sure found the enemy.

Merl's stomach announced its desire with a loud growl. It followed with several sharp gurgles and a slow whine. The girl behind the counter giggled. Merl patted his belly.

"Always trust your gut," he said. He headed back to his cruiser and drove toward the hospital.

Chapter 51

Jack Thompson knew how to be found. Such a creature of habit—he frequented the same places on the same days at about the same times—it didn't take much guesswork to locate him. The Waffle Griddle in the morning, the library at mid-morning and Becky's Place in the afternoon before circling around. On Tuesdays, he wandered about town.

Being so structured, Jack grew attuned to the town's rhythms. He recognized its occupants' patterns. It was the reason he bumped into Merl like an unintended game of tag. It was why Jack came straight to the Griddle from the library. His friend would come here next. No fast food in the squad car. No early dinners. It was the only sit down restaurant near the hospital. Merl would show.

Jack believed his friend could make a difference. Believed he'd make the leap of faith in time. *He just needed these.* Jack fingered his shirt pocket. He needed Merl to show. He also needed Wacky Jacky to shut up. He kept getting in the way.

So did Cindy Horner. Every few minutes, she insisted Jack order something or leave. Although he'd been seated long enough to memorize the menu, he told her he hadn't decided yet. She fumed. In the near empty restaurant, she complained loudly that paying customers needed the booth.

Mike Butler waved a dripping spatula at her.

"Let him be," he said. He turned his attention back to three strips of bacon.

Jack ducked down in the booth. He set his chin on the cold table. He counted the sugar packages in the white mug. Six pinks. Three blues. Two whites. He scanned the words on the menu for letters, seeing how fast he could run through the alphabet. If he lacked a letter, he scrutinized the words painted on the front window. He examined the license plates in the parking lot. Even the blue nameplate on Cindy's breast pocket. He grinned at what was engraved on it, "Serving more than smiles. CINDY."

There he is! Finally!

Merl pushed through the entrance.

"Hey, Merl," Cindy said. "Mind arresting Penniless back there for loitering? He refuses to order anything."

Merl saw Jack's head pop up from behind the booth bench. They gave a knowing nod at each other.

"I'll see about correcting that situation."

Merl moved swiftly to the booth. He slid across from Jack.

"You stalking me?"

Jack ignored his question.

"You gonna see ... Robbie ... soon?" he asked.

"Heading that way now."

"Got something ... you need to give him ... It's important," Jack said. He reached for his shirt pocket.

Cindy interrupted.

"Can I get you anything, Chief?" She called anybody with a badge "Chief." She tossed different salutations at different folks. Some she called "Pal" or "Babe." If she liked you it was "Sweetie." Merl contemplated if she devised her own class system for customers, considered if he weren't wearing a badge whether he'd be a "Pal," "Mister" or "Sir." *Be nice to be called "Count."* Merl shook away the thought.

"You hungry?" he asked Jack. Jack nodded.

"I'll have two scrambled eggs, grits, two sausage links and whole wheat toast, hold the butter," Merl said. He pointed to Jack for his order.

"The same," Jack said.

"Anything to drink?" Cindy said.

"Coffee," Merl and Jack said in unison. She turned over the mugs on the table. She filled each a thumb below the brim.

"Order will be right up," Cindy said.

Merl tore open a cream cup. He upended the contents into his coffee. He watched it create a tan trail in the black liquid. He repeated it twice more before unrolling his napkin. His silverware clattered onto the table. He picked up the spoon. As he poured in the sugar, he stirred slowly.

"Been thinking about Bobby Callahan," Merl said. "How he believed there was something out there."

"Don't you?" Jack said. Silently, he wondered how many times Merl was going to swing at the same pitch.

Merl paused.

"I don't need to believe in Santa Claus or the tooth fairy to know others do," he said.

"They're ... not ... real," Jack said.

Cindy interrupted them. She slid two plates of food onto the table. Merl was always impressed how fast it arrived. He centered his plate. He watched Jack immediately salt his eggs. *How impulsive.* Merl scooped a bite. He reached for the salt shaker himself. As he exchanged it for the pepper, he realized Cindy still hovered. He looked back up at her.

"Is it true?" she asked.

"Is what true?"

"Someone's murdering little boys."

"Where in the world did you hear that?"

"Harry and Neil were talking about it."

"Well, consider the source," Merl said.

She looked at him like he reprimanded her.

"Nobody's murdering little boys," Merl added to appease her.

Cindy flashed a smile.

"You need anything else?" she asked.

"I'm fine," Merl said.

She didn't ask Jack. He was almost finished. He had a few specks of egg and some melted butter left on his plate. He munched on his final piece of toast. Merl poked at his pile of eggs.

"How come all these years, there's no evidence?" Merl asked. "I've read all the stories. I've checked the police files. Everything is hearsay. It's 'he said that; she saw this.' But there's never any hard evidence. Everything can be explained away. I mean, some folks believe Bill Talbert was attacked by a bear drawn to the smell of those fish sandwiches. No offense, but that's the town's most credible sighting."

Jack shook his head, wishing Merl was way past this point.

"Do I doubt you ... because you ... have no pennies?" he said.

Merl smiled crookedly. Point taken. He stabbed his lumpy grits.

"Do I doubt you," Jack continued, "because ... I wasn't there ... when Bobby died?

"Or Bill ... Tal ... bert?"

Merl set down his fork. He searched for a rebuttal. All he could find was "Doesn't it strike you as strange that everything can be explained away?"

"We already slew this dragon!" Jack yelled. His angry retort stunned Merl. It silenced all other conversation in the restaurant as well.

"Most legends ... ignore the facts," Jack said with his jaw tight, his eyes hard. "You must believe ... beyond reason. ... Hard evidence? ... It's there for those who see. ... But how many ignore the truth? ... How many think the moon landings ... were staged? ... How many think ... the holocaust ... never happened. ... How many argue ... argue that Moses ... parted the Red Sea ... where it was ... only a couple of feet deep? ... Even they miss ... the greater miracle ... That God drowned ... Pharaoh's army ... in shallow water."

Jack pounded the table once, rattling the silverware and jostling the cups. "Facts are facts! ... Change them? ... They still hold truths."

He glared at Merl, his anger and voice rising. Only sausage sizzling on the grill provided background noise.

"'All that glitters ... is not gold. ... All those who wander ... are not lost,'" he said. He learned forward. His speech quickened. Jack wanted Merl riled, too, because he knew he'd dwell on it. He knew retreat pushed Merl's buttons like nothing else. Jack lowered his voice and growled, "You can't fight this. ... There's no way ... to fight fate. ... Sometimes, a good run is better ... than a bad stand."

Merl's jaw set. He knew Jack didn't want him to let another die and be done with it. He rose to the bait. He spat back, "Better to shoot for the moon and get off the ground than to aim for the ceiling and never leave the floor."

"Amen, brother," Wacky Jacky said. He chortled.

His appetite lost, Merl pushed his plate back. Wacky Jacky rocked. He hummed. He eyed Merl, sideways.

"You ever ponder the phrase 'doggin' it'?" he said. "Comes from the big saws cutting trees. They'd get caught biting into the wood and it made it look like two dogs gettin' it on. Gettin' it on!"

Merl cursed under his breath. He didn't need this. He wanted answers. Frustrated and irked, he slid out of the booth. He stood. Wacky Jacky grabbed Merl's wrist. He reached into his shirt pocket and extracted three pennies. He planted them into Merl's hand. He folded his fingers over them.

"Everyone thinks they have more than enough common sense, but everyone else thinks it's not enough," Merl heard Wacky Jacky say.

Merl didn't disagree. *What does that have to do with three pennies?* Merl thanked him before thinking it might be Cindy's tip. Wacky Jacky held his gaze. His eyes hinted that Jack was still home. "Everyone thinks they have more than enough common sense, but everyone else thinks it's not enough."

Again, the look. This time, another line, "People who tell you about doom are probably the least interested in your welfare."

"What's your point?" Merl said.

Wacky Jacky tightened his grip on Merl's closed fist. He glared at Merl and then the fist. When he looked back up at Merl, he said, "Common C-E-N-T-S."

Merl mouthed the line he had misinterpreted before, "Everyone thinks they have more than enough common cents, but everyone else thinks it's not enough."

Wacky Jacky opened his hand as if to ask for the coins back. He repeated the line, "People who tell you about doom are probably the least interested in your welfare."

Cripes, Merl thought, *this is like talking to Lassie. Is Timmy in trouble out by the barn?*

Merl dumped the coins back into Wacky Jacky's hand. Again, he was offered them. Wacky Jacky dropped them back into Merl's palm. He closed his fist. Merl read the repetition as a lesson. But what was he supposed to learn?

He looked down at his fist. He opened it. Three pennies. All tails. He flipped each to check the dates: 1974, 1990 and 2004.

1974: The date Becky Danforth, Bill Talbert and Marvin Reynolds saw Old Coals. And three died.

1990: The date Bobby Callahan saw Old Coals take Becky. And two more died.

2004: The date Old Coals took Bobby, Alex and ... Merl snapped his head toward Wacky Jacky.

"Are these for me," Merl said, watching him nod slightly.

"Or Robbie?"

Wacky Jacky nodded wildly.

Merl noted the change in intensity.

"Are these for me to give to Robbie?"

Wacky Jacky offered two thumbs up. He slid out of the booth and started singing, "Come sail away. Come sail away. Come and sail away with me." He danced and sang his way out of the restaurant.

It took a second for the song to register. Merl debated if it were a joke or another clue. But Jack had not been joking. *Somehow he's taken advantage of Wacky Jacky's knowledge. He's trying to help me. Was the song choice a hint?* He stabbed at the obvious. It was a hit single from the rock group Styx. Styx was the river the dead crossed to get into Hell. The ferryman had to be paid. It was the reason coins were placed on the eyes of the dead.

Was he supposed to put these on Robbie's eyes? If so, why had Jack given him three?

Chapter 52

Merl climbed into his cruiser more confused than ever.

None of this makes sense. S-E-N-S-E. Other than these pennies were for Robbie. That might settle the "who" and "what" but it left the "where" and "how" open for discussion. Merl had no desire to talk about the "why."

He didn't want to accept the absurd. The concept ran counter to who he was. Reality had to be based in reality. Stepping beyond that border meant releasing an anchor, weakening the foundation of principles that guided his life. Like experiencing a quake for the first time and learning that the earth is not stable. For Merl, accepting that Old Coals really existed would be like believing gravity no longer held sway, that sometimes it simply let go. That one plus one equals a shoe. Merl preferred sanity, but sensed that side of the debate was losing, that his resistance was eroding. He recognized he was following his mother's admonition about sin. That first one tolerates it. Then one accepts it. Then one embraces it. He was grappling with step two.

The car radio squawked. Merl heard dispatcher Betty Trumble's dispassionate voice.

"All units. All units. Suspicious subject at one-niner Kinard's Ferry Road."

Merl heard Andre Waters respond to the call.

"10-4. I'm 10-17 to her house."

Merl stayed off the air. He didn't feel the need to respond. A potential prowler at Alva Galveston's place probably didn't require the bulk of the Soke Police Department. *Probably some fox nosing around near her hen house, stirring them up.* His mind wandered until Betty told Andre not to let Old Coals get him. Any other time, Merl would have written it off with a "here we go again."

Instead, he did a double take at his radio. Had he just heard what he thought he heard? He asked for a repeat.

"10-9 your last transmission."

Back at the station, Betty cringed. She knew extraneous comments were frowned upon. Expecting Merl was about to chastise her for her breach of protocol, she debated whether to repeat the line or apologize. Her hesitancy prompted another inquiry.

"What was the information about Old Coals coming to get you?"

Betty played it straight.

"Car 8. Asked Car 3 not to let Old Coals get him."

"10-4," Merl said. He called for Andre Waters.

"Car 3. Car 8. What's your 10-20?"

"Car 8," Andre responded. "Car 3. I'm on Day Drive, coming up on Oak."

"10-4. Meet me at Hansen Way and Hallman."

"Come again?"

Merl knew that was Andre's way of questioning the request. Merl knew Andre wanted nothing more than to zoom through town with the siren wailing and test how high he could tip the speedometer as he raced down Highway 37. Merl also knew he was closer to the scene than Andre right now. He could wait the 30 seconds for him to catch up because this might be a situation where Merl wanted eyes and ears seeing and hearing the same thing at the same time. That meant riding in the same car. Merl repeated his request more sternly.

"Meet me at Hansen Way and Hallman."

"10-4. Be there in five," Andre said.

Andre made it in four, taking seconds to park and secure his cruiser behind the post office before piling in with Merl.

When they reached Alva's place, the dirt road was still wet from the afternoon rain. Switching off the siren and bubble lights, Merl noticed no tire tracks in the thin mud. When he spotted Alva, he stopped the cruiser at an angle in the road. He left the headlights burning.

She paced at the end of her muddy drive. Waiting. Cradling a shotgun. Although she patrolled armed, her posture portrayed the attitude of a whipped hound, hoping a low growl would be enough. When asked, she handed possession of her weapon to Andre, her hands unsteady. Her words babbled, almost incoherent. Something about a giant alligator. A man's head. Eyes like volcanoes. About 10-feet tall. Attacking branches, coming for her. Old Coals. At least that's what she thought she saw. She'd been too afraid to draw close. Too fearful to watch it for long. But scared enough to dial 911.

Merl wondered how someone that frightened could be at the end of the driveway instead of cowering under the bed. When she spoke Merl thought he understood. He could smell her breath. Catching a whiff of liquor, Merl relaxed a bit. He tried to calm her. She refused to move. Anger welled in her now. Her eyes remained wild, no longer fearful, but defiant. Yet, she refused to accompany them to where she thought she had seen the creature. Merl beamed his flashlight to the area she indicated. He saw nothing out of the ordinary. She told them to check it in the morning when it was light. She told them Old Coals was not going to get her. She'd lash his butt six ways to Sunday if he showed his face around here again.

When Alva calmed down, Merl guided her by the arm back to her house. He telephoned her nephew. Even though she no longer seemed frightened, Merl preferred someone else there, not willing to risk her firing off a shotgun at shadows in the dark. Her nephew made good time. He lived only a couple of doors down the road.

With Alva cared for just a few houses away, Merl and Andre headed back down the drive to the car. Merl listened to their footfalls squishing in the mud.

"Homebrew will make you see some strange things," Andre said. "That old bat was 10-68, wasn't she?"

"Yup," Merl said, believing she was a bit crazy. After a pause he asked, "So you don't believe her?"

Andre laughed.

"Do you?"

Merl shrugged. "Worth a look."

A few steps and slides in the oozing mud brought them almost to the car, to where Alva claimed she saw the creature. Merl swept his flashlight's beam up the nearest pine tree. Its trunk was bereft of branches except for a broken one about 12 feet from the ground.

Snapped.

Merl flicked the light to the next tree. About the same height, another snapped branch. Another tree. Snapped branch. The bark was undisturbed. None of the branches snapped to the side, indicating a passing truck may have done this—not that any large trucks even could use this road. Instead, all the branches hung by their top layer of bark as if each had been bent upward to snap the wood so it would fall flaccid against the trunk.

But why?

Merl whipped his light to the other side of the road. Same height. One branch on each tree, snapped, but not off.

With the exception of one. The bark on that pine tree had peeled back to expose what looked like an open wound, a split in the wood where something seemed intent on forcing its way out. Merl stepped closer. He expected to see sap oozing from such an ugly rent. There was none. He felt a chill in the air. He reached out to run a finger along the pine's scar. When he touched the tree, the image of Wendy Sullivan's mangled body flashed into his mind. He recoiled. The vision vanished, but it left a rotting memory. It dragged Merl to the last time her image came unprovoked—the night Bobby Callahan died.

Merl staggered back. He swallowed hard. He tasted copper. He wondered if he would have felt this way had he not spoken to Jack, if he hadn't just heard Alva claim Old Coals had been here. Would thoughts of some supernatural menace be dancing in his head now?

Behind him, the cruiser's engine popped and sizzled as its joints and pipes cooled. That's not what Merl heard. He heard silence. No crickets chirped. No dogs yapped. No frogs. The frogs. He'd never been out here without hearing that incessant croaking. Even this late in the season. Especially after a rain.

Something wasn't right.

At just above a whisper Merl told Andre to get back in the cruiser. Andre didn't question the request. Both men edged toward the car. Both men eyed the darkness. Merl left his weapon holstered. This tense, he didn't trust his trigger finger. He explored the darkness as he neared the vehicle. He and Andre climbed into the car. They firmly closed the doors. Merl hit the automatic locks. He calmly started the engine. He shifted into reverse. Inching backward, he kept checking the road in front of the car. He withdrew more than a car's length when he stomped the brake pedal and froze.

"What the?" he said.

Andre scanned the scene. He saw nothing.

"Look," Merl said, seeking a second opinion. Andre squinted into the darkness. He hunted for something to emerge from beyond the headlight's illumination. From out of the blackness.

"Lower," Merl said. "Look at the road."

Andre's breath caught.

Confirmation.

Merl reached up to adjust the rear view mirror. He pressed harder on the brake as if it would improve the illumination behind the car. It didn't. All he could discern were the trunks of pine trees basking red in his brake light's glow. He flicked on the bubble lights. Their blue sweep registered the same. In front of the car, imprinted in the mud between the cruiser's tire tracks, were sets of claw prints.

Large.

Three-pronged.

That hadn't been there before.

Merl felt dread flow over him like a fast-filling bathtub. He knew if he didn't react soon, it would drown him. All his training mattered little now. It evaporated as panic robbed him of reason. Merl floored the gas pedal, slinging mud and gravel. He relied on his recall of the road and his skills at driving in reverse. He possessed one thought—*GET OUT OF HERE!*

He raced the car backwards down the lane. He skidded and spun it into drive when they hit pavement. It was miles before his adrenalin ebbed, miles before reason returned. Neither said a word on the twisting route to fetch Andre's squad car. It was as if each officer first needed time for his brain to process what he had seen. Needed a moment to piece together a rational explanation before discussing it. None came. Even after they circled back to scan the scene again, neither spoke. Neither acknowledged that the rain erased everything. Including their own tire tracks.

It just didn't make sense. There is always a reasonable explanation.

Always.

They neither found nor discussed one. None came to Merl after he dropped off Andre. None came as he drove slowly through town toward the hospital. Instead, Merl questioned his sanity. He questioned if the power of suggestion were enough to induce a leap of faith. He didn't question whether he'd just been struck blind on the road to Damascus. He accepted the truth.

Someone was going to die in Soke tonight.

He knew the killer was no myth.

He had to find a way to save Robbie.

Chapter 53

Merl raced into the hospital parking lot. His heart sprinted. His mind pinballed. From Robbie to Jack to Old Coals. Manic, he kicked open his car door. It swung back with force. He impeded it with his size 11. His leg then dropped weakly to the pavement. His whole body sagged. Exhaustion walloped him. Drowsiness besieged his senses. He regretted only taking a bite or two of his meal at the Griddle. It wasn't enough. The strain and his lack of nutrition goosed the aftereffects of his adrenal rush. He slumped back in his seat.

His uniform, damp from sweat, pasted to his skin. It stank like burnt eggs. He tasted bile specked with pepper. His muscles ached. His hamstring knotted. His mind volleyed between lucidity and absurdity. He wiped his nose on his sleeve. Aware his energy level red-lined, he wolfed down a pack a peanuts like a drunkard.

Although Merl thought his mind had never been more clear, he couldn't understand why the hospital looked blurry. He blinked hard. He rubbed his eyes. His left leg felt cold and wet. He glanced at it and noticed the misty rain. He left his leg in the rain and flicked on the wipers. The windshield cleared.

Nothing wrong with my eyes.
Nothing wrong with me!
I came here with a purpose!

Retrieving the three pennies from his pocket, Merl recalled the myths and hearsay. He steeled himself to face the creature that terrorized this town from the shadows for hundreds of years. He raised his hand.

Armed with these pennies.

He girded himself for battle with a wraith that possessed the unfathomable power to pervert nature and siphon souls. He raised his hand again.

Armed with these pennies.

He laughed like he didn't get the joke.

What kind of monster turns pets rabid? What contorts a face in such horror? Can force a victim to swallow poison? Set oneself on fire? Pull a trigger? Drown? How can it convince a mother to smother her child?

Merl wanted to weep. Instead, he cackled. He raised his fist. He couldn't believe the only weapons Jack offered him were three copper pennies.

Three dumb pennies.

Merl ignored his exhaustion. He convinced himself he was fit and rested. He strode across the lot and bounded up the short flight of stairs rather than mount the slight incline. He didn't slow for the automatic lobby doors to open. They cleared a path in time.

Jack Thompson stood in the lobby. Merl stopped in disbelief. He dismissed it. Didn't really care that dumb luck strolled in minutes ago to check on Robbie. Merl cared about one thing.

"How do I stop it?" he blurted.

"You can't ... and you can," Jack said. "Somebody ... always ... has to pay."

"C'mon," Merl said. "You can't be telling me three pennies is going to save Robbie. Like killing Dracula with a stake. Or a werewolf with a silver bullet. And that snake lady with a mirror."

"You mean ... Medusa?"

"Yeah, her."

Merl smirked. "Why not try swamp moss dabbed with Tabasco sauce?"

Jack scowled at Merl's lack of faith.

"Payment ... in ... threes," he said. "Three pay. It goes. Case closed." Jack's face beamed. Merl knew Jack Thompson departed before Wacky Jacky said another word.

"My uncle had five kids," Wacky Jacky said. "None of them were matched in looks or personality but when they talked. That always got me."

Merl tuned him out. He knew a rambling dialogue would follow. He fingered the pennies in his pocket and decided he was out of options. He asked at the desk for Robbie's room number. He poked the elevator button. He now felt silly, like he was sneaking around. All the way up the hospital elevator, he played with the coins in his pocket. He tried not to. He tried to think what he would say to Mal if she asked. He couldn't think of anything other than the truth. He figured that wouldn't fly. Even if logic no longer mattered. His palms sweated.

Merl trudged toward the nurse's station. He couldn't suppress the nagging feeling that everybody knew what he was doing. He greeted Gretchen Cassidy. He remembered when she was in grade school. She executed a beauty pageant smile. They exchanged courtesies. She didn't rise from her station.

"Is it okay to step in and see Robbie?" he asked.

"Go right ahead," Gretchen said. "You know which room, right?"

Merl pointed. Gretchen nodded.

"Mal's gone downstairs to get something to eat. She should be back in a few minutes. I think she'd like to know you stopped by."

Merl nodded, grateful for the minor miracle. He pushed open the door. The lighting cast a pale luminescence over the room. In here, Robbie looked ... like he was dead.

I'm too late!

Merl chided himself. The steady beeps and puffs of oxygen rendered that conclusion moot. But Robbie looked worse than asleep. Merl entered cautiously. The pale green paint on the walls hinted of mint. Instead, the aroma of antiseptic assaulted the olfactory system. Merl noticed the sweat from the water pitcher pooling on the tray. He glimpsed up at the muted TV rattling off the headlines to an inattentive viewer. A CD player rested next to the sink. The chair in the corner provided haven for a blanket, pillow and jacket. Merl opened the bathroom door. He peeked at the sparse but pristine facility.

He moved to the far side of the room. He proceeded quietly, not wanting to wake Robbie. It never dawned on him that everyone else wanted to wake Robbie. He didn't check his reflection in the mirror. If he had, he'd have been surprised that it looked better than he felt.

His eyes darted to the door. To Robbie. To the curtained windows. Merl had no plan. No idea what to do. He just wanted to hurry. Get this done and be gone before Mal returned.

Instead, he fiddled with his pants pocket. The coins jingled. They sounded so loud he feared it would summon the hospital staff. He broke into a sweat. He pulled the pennies from his pocket. It seemed irresponsible to place them on Robbie's eyes. Dwelling so much on what to do with the third coin, he still hadn't connected that they were placed not on the living, but the dead.

So where?

He scrutinized Robbie's left hand, clutched tightly. He poked it. It remained closed.

This feels like such a violation.

Merl wiggled his index finger like a crowbar to nudge Robbie's thumb open.

Nobody will find them here.

He jammed one penny after another into the closed fist like coins into a piggy bank. He checked the door again. He felt the urge to say something. He had nothing. He leaned close. He whispered into Robbie's ear the first thing that popped into his head, "Return these if you meet anybody."

Feeling guilty, Merl jerked back when the door opened.

Chapter 54

Something touched Robbie's hand. It was fleshy. Cold. Clammy. It felt real. It touched him again.

WAKE UP!, his mind screamed at him. *WAKE UP! This is not a dream.* He felt himself bolt upright. His teeth snapped at whatever assaulted his hand. He heard his teeth click. He nipped only empty air. In a dream. His body remained inert, but his heart rate quickened. His jaw clenched. He heard a siren in the distance. Robbie thought his eyes were open, that he was awake and awaiting what terror lurked. He knew he was alone in his bedroom. But something was in the house. He hushed his breathing, stilled himself until he became so quiet he could hear dust shifting on the downstairs rug.

He recalled the time he had been awakened in the middle of the night by a monster in the kitchen. He had held his breath awaiting its approach. He had listened to the thwock, thwock, thwock of its suction cups propelling itself across the linoleum. Getting closer, getting closer. Moving into the hallway. Up the stairs. Outside his door. Eager to devour him. When it never entered, Robbie had followed his Dad's lessons. He broke down his fear. Maybe this wasn't the Creature from the Black Lagoon or some tentacular sea monster. Could it be something else? Should he confront it?

Robbie was back in the moment, climbing out of bed. He reached for his Wiffle Ball bat. He secured his army helmet. If he were going to war, he wanted to be ready. He paused at his door and listened. The sound had changed.

Tu-loop, tu-loop, tu-loop.

It was not getting closer. Maybe the monster had morphed. Robbie edged to the stairs. They yawned into darkness. Robbie's eyes peered into it. He saw no movement. He knew whatever awaited might know he was coming. He froze. The sounds persisted.

Tu-loop, tu-loop, tu-loop. From the kitchen.

Robbie crept down the stairs. His socked feet muffled his passage. He moved lithely, willing the stairs not to creak. He angled away from the wall and toward the banister. If something grabbed him from between the railings, he could break free before being squeezed between the posts. But if that gnarled slimy claw snatched him from the dark of the dining room at the base of the stairs, he'd have no chance. He would be lost forever. Robbie paused three steps from the bottom. He listened.

Tu-loop, tu-loop, tu-loop.

His mind imagined something gruesome lurked behind the wall. Waiting. The sound from the kitchen was a distraction. No, he reminded himself. Face this fear. Beat this fear.

Tu-loop, tu-loop, tu-loop.

He leapt the final stairs, slid on the entry hall's floor into the front door—making a soft thump—before darting through the den into the kitchen.

Tu-loop, tu-loop, tu-loop.

He snapped on the light. He dodged away from the door. The kitchen blazed empty.

Tu-loop, tu-loop, tu-loop.

Any creature creeping across the floor flittered into nothingness. Coffee burbled in the automatic maker.

Tu-loop, tu-loop, tu-loop.

Robbie chuckled. He snapped off the light. He headed back to his bedroom, a conquering hero. But as he passed the dining room, he blurted, *"I know you're there."* He sprinted up the stairs, his imagination picturing a slimy talon snatching only air.

That was months ago. Robbie feared this cold touch on his hand was something more sinister. He strained his ears for any sound. He waited as his eyes absorbed the dark, turning slightly for a better view of the doorway. No movement. He tensed when the back door creaked as it adjusted to a change in wind pressure. He debated if something were checking the locks. The screen outside his window banged. Was something reaching to lift the sash? A floorboard creaked. The sounds retreated. A muffled pat on the roof. Then another on the side of the house. Were creatures gathering? Prodding and poking for passage? Or was that rain sprinkling its first few drops. Robbie anticipated more. None came. A shoe squeaked. Blinds shuffled. A door closed. Robbie ducked under the covers. He trembled in the darkness. He took a deep breath and inhaled dust and dirt. He coughed and spit grit. It took him a moment to gain his bearings.

What am I doing here?

He knelt in the graveled parking lot of Ray Ray's. His mom never had a good thing to say about this place. She made the bar sound so bad that Robbie pictured it like Mos Eisley Space Port on Tatooine. Obi-Wan Kenobi crossed his mind, *"You will never find a more wretched hive of scum and villainy."*

"What did you say?"

Robbie pivoted toward the slurred voice. It was an adult.

"Get in the truck, now!"

Robbie knew better than to climb into any car with a stranger. But he knew who this was. Robbie had met Officer Westbrook before. The highway patrolman had been to his school often. He seemed nice. Robbie grew worried. What if something were wrong with Mom and he were needed at home? He piled into the driver's side and scooted to the middle of the cab. He hunted for a seatbelt buckle. He couldn't find one. The passenger door swung open. A man Robbie didn't know got in. He clutched a red hankie and kept swiping it across his face. He didn't look well.

"Can't hold his liquor," Westbrook said. *"And he better not PUKE in my truck!"*

The man with the red hankie wiped his face. He gazed straight ahead. Robbie watched him. Even with both windows down, the smell of whiskey hung in the cab as the pickup barreled down the road. It slowed to turn onto Old Coals' Alley. Robbie saw the man with the red hankie retch. He leaned out the window. He vomited. Westbrook swerved the truck off the road.

"*Better not get any on MY highway!*" he yelled.

The man with the red hankie dropped back into his seat. His head was missing. Robbie's eyes flared in horror. Before he could scream, Westbrook elbowed him.

"*He loses his head when he drinks,*" he said. He cackled madly.

When Robbie turned, the decapitated rider lunged for the radio dial. Music blared.

"*Midnight at the Oasis ... Send your camel to bed.*"

Chapter 55

Mallison Callahan munched on the tomato slice from her salad. She savored the zip of the Ranch dressing. She sampled the rice. Too drab. She picked over her Salisbury steak. As she chewed a bite, she had a premonition of alarm in her son. She dropped her fork.

Despite her hunger, she rushed back upstairs. She poked the Up elevator button. The door opened. It was Down. She stepped toward the stairs when she heard another ding. She darted to the door. The car was full. Eager to enter, she stepped back to let it unload. She held the door, determined not to let it depart without her. She hurried aboard and jabbed her floor. The doors took forever to close. Thankful she was alone, she welcomed the idea of an express ride. The elevator halted at the second floor. Nobody waited to board. She popped the Close button. The doors took forever to close. The elevator stopped at the third floor. Mallison groaned. The doors opened.

"Going down?" a woman asked.

"Up," Mallison barked. Close button again. The doors took their time shutting. The elevator rose past the fourth floor. Mallison exhaled, only to be halted on the fifth. The doors opened. Again, she saw no one.

"Hold it please," someone said. Mallison seethed. Against her wishes, she held the door. An orderly pushed a wheelchair occupied by an elderly gentleman.

"Thank you, young lady," the elderly man said. Mallison blushed guiltily. His wheelchair jammed in the door slot. The orderly struggled to shove it across without dumping him. Seconds dragged into minutes. Finally aboard, the man wanted to go down. The orderly poked "L" for the lobby. Mallison kept silent, not wanting them to exit in favor of another elevator. *You'll just have to wait.* The doors closed.

Finally, her floor. Harried, Mallison raced to Robbie's room. Even though she knew she needed to eat, she felt guilty at being away for long. She'd never forgive herself if Robbie woke and she wasn't there. Yet, every time she opened the door, she hoped he'd be sitting up, playing with the TV remote.

She opened the door and caught her breath. She never expected to see Merl Burt here, much less see him flinch. Unprepared to see him, all of her memories of Bobby welled up. They overtook her.

"Get away from my son!" she spat. "Get out of this room!"

Merl, like a criminal caught red-handed, fumbled for an excuse he didn't need.

"I was, I was just ..."

"I don't ever want to see you again!" Mallison said with force.

"I ... I was just ... checking up on him," Merl said. "Ah, seeing how he was doing. H-h-how is he doing?"

Mallison broke into tears. Merl shifted gears. He thought she looked defeated. Her eyes were baggy. Her hair was mussed. She seemed out of hope. He wanted to give her some good news fast. He had none. He wondered if he should mention the pennies. What could he say? Mentioning them wouldn't lift her spirits.

"How is he doing?" Merl asked again. He moved closer to her.

"We still don't know," she said slowly. "Dr. Tyson's hopeful. But ..."

She draped herself around Merl.

"I'm sorry," she said. "I'm so sorry. It's just ..."

She buried her head in his chest. She sobbed. He put his arms around her. He let her cry.

"I'm sorry," she said. "It's just been too much."

Merl nodded. He said nothing. Could think of nothing. "Everything will be fine" sounded so inadequate.

"I always thought life was a Disney movie," Mallison said.

"You meet Prince Charming and live happily ever after.

"But I lost Bobby. And now …"

Merl patted her on the back. She looked directly up into his eyes.

"Where's my happy ending?" she asked.

Merl didn't know. He once thought there was somebody for everyone, but the love of his life married someone else. He once thought good triumphed over evil, but how could you explain innocent children like Wendy Sullivan murdered? All he could think to say was "It will all work out for the best."

He didn't believe it. It, too, rang hollow. It just sounded like the appropriate thing to say. The sentiment didn't last.

Robbie began twitching. Beeps filled the room.

Mallison sprang to his side. She patted his chest. She spoke softly to him. Merl retreated. He felt a flash of panic. He feared Robbie's twitching was a reaction to the copper in the pennies. He knew better, but still felt silly at trying something so unorthodox.

Gretchen Cassidy entered. Merl exited. He could wait out by the nurses' station until things calmed. Once outside the room, he slid down the hall and headed for the cafeteria downstairs as Gretchen tended to Robbie while Mallison hovered.

"What's happening?" Mallison asked. "What's wrong?"

"Not sure," Gretchen said. "We need to make sure he doesn't yank his IVs out. Just a little something to settle him down."

Unaware Robbie was one of those rare few who reacted adversely to the drug, Gretchen added Haldol to his drip. No sooner had the sedative coursed into him that the monitor beeps sped from a slow stroll to a sprint. Robbie's temperature climbed with it.

"What did you give him?" Mallison shouted.

Gretchen tapped a few buttons. She initiated an IV hydration. She rang for the doctor. The beeps soon returned to a less stressful interval. Robbie's temperature, however, continued its rise from 97. Past normal. Past 100. Mallison watched sweat beads form on Robbie's forehead. She dampened a washcloth. She daubed his brow while Gretchen noted the number stall at 104. She awaited the doctor.

Dr. Benton Tyson paraded into the room, chomping on gum like he was working the speed bag at the gym. Ignoring Mallison's request to know what's wrong, he raised a finger. He wished to silence her long enough to hear Gretchen's summary. Once heard, he instructed Gretchen to secure some blankets.

"Blankets?" Mallison said. "He's burning up!"

Dr. Tyson didn't feel like explaining. He felt like smoking a Marlboro. He felt like booting her out of the room.

"Why don't you get him some ice chips?" he said.

Dr. Tyson knew Gretchen's hydration would rid Robbie's system of the Haldol. He knew cooling blankets would be the most effective deterrent to his high temperature. But ice? That was playing fetch.

"Ice?" Mallison said.

"Ice," Dr. Tyson said.

"Ice!" Mallison grabbed the thermos. She raced down the hall. It would long be melted when Robbie threw his next scare into her.

Chapter 56

Robbie heard voices. The drug may have succeeded in calming him, but it failed to muffle his dreams. His mind keyed on one word as he drifted off.

"... you get him some ICE chips?"

Robbie visualized ice—a glazed rink with blue lines, red lines and face-off circles. He glanced around. He realized he was at Philips Arena. This irked him. Not because he didn't want to be there, but because he wasn't wearing his hockey sweater. He always wore it to games. How would the team know he was pulling so hard for them if he weren't wearing their colors?

Wait a sec! If there's a hockey game, where is everybody?

Robbie inspected the well-lit stands. No seats held an occupant. No blue-jacketed ushers manned the aisles to help incoming fans. Robbie glanced back at the ice. It glistened as if anticipating whirling skaters with sticks. The scoreboard hanging over center ice that flashed video or scrolling messages offered a black screen. No rock music blared. Only the whirr of the building's air conditioning disrupted the silence.

We must be here really, really early.

Robbie loved it when he and his dad arrived before anybody else. It meant nobody had searched the stands yet for practice pucks. Robbie started down the aisle. He scanned the adjoining rows of seats. Step down. Scan the adjoining rows. Step down. One season, he found four pucks—NHL Center Ice Official Practice Puck. He had them stacked on his dresser.

Robbie almost reached the section's bottom row when someone shouted his name. He didn't recognize the voice. Just its direction. He looked toward the corner of the rink where the Zamboni entered to resurface the ice. He caught his breath.

Is that Danny Snyder?

Robbie remembered opening night when they played bagpipes in honor of the forward's death. Robbie remembered it was the first time he had seen his dad cry.

The hockey player, dressed in a white road sweater with 37 on the back, suddenly stood next to Robbie. He balanced a stack of pucks that zigzagged to the arena roof.

"I thought you might like to have these," the player said.

Robbie smiled, but unsure now, he asked, *"Are you Danny Snyder?"*

"What do you think?" he said.

"You're my dad's favorite player."

The player flashed a crooked grin. *"Who's yours?"*

Robbie blushed. He glanced guiltily at his feet. *"Ilya Kovalchuk."*

The player fluffed Robbie's hair. He chuckled. *"Awesome,"* he said.

"My dad likes you cuz you weren't that talented. He said you made up for it with hard work."

The player chortled at the back-handed compliment.

Robbie stared at the balanced stack of pucks. He babbled.

"Dad said every team needs a player like you. Dad said you learned from what you did wrong. He said I should learn that. Dad said you know that 'Can't never could.' Dad said you gave it everything you had."

Robbie shifted his gaze from the pucks. He dipped his head.

"Do you have any broke teeth?"

The player grinned like the Cheshire Cat. Robbie peered intently. They all looked real.

"Dad said if I turned out like you, he would be proud."

The player leaned toward Robbie.

"*Kid, don't be afraid of anything. Great men became great men by doing what they didn't want to do when they didn't want to do it. So always take one more step than you think you can.*"

Robbie's eyes widened in amazement.

Dad said that too!

The player handed Robbie a puck. It was ice cold. Robbie read it: Official Game Puck. Stamp signed by the commissioner. Robbie turned it over. It displayed the Thrasher logo. It was autographed in white ink with the message, "Give this away and you can overcome your fear."

Fear? That puzzled Robbie. What did he have to fear here? He grew anxious.

Robbie flashed hot and cold. He could feel his body sweating. He shivered with chills. He plunged into darkness. He heard water lapping. He heard his heartbeat accelerate. He clutched the puck hard. He heard a strange buzzing. He thought he heard his mom's voice, thought he felt a rustle of activity. Something forced his eyes open. A bright light flashed. He wanted to squint but couldn't. The light hurt as his pupils contracted to minimize his pain. A soothing sensation washed up his arm. It flooded his body.

Robbie shivered. So cold. So cold. Why so cold?

Chapter 57

Chilled, Robbie crossed his arms. He hugged himself for warmth. He inhaled quickly and felt even colder. He wished he still had his jacket. He rubbed his biceps furiously to generate heat. The wind gusting at this height stole it. It left an ill scent that only an old salt could detect.

From the 16th floor balcony, Robbie gazed at the whitecaps in the Atlantic Ocean. He listened to the roar of the waves as they smashed the shore. He edged toward the railing. He'd never been so high up before. The cars in the parking lot appeared the size of small Tonkas. The distance spun him. Dizzy, he tightened his hold on the wrought iron rail and remained an arm's length from it. He still felt unsafe. It wasn't so much the height. He knew the distance didn't faze him. He'd tight-roped across the Marshall Cypress branch to cross Landfalls Creek. On a dare, he scaled the water tower, perched on the hand rail and stretched to touch the blue star. But such bouts of bravado seldom dodged the overpowering feeling that if he slipped, he couldn't save himself.

Until that day with Grandpa, he never worried about losing his balance. Never considered falling. Never questioned his ability to grab onto something. That day with Grandpa, Robbie learned nothing could save him but himself.

No rails. No ropes. No walls. There was no safety net below.

The lesson came just after he turned six. It was a good day. Like all days when he rode to town with Grandpa. They came free of restrictions. Nobody counted how many sodas he drank. Nobody limited how many watermelon Jolly Ranchers he ate. But this trip differed. Grandpa first stopped at an abandoned building to meet a business friend. Before they disappeared behind a door with frosted glass, Grandpa's friend spoke to Robbie.

"I hear you collect baseball cards, young man," he had said.

"Yes, sir," Robbie said.

"If you can wait patiently, you can have this."

He presented Robbie a baseball card. Robbie accepted it. He didn't recognize the player. The stripe in the upper corner claimed he played for the Braves. The stripe at the bottom identified him as Woody Woodward, shortstop. Robbie recalled no player by that name. He sported a military-style haircut. Robbie flipped the card over.

It was from 1966!

Wow! It's older than my dad!

Robbie studied the statistics on the back. He memorized the bio. He couldn't understand why the card indicated Woodward was with the Braves when the yearly stats showed he played for Milwaukee. Robbie didn't know that the franchise had moved from one city to the other. Engrossed, Robbie didn't notice Grandpa approach until he spoke.

"Whatcha got there?"

Robbie held up the card.

"Woody Woodward," Grandpa said. "Good little shortstop out of Miami."

Robbie was stunned. How did Grandpa know Woodward was from Miami? Robbie read the card's front again. He saw nothing to indicate Woodward was from Miami. He bet Grandpa also knew that Woody was an excellent golfer like the cartoon on the back indicated.

"We're going to take a look upstairs," Grandpa said. "You can wait down here or come with us."

Robbie hopped out of the chair. He pocketed the card. He grasped Grandpa's hand as they strolled over to an iron gate. To Robbie, the elevator's outer door looked like a small prison cell. Grandpa's friend threw it open. He unhitched the inner door. He shoved it back. He stood aside until they entered. Following them in, he yanked the gated door until it clanked shut. He tugged the inner door. He re-latched it.

"Push the top button," the man said.

Robbie poked it. The elevator jarred and shook. With a whine from the engine, it climbed and clanked. Through the grated doors, Robbie watched the floors go past. Dust and sheets covered decaying furniture deemed too worthless by others to steal. Robbie heard the engine calm before the elevator halted with a jerk. Robbie nearly tumbled. His Grandpa steadied him to prevent a fall.

"Ladies underwear," the man said with a chuckle before opening the door.

Grandpa chortled. He stepped off with vigor. Robbie didn't move. He wasn't about to exit on the floor with women's underpants. He'd stay right where he was.

"You coming or not?" Grandpa asked.

Robbie eyed the vacant room. He shrugged. The thick red and gold stripes on the worn carpet before him sprinted out like lanes on a track. Robbie raced down one toward the window. He puffed out his chest to snap the imaginary tape and braced himself for a bump into the wall.

"Be careful. This place is old," the man said.

Robbie paid no heed. He looked down past the windowsill in amazement.

We're moving!

"I wouldn't stand too close," Grandpa said. "Place is condemned."

Robbie didn't know what that meant. He couldn't understand what was happening. He focused on the floor. It didn't move. His eyes darted to the baseboard.

Yes! The wall is breathing!

As it inhaled, Robbie peered through the exposed space to the floor below.

"Hey, the wall's alive," he announced. The news surprised no one but him.

"It moves with the wind," Grandpa's friend said. "You get up this high and the whole building sways."

Robbie's belief system staggered. *Buildings don't move. They're solid.* His imagination flashed, shooting a chill up his spine. He flinched. If he hit that wall any harder, it could have dropped away unexpectedly. He pictured himself falling completely out of the building. Or at least tumbling down a floor. Or being grabbed from below by whatever lived under those sheets. Feeling insecure, he hugged his Grandpa's leg. He said nothing.

Such a fear of heights incubated as Robbie matured. It sprang forth on its own whim. It stayed hidden for the same reason.

But on the 16th floor balcony, it raged as Robbie gripped the wrought iron railing. He shifted his weight back like a hissing cat. To calm himself, he calculated the distance.

Sixteen floors up, that's 10 feet a floor. That's 160 feet high. More than a football field and a half! That's a long way down. Wait, that's yards, not feet.

Robbie swayed. He tried to figure how far 160 feet was on the gridiron. The wind shifted. It nudged him off balance. Before he could counter his weight, the iron grating wrenched free. Robbie released it. He tottered near the edge, nothing impeding a plunge to the death.

As the fallen grate flipped and swiveled away, Robbie crouched and leaned to watch. Instead, he felt the ground tug at him. In his mind, the beach rushed up and kissed his face before receding. Disoriented by the yoyo-like hallucination, Robbie noted the falling grate strike the building's façade before he pitched over where it used to be. Instinctively, his arm reached out. His hand snagged the bottom rung of another section of rail. As the grate below now cart-wheeled, Robbie's momentum swung him down. He smacked into the wall. The impact knocked his breath out. Robbie held firm. For now, so did the bolt securing his rail to the balcony. Robbie watched the other impale itself into the concrete below. He dangled one-handed. About 155 feet of air dropped below him. He gasped.

Don't look down!

Robbie looked up. As he swung ever slower, his arm ached. He noticed his weight and movement had loosened the lone bolt. Its ridges excavated concrete, piling the white dust like ants shifting building supplies.

Don't look up!

Robbie looked over. He debated whether to swing himself high enough to sling a leg back onto the balcony. He didn't trust the bolt to hold. If he climbed up the railing, he'd slide back down because it was so smooth. He knew he couldn't swing himself onto the floor below because the balcony recessed too far and he didn't hang low enough to clear his floor.

Don't look down!

Maybe he could …

Robbie heard metal groan. He looked down. He hyperventilated. His heart felt as if it wanted to leap back onto the balcony and let him fend for himself.

Mommy!

The railing jerked, jarring Robbie. It altered his grip.

Maybe I can make my shirt into a parachute.

Robbie's grip faltered. He fell. At first, it felt like slow-motion.

I love you Mom!

Then fast forward.

I don't weigh enough to be falling this faaaassst.

Daaaaadddddeeee!!!!

The ground zoomed closer. If this were a dream, he had to wake before he hit. If he didn't, he'd wake up dead.

If this were a dream …

A dream?

You can change your dreams!
You can dream anything!
You can—
He slammed into the cement.

Chapter 58

Robbie's body seized.

The room blared at the incongruent behavior with the cacophony of beeps and buzzers. Mallison sprang toward her son.

"What's wrong?" she blurted at him.

She knocked over his ice pitcher. The sweaty jug toppled to the floor. Water splattered. It raced toward the baseboards and around the equipment.

Seconds before, Robbie lay trance-like. Peaceful. Now, sweat drenched him. He twitched.

"What's wrong?" she asked again to no one in particular.

Dr. Tyson, Gretchen and Maggie had all said he was fine. They said his Haldol reaction had been controlled.

"What's wrong?" she pleaded to the empty room.

Robbie wasn't moving. He wasn't breathing.

Mallison placed two fingers on his neck. No pulse. She placed her ear to his chest. No heart beat. She pounded his chest with the bottom of her fist. She set her ear against his chest. It returned a reassuring thump, thump, thump. She heard the EKG beeping normally. The room seemed normal. Had she just imagined what happened? Was she dreaming?

Maggie Peterson burst into the room.

Chapter 59

Darkness. Robbie drifted. More darkness.

Beep.

He welcomed it. This blindness produced no fear. It conjured no haunting memories.

Of the swamp.

Of the creek.

Of the closet.

The gloom beckoned with respite. Robbie desired rest. He felt so tired he believed his hair would hurt if he made any effort to move. He bobbed weightless, like in space. He wanted to drift away again before the bumblebees caught up with him.

Beep.

Drifting. Floating. Sailing. His chest constricted under intense pressure. No bumblebees. He took a punch. The pressure vanished.

So that's what it's like when G-forces quit. I just left Earth's atmosphere.

Robbie never expected it would be so dark in the capsule. He contemplated if his eyes were open. He arched his eyebrows. He waved a hand in front of his face. Nothing. He blinked. He noticed no change.

Beep.

Why can't I see any stars?

Blink.

Why are no panel lights on?

Blink.
Beep.
What IS that noise?
Beep.

Robbie giggled. He figured out just where he was. *That beep's from the Command Module. I'm on a space walk in its shadow. That whooshing's the oxygen feeding through the tube to my suit and helmet.* He moved his hand toward his face. He struck a hard plastic surface.

Beep.

Jeez, you numbnut, wear a visor often? Sun shield's probably down too. Where's that darn switch for night vision? He poked the button near his hand. Nothing.

Beep.

Could this be space blindness?

Beep, beep ...

Panic bloomed in Robbie.

Beep, beep, beep ...

I don't want to die out here.

Beep, beep, beep, beep ...

"Houston, we have a problem!"

Beep, beep, beep, beep, beep ...

Something grabbed Robbie's wrist. He flinched. A voice boomed.

Beep, beep, beep, beep, beep, beep ...

That voice again, "Everything's fine. Relax. Calm down."

Calm down? Mission Control wants me to calm down? Then, quit yelling at me! Adjust your volume control! It's like you're right next to me.

Beep, beep, beep, beep ...

"Roger that."

Robbie didn't recognize the voice. He always imagined his dad working CapCom. *Maybe he was on break.*

"This is CapCom. The docs in the back room say you need to cool your jets. Looks like you're pushing too far into the red out there. We suggest you throttle back, take a deep breath. Maybe think of your mom's strawberry cake."

Mom's strawberry cake? That made no sense to Robbie.

Beep, beep.

The scent of Mom's cooking enveloped him. He could almost taste the icing he often licked off the beaters. Could smell her nearby. He regrouped.

Beep.

Check. Gather your senses. Check. Nobody on Apollo lost control. I won't be the first. You could bank on that, Bub!

Beep.

Robbie still couldn't see anything. *How to ask for help without sounding stupid?* He was glad Dad taught him ways to think around a problem.

Beep.

"CapCom, My sun shield appears to be stuck. I'm currently in the dark here."

He anticipated CapCom's reply would contain ridicule and mirth.

"Ah, not a problem. Advise to take your sunglasses off at night. Fellas down here concur that the ladies know you're a cool cat. You're behind the moon right now so everything in that direction is pitch black. Either enjoy the solitude or you might want to roll over and take an otherworldly view. It'll get real bright again soon enough."

Beep.

Robbie rotated away from the darkness. He never saw so many stars so brilliantly lit. The universe winked crystal clear. He picked out the Big Dipper. He identified the North Star. It never dawned on him that Mission Control couldn't reach an astronaut on the dark side of the moon.

Chapter 60

Orbiting with the Command Module, Robbie surveyed the cosmos. He relished his view of Mars. The Red Planet looked redder than ever to his naked eye. He had never seen it this close. Not even through a telescope. He could see the canals crisscrossing the surface. The ice caps on the poles. As he scrutinized the planet, it seemed to split and separate. Robbie stared in disbelief.

Why were there now two red planets?

Robbie decided his space visor reflected a second Mars into his vision. He moved his hand toward his face. His fingers found his forehead.

How could that be? Where's my helmet?

In this environment that meant instant death. Too frightened to inhale the cold of space, Robbie watched the red planets enlarge. The stars, so brilliantly lit before, blinked out. The atmosphere thickened. As the scarlet orbs hung still in the darkness, Robbie shuddered. Thoughts of his father's ashen face resting peacefully in satin emerged. Robbie sobbed. He knew the very thing that terrorized his mother had come for him.

Old Coals.

It hovered over him. It absorbed all light so that only two crimson eyes pierced the black. They pulsed with malice. They throbbed with despair. Robbie gasped a chilled breath. It terrified him too much to try another for fear his next inhalation not only would fail to supply oxygen but also suck in the creature. Robbie's ears popped. His chest constricted. His blood gurgled through his veins as other sounds suffocated in the inky cloak enveloping the creature.

Robbie looked up.

When their eyes connected, Robbie was all alone. Sight. Sound. Mind. All were eviscerated. Robbie's memory tried to flee but couldn't remember why. It simply stepped aside.

Images tore through his brain like shrapnel, each jabbing toward weaknesses, probing for dread, mining for despair. Those crimson eyes became Robbie's entire universe—his past, present and future. He stared, so magnetized by the dark pupils that he became a part of them, a victim in the relentless assault.

He spotted himself peeking out of the command module window. Recognizing his Apollo crewmates on the moon returning to the lunar module, he prepped his ship for its final pass before rendezvousing for the return home. Something hurtled past the window. It spanked against the hull. Robbie released his procedure checklist. He unbuckled and glided toward the skylight. He pressed against the glass to inspect any damage. The face of a crazed chimpanzee flashed into view. Robbie jerked back. The simian's eyes raged. Its dripping incisors chattered in malevolent glee. Another winged monkey joined it. And another. They snapped at each other. They pawed at the window. They banged on the hatch. They tore at everything attached to the capsule. If Robbie did nothing, they would breach the hull and devour his remains. Robbie hurriedly reset his coordinates and ignited the thrusters for trans-earth injection. Heading home, he sentenced two fellow astronauts to die on the moon, their bodies there forever as a testament to his weakness. He saw the disbelief on their faces. He caught the disapproving looks of revulsion from the Navy frogmen who retrieved him after splashdown.

All had witnessed his failure.

Robbie flushed with shame.

The scene changed. He recognized himself as a sentry in the trenches at Bastogne during the Battle of the Bulge. He rubbed his mitten-clad hands together. He struggled to stay warm. He shivered in the night air. He listened to snow falling in the trees. So peaceful. Hearing a crunch and jangle of metal, he peered from his foxhole. Movement! An enemy unit charged his outpost. Rather than man his machine gun post, he cowered before the approaching soldiers. Rather than fire on the foe or cry for help, he remained mute. Stay quiet. Stay alive. Maybe they would go for someone else. Robbie covered himself with a blanket. He trembled as enemy soldiers swarmed his buddies' foxholes. Bayonets jabbed into flesh, the gurgled screams of men dying in a guttural slaughter echoed. Robbie fled. He raced to save himself without a concern for his buddies. He sprinted toward what looked like a historical marker. He slowed to read it. "On this date in 1944, Robert Wilson Callahan shirked his duties in a brazen act of cowardice that cost the lives of 37 men."

Robbie's depression grew. He wept.

He found himself in kindergarten. He waved at the little girl in the red dress, the one that held such a special place in his heart. She kissed another boy. They held hands.

Robbie's heart broke.

He saw himself as an adult. With a wife, a family, a Beagle puppy. They lived in a mansion. He lounged downstairs watching television. He heard glass break in the back room. He muted the set. He retrieved a loaded pistol from his lock box. Rather than charge upstairs to protect his family or call the police, he slunk into the garage. He hid. Three shots blasted. His wife? His son? The puppy? The newspaper headline exposed the truth, "Father hides while family slain."

Robbie never wanted to grow old.

He saw his new jacket all bloody. He saw his clothes torn and wet. He saw his mom. He wanted to run to her. Fall into her arms and never let go. Instead, she stopped him. He heard her say no son of hers would ruin his clothes. She told him time and time again to take care of his things. He hadn't. She didn't care that he was hurt, that he was frightened. She only cared that clothes cost money. She glared at him.

"Don't bother to come home ever again," she said. Robbie had nowhere else to go.

He saw his dad emerge. Dad would make things right. He'd understand. Rather than relief, Robbie found more despair.

He heard his father call him "Robert Wilson Callahan, Jr."—a sure sign of trouble. *"You have displeased your mother. That's one thing I cannot abide. My son would never do it."* His dad's eyes grew intense. *"You know, you were a mistake. We never wanted you. Why do you think we never had any more children?"*

Crushed, Robbie lost hope. He had nothing left. This hurt too much. Life was too painful. Robbie wished he were dead. That would make everybody happy. Make the pain go away. Darkness smothered him. His pulse weakened. His heart slowed. Robbie wanted to give up. The beep became a single, uninterrupted tone.

Chapter 61

Robbie felt so alone as Old Coals extended a hand. He felt if he took it, all his pain would abate. He would be released. He would be loved again. All would be right. As Robbie reached to shake with his right hand like his father taught him, he stopped. He misread the reflected image in the creature's eyes and believed he offered the wrong hand. He sure didn't want to disappoint his dad any further. Seeking Dad's approval, he shifted to his closed left hand. His dad emerged again in the creature's eyes. He shook his head disapprovingly. The image of his father said, *"I never loved you."*

The words smacked Robbie like a sledgehammer. He reeled back. He heard them not as truth, but as warning. He remembered his father's promise,

"No matter what you see or what someone says, I will always love you. Nothing can change that. And I will never say otherwise."

Chapter 62

"... *And I will never say otherwise.*"
That's not Dad!
Hyperventilating with excitement, Robbie slowed his breathing. He thought of Josey Wales.
"*If you give up, you neither live nor win. That's just the way it is.*"
The darkness pressed hard. Robbie pushed back.
One step more.
Movie scenes filled his head—*Aragorn rode a stallion. He exhorted, "A day will come when the courage of man fails, when we forsake our friends and break all bonds of friendship, but it is not this day."*
Gandalf stood on the Bridge at Khazad-dum. He screamed, "You shall not pass!"
Josey smiled and said, "I reckon so."
Emboldened by the images, Robbie girded himself for battle. *Great men became great men by doing what they didn't want to do when they didn't want to do it.* He wanted to face the images again, the ones that nearly destroyed him, that wielded such an oppressive air. He needed them on his side, not in opposition.
Robbie summoned them from the creature.
He beckoned his father's image in Old Coals' eyes. He remembered the countless movies they watched together, their spirited battles with dialogue, the feeling his dad instilled that he could do anything if he set his mind to it. He saw his dad salute and vanish.

He summoned his mother's image. He turned her scolding into one of happiness. She could care less about his jacket. Expressed joy at his return. He could smell a strawberry cake baking in the kitchen. She offered him the mixing beaters to lick free of icing.

If that were his future family he abandoned, he muted the television. He retrieved his pistol. He stalked the intruder. He caught him on the stairway without firing a shot or waking his family. He held him until police arrived. The headline read, "Sleepless dad surprises burglar."

He kissed the little girl in the red dress. Walked right up to her, took her hand and planted one right on the lips. She beamed. She hugged him. His confidence rising, he kissed her again. His heart soared. He circled the moon. He spotted his crewmates' ship floating closer and closer for rendezvous. They docked. He heard the bang-bang of the locks clicking into place successfully. He opened the hatch. He saw two dusty astronauts. They never looked so good.

He crouched in the cold of a small French town. His finger wrapped on the trigger of his machine gun. He waited patiently for enough enemy to near. He opened fire. Not a member of his unit absorbed a scratch. He earned a Medal of Honor for repulsing an enemy offensive. Said so on the plaque outside Bastogne. Patton? Who needed his help?

As Robbie pictured himself hailed as the conquering hero, marching forth as rose petals fluttered down upon he and his white thoroughbred mustang, his triumph turned tail. A counterattack commenced. Almost before he quashed one concern, others charged. They lured Robbie's fears to the surface. Scenes morphed too fast for Robbie to master, let alone stifle. By the time he identified his fear, another ignited as sparks blazed into a firestorm.

The shift from triumph to retreat materialized suddenly. One moment Robbie soared in complete control of his destiny. The next, he crashed to earth, broken and bent. He landed first in a darkened room. When he caught his breath, he explored his surroundings. He moved his hand forward to test the space. He felt the cling of a broken web. His arm tickled with movement. Before he realized spiders were swarming up his arm, it exploded with pain. He screamed. He tried brushing them off. They were legion. They swarmed his other arm. It burst into pain. They raced for his head and body. Their passage seared his skin. His terror grew. His mind kicked toward the repetitive lessons his father taught him.

Break down your fear.

Spiders gave Robbie the creeps. He wished they feared him like he feared them. *Wait a sec.* Robbie calculated quickly. His mind charged toward his dad's garage shelves. Looking for that aerosol can, the one next to the top, out of reach. He strained to read the ingredients on the side. It was too high. Spiders swarmed up his shoulder. In his mind, Robbie pinched his fingers together. He peered through the pinprick hole it created to improve his vision. He spotted the word he couldn't remember. Robbie pretended to give his skin the taste and scent of Dursibane. The spiders fell away.

Whew! At least they weren't...

Snakes.

Small ones, medium-sized ones, large ones. In the growing light, Robbie spotted them writhing over the floor. He didn't move a muscle. They slithered over his shoes. They wound around his ankles. He spied what looked like a mound of water moccasins move toward him, like a wave out at sea. He wondered if something under the floor bowed the boards. It came toward him. Copperheads rode along with it, oblivious to the movement. Robbie didn't perceive until too late that an anaconda caused the wave. It rose before him, rattlers toppling off its scaly skin. The huge reptile flickered its tongue. It wavered. It circled as Robbie stared. He watched, mesmerized as it curled itself around him. Before Robbie realized it wouldn't strike, he was entrapped. It prepared to squeeze the life out of him. He felt the weight of its body crush his small chest. He felt its muscles constrict with each of his exhalations. He was too young to fathom the irony of each breath bringing him closer to death. Inhaling less and less air, Robbie started to black out.

In his dreamlike state, he imagined a trick Merlin pulled from *The Sword in the Stone*. *If this body wouldn't do, find another. Picture yourself differently.* Robbie imagined himself a porcupine. His quills jabbed into the reptile's skin. The crushing pressure abated. He plopped free.

As the snakes squirmed, the room swirled. Robbie's mind cleared. Visions arrived too fast to solve. Frustration mounted. Robbie felt as if he were so close to that first breath upon breaking the surface only to discover they put more water in the pool.

Now what?

Robbie rested in the hospital. Doctors hovered. They waved giant syringes. Robbie recoiled. He hated needles. Both times doctors had taken his blood, he'd passed out. Each time, he blacked out before the needle found his arm. His fear was so great that he got queasy if he saw a bloodmobile. Needles. He watched the doctors close in. They assured him this wouldn't hurt. Their fingertips sprouted needles. They were going to insert them into his arms, his neck, his stomach, his eyes.

He remembered passing out at the dentist when they showed him a needle of Novocain. Robbie now sat strapped to a dentist's chair.

Noooooo!

The whine of the drill intensified. It bit into his tooth, into an un-numbed nerve. Robbie's mouth filled with the taste of copper. Pain blasted through his jaw. *One step more!* His fingernails dug so hard into the palms of his clenched fists that blood dripped free. He watched the drops fall.

Into water.

Not water! Bad things in water.

Robbie tried to move. He remained strapped tight. His clenched fists still bled. He stood chest-deep, lashed to a pier piling. The incoming tide sloshed water into his face. He timed his gulp for air to prevent swallowing saltwater with each incoming wave. He knew his blood would attract sharks. *If I survive long enough, I'll probably drown first.* Looking up, he discovered a more pressing worry. A giant pincher menaced. It rose and fell as if trying to disorient its intended target. It was as large as Robbie. The crab that wielded it looked prehistoric. It edged partway down the piling. It raised and lowered its pincher again, testing. Its smaller pincer snapped off whole barnacle clusters from the piling. It fed them into its maw. Eyes on thin stalks both inspected Robbie. Robbie watched them transform to red. He heard the giant claw snap shut. Before his bindings fell loose, the smaller pincher clamped around Robbie's torso. The vicelike grip jettisoned the breath out of Robbie so fast he couldn't scream. The large crustacean tried to ram him down its throat. A wave slammed into them. Robbie shook his head to clear the water from his eyes. Somehow, he floated free of the crab. He sucked in a deep breath. He grew light-headed again.

Darkness fell. Sweat trickled down his forehead. He tried to wipe his face and realized he wore a mask. Robbie pulled it down so his eyes could see more clearly through the slit. He squinted as the sun broke over the horizon. The rest of the valley remained shrouded. Robbie was no longer alone. He stood amid a crowd. Not a crowd, an army. He looked over. He observed what he thought was a stone keep. It looked familiar.

Was this ...

* * *

He spotted Legolas and Aragorn upon the battlements above.
Was this Rohan? If so, why are they up there? Why am I down here?
Robbie froze. If he weren't inside Helm's Deep, he milled among the enemy. Any second, they would discover him. They'd tear his limbs from his body. Like the ant in his ant farm. He shifted to the right. The foul smell of orc breath gagged him. *I'm not one of them. How come they can't tell?* He shifted left. That orc grunted. It cowered. It rattled its battleaxe. It repeated the gesture. Robbie heard a whirr. The orc fell. Robbie watched him tumble. Another whirr. He felt a breeze.

Something just flew past my face. They're shooting arrows! At me!

Robbie raised his battleaxe. The sound he uttered could not have come from his throat, but it did. He strode toward the scarred refuge. He screeched amid the tumult. He swung his axe. He sliced through the leafy armor of Elvin knights. He reveled in how good it felt. He stormed through the walls. He brandished his weapon at all comers. Many fled. Most cowered when he raised his arm. It held not an axe but a scepter. Robbie relished their terror. Knights bowed before him. Soldiers cleared a path for him to pass. Damsels fainted. The feeling of power intoxicated him. He didn't understand why.

Why do they fear me so?

Robbie shifted his focus from the whimpering masses to the bejeweled rod he clutched. His jaw dropped. It wasn't the scepter they feared. It was the other object Robbie possessed.

It can't be!

Robbie howled. His anguish shredded through malevolent glee. His revulsion vomited up depraved delight.

He wore the one ring, the ring of power, the one ring to rule them all.

He was Sauron.

He was the embodiment of all evil.

Noooooooo!!!!!

Chapter 63

Maggie Peterson's shoes squeaked on the just-mopped floor. After all the recent excitement, she plumped Robbie's pillow, scrutinizing his face as she did. She wished she had his skin. It looked so fresh and supple. Not a blemish to be found. Its lone imperfection a slight nick just above the left eyebrow. *It'll heal without a scar.* His cheekbones set high and sturdy. She wondered if he dimpled when he smiled. She bet his eyes dazzled the young girls in his class but she only knew they were blue from his chart. The oxygen mask covered his sleek nose. Maggie bent close, not recalling it if buttoned. When Robbie spoke, she jumped.

"Nooooo," he groaned.

It was as if the world paused and all took notice.

"Did he just say, 'no?'" Mallison said. Her voice rose with excitement. She prayed she hadn't just dreamed it.

Not sure if it were a command, Maggie ceased fluffing, still stunned by the word. She nodded at Mallison. She rang for the doctor in slow-motion. Mallison paid no attention to her. She locked Robbie's right hand in hers. She patted it with her other.

"Robbie, it's Mommy. Wake up, Honey," she said. She touched his forehead. It was damp. She felt his chest. His heartbeat felt strong, but a tad rapid. She felt overjoyed. She giggled.

"Keep talking to him," Maggie said. She felt so elated she wanted to laugh out loud. She rang again for the doctor. The door opened.

The blinds banged and rustled when Dr. Tyson bumped into it as he entered. He nearly stumbled.

"You okay?" Maggie asked.

He ignored her.

"What have we got?" he said. He casually braced himself against the sink counter. Feeling slightly nauseous, he bit it back with a hard swallow. He plucked the gum from his mouth. He pushed it into the trash bin. As Maggie offered him a curt summary, he raised his shirt. He ripped two nicotine patches from his skin. He dropped them in the medical waste bin.

"You okay?" Maggie asked again.

Dr. Tyson flipped his hand dismissively at her. With more than a hint of exasperation, he mumbled, "I'm fine."

Maggie didn't think so. But she'd worked long enough as a nurse to know that questioning a doctor's judgment meant stepping into treacherous territory. Although Dr. Tyson already sounded on edge, she stepped anyway. Trying to be discreet, she leaned close so that Mallison couldn't overhear. She whispered, "Are you sure you're okay? You don't look well."

Maggie nodded her head toward the mirror as if to encourage Dr. Tyson to examine himself. He bristled.

"I'm sorry. I didn't realize I asked for a consult," he said.

Maggie felt his sarcasm suck the joy from the room. *Well, thank you, Dr. Sunshine.* When Dr. Tyson didn't speak further, Maggie anticipated he'd play the arrogance card. *Fine by me.* At least she could attend to Robbie without hassle. As she monitored Dr. Tyson rinsing his hands in the sink, she prepared herself to be completely overlooked. His next move knee-capped her.

Feeling anything but fine, Dr. Tyson wanted Maggie out of the room. Not so much to punish her for questioning him but to save face. After stepping all over her concern, he didn't want to give her the satisfaction if he took ill. Taking a deep breath, he convinced himself he was well enough to care for this patient. Fishing for an excuse to dismiss Maggie, he looked over at Mallison.

"Go get some ice," he told Maggie.

"Ice?" Maggie said, feeling he had challenged her.

Dr. Tyson glared.

"For Robbie?" she said.

"You heard me," Dr. Tyson said.

Maggie backed down. She decided not to fight this battle without re-enforcement. She glanced at Robbie, then back at the glowering doctor before brushing past him with a scowl. She hurried to the nurse's station to recruit Gretchen.

With his stomach pained, Dr. Tyson shuffled past Mallison to the far side of the bed. It presented a clearer path to the bathroom. *Just in case.* He retrieved his penlight to examine Robbie. He lifted one of Robbie's eyelids. He flicked his light across the iris to test its responsiveness. It immediately constricted.

"Wake up, Sweetie," Mallison said.

Robbie opened his eyes. He was now awake. His eyes darted fearfully around the room. At the doctor, who backed up and froze. At his mom, who started to smile but stopped. He noticed the closed window curtains jostle as the air conditioning kicked on. He heard the bathroom door creak slightly, heard the blinds on the room door rustle. He glanced at the flickering television as it mutely sold an icy cola.

Parched, Robbie licked his chapped lips. His throat constricted.

"Water," he rasped, arching an eyebrow. He wondered why his mother didn't move. *Not again! Not another stupid dream! Is NONE of this real?* He concluded incorrectly.

Robbie saw the mirror behind his mother fog as if a breath caressed it and vanished. He saw her face drain of color. Her eyes grew wide. Tears welled in them. He sensed what she knew.

It was here too!

Robbie shivered at first, but then his anger rose. *Not Mom. You're not messing with my mother!*

The creature's presence defiled the room.

For Dr. Tyson, standing bedside opposite Mallison, his nausea gurgled as he grieved silently that the love of his life—his turbocharged Porsche—bore three long and ugly scratches down its emerald-glittered body, inflicted by a malicious key.

For Mallison, all joy at Robbie's recovery evaporated. She surrendered to memories of Bobby's death. Her recollection breached unhealed wounds. She ached at them: Robbie's funeral salute, Merl's heart-wrenching news, Bobby's retreating eyes. She found herself trembling by the creek.

For Robbie, life hadn't vanished from the room. Despair hadn't rushed in to fill the void. Amid the terror, despair and woe, a sense of peace, instead, washed over Robbie. He felt mighty. Having beaten back so many fears, Robbie felt he had nothing left of which to be afraid. Had refused to accept the evil his future held. But now it was attacking his mother. He placed his full faith in the three facts that he was positive—certain beyond doubt—had saved him so far, *What's not real can't hurt me. I am only defeated if I give in. I can overcome anything.*

Robbie bet his life on it.

The foul odor that had assaulted his senses before intensified. Robbie nearly gagged. He trained his eyes on the source—the darkness billowing behind his mother. As she started to turn, Robbie spoke.

"Mom," he said softly. She grabbed his right hand. "Look at me."

Mallison's eyes locked on his. He felt pulled into her. Her fear surrounded him. It was paralyzing, but Robbie felt strangely secure. *I'm right here with you, Mom.* He let her lead him into her past. *She thinks I'm gonna die. I'm not gonna die, Mom, I swear. Where are we going? There's Dad! How come we're not stopping? Can't we? Pretty please?* Deeper into the past they raced. *Not there, Mom. Please not there. Don't look, Mom. Keep watching me.*

Suddenly, they stood on a creek bank and peered across the water. *She's showing ME not to look!*

He squeezed her thumb and smiled.

"I love you, Mom," he said. Tears welled in her eyes. "Watch me. Are you watching? Promise?"

She nodded.

"I love you so much, Sweetie," she said.

Robbie shifted his gaze toward Old Coals. When his mind filled with broken bicycles, torn jackets and long-dead pets, he fought through it. *That game won't work anymore, Buster. You got anything different? You just bring it on.*

He stared down the fiend that haunted his dreams. It glided to the edge of the bed, obscuring almost a quarter of the room. It had never appeared so vivid before. This time its eyes were vacant. Robbie watched wrinkles harden into crevices, then crack or burst with pus. What looked like whiskers curled and withered from out of gray skin, which hung in flaps from the cheeks like unsecured tent canvas. Two hollows flared where a nose should have been. An ashen tongue flicked at wiggling roots that teeth once hid. It fanned breath infected with a sweet gangrenous stench as it leaned closer.

Everything seemed to slow as its dark form drifted until it nearly covered the foot of the bed. Even under a heavy blanket, Robbie felt his toes chill. He pulled his legs toward his body, his knees creating a barrier of bedding between him and Old Coals. Robbie could no longer see half the room. He tugged his mom's hand into his lap, cradling it there.

"Whatcha got this time?" Robbie said. He felt his mom's grip tighten, her palm slick with sweat. She jerked when Dr. Tyson's dropped penlight clattered to the floor. They both heard him vomit and curse. Robbie grinned. He glanced to catch her eye.

"It's okay, Mom," he whispered, giving her thumb a reassuring squeeze. "Keep watching me like you promised."

"I'm watching," she said.

With a bold turn of his head, Robbie challenged the creature.

"Bring it on, Bub," Robbie said.

When its milky eyes flared in response, Robbie shrunk. He wished he'd remained silent. He wanted to scamper away, to run and hide. But an arm stretched out abnormally with a pop of bone and snap of tendons. Skin tore. Feeling trapped, Robbie felt so insignificant, so alone. He stared as the grotesque face morphed. It colored. It assumed a shape that tore at Robbie's heart. The face no longer was unrecognizable.

It was his father's.

Robbie knew better. He reminded himself this wasn't real. That it was a cruel trick from his imagination.

Until the creature spoke.

When Robbie heard his dad's voice emanate from what used to be such a foul-looking mouth, his eyes blurred with tears. Only his ears heard what passed from newly-formed lips.

"Son, I'm here because of you."

Robbie gazed deep into eyes that flashed from gray to blue.

"I loved you so much that I let this creature take me ... instead of you."

Robbie swallowed a sob.

"It's your fault that I'm dead."

Robbie inhaled sharply. His tears fell.

"For Thou art with me," Robbie whispered. *This isn't real. Don't give up. I can overcome anything.*

His mother slashed away all that with one word.

"Bobby!" she said.

Robbie's stomach knotted as he gasped.

Oh, no, Mom looked!

The creature leered before Robbie tore his gaze from what he thought was his father's face toward his mother's. *Is this real?* She glanced back, smiling sweetly, tears dribbling down her face.

"Your Daddy's back," his mom blubbered.

"Mom, no!" Robbie blurted. *This is real?* "You weren't supposed to look. You promised."

"I know, Sweetie," she said, patting his hand. "But it's Daddy. He's back."

Mallison leaned in and kissed Robbie's cheek.

"It's all right," she said.

Robbie shook his head. *This is real.* His tongue retreated. He grew dizzy. He felt the room start to spin and clamped his teeth to stop it while his belly churned as if ravenous worms suddenly hatched there and sought freedom. *This is real.* He saw the creature flash a malicious grin before morphing back into his father's face. It mouthed the words "I love you more than life itself." Robbie heard them in his Dad's voice.

"I love you more than life itself," his mom echoed.

She leaned forward and snuggled, her arm wrapping around his still bent knees and her head pressing against his chest. She saw Dr. Tyson grab the bedrail and steady himself as he stood. He wiped his mouth with his sleeve and exhaled deeply.

Wincing at the sickening smell, Robbie shifted slightly to keep his line of sight on the creature. It stared back. In a flash, all the dreams, all the lessons, all the pain, everything zipped through Robbie's mind. *Red triplanes, blue stars, needles, outer space, Dad, winged monkeys, dentist drills, a line from Josey Wales, "If you lose your head, you neither win nor live. That's just the way it is."*

Old Coals curled an elongated gnarled talon toward them.

"Oh, Bobby," Mallison said. She leaned back and lifted her arm from Robbie's knee to meet the embrace.

Robbie reacted swiftly, trying to keep her close, keep her safe.

Using his clenched left hand, he pushed himself up and toward his mother. The pennies that were jammed into his fist dug painfully into his flesh. Frightened, Robbie released them and quickly threw his arm around his mother in a protective hug.

"I love you, Mom!" Robbie said.

Reflexively, Dr. Tyson snagged the cluster of coins that tumbled free. He glanced at Robbie hugging his mother. He looked back down at the coins in his palm. *Why three pennies?* He shrugged.

Must be good luck.

He was wrong.

His own hand now rested in a gaunt upturned palm, the skin ashy, the fingers skeletal, the nails jagged, cracked and torn. What invaded his mind made Dr. Tyson's jaw drop. His eyes widened. His breath came in gulps. He watched the hand close around his. He felt no touch but followed it as if tugged. He turned. As a savage grin jagged across the most hideous face he had ever seen, Dr. Tyson's eyes merged with Old Coals'.

Dr. Tyson trembled. He tried to scream. No sound issued forth. The anguish of all his dead patients—like lit faces in a mirror—flooded his mind; their pain tearing into his soul like a dull saw; the grief of their families ate into his conscience like spilled acid. He swallowed bile. His blood raced like a rollercoaster never reaching the bottom. The nicotine coursing through his system accelerated his heart into overdrive. He felt his left arm throb. He saw the cadaver he made such fun of in med school rise off that university table. It howled in delight and reared back its dissected arm and punched him in the sternum.

Dr. Tyson's chest exploded in pain like it had been crunched with a Louisville Slugger. He wanted to wail for release, but had no air.

His mind broken, he couldn't sever his gaze from dead gray eyes so cold they burned.

They wanted him.

Invited him.

Sliced into him.

Dr. Tyson's heart quit.

Chapter 64

Out at the nurses' station, Maggie Peterson started her pitch.
"Does Dr. Tyson look good to you?" she asked.
"Jonesing for a doctor tonight?" Gretchen said with a laugh.
Maggie frowned.
"Get real," she said. "That's not what I meant. Does he look sick?"
"Wasn't paying him any attention. Why?"
"Something's wrong with him. He jumped down my throat when I asked if he were okay."
Maggie reached under the counter for a plastic pitcher.
"Oh! I think Robbie's waking up." Maggie couldn't believe she hadn't blurted that out immediately.
"You're kidding," Gretchen said.
"Maybe you could go in there and check on Robbie and, you know, see if I'm wrong about Dr. Tyson. Make sure I'm not—"
A loud crash halted her request. She and Gretchen turned toward the sound. They looked at each other.
"Tyson?" they said in unison.
They rushed to Robbie's room.

Chapter 65

Once again, Merl Burt arrived too late. Returning from the downstairs cafeteria, he found the floor alive with activity outside Robbie's room. His eyes raced to the stretcher with the draped white sheet. He cursed himself for abandoning his post. Just as quickly, he realized the body was much too big to be the 11-year-old's. Pulling back the sheet, he immediately recognized the tortured expression on Dr. Benton Tyson's face. He'd seen it earlier in the day. Even stranger were the hands. Each empty upturned palm displayed fingers rigidly splayed.

When Merl inquired, Maggie Peterson filled in the details. Dr. Tyson apparently died of cardiac arrest. They couldn't revive him. They suspected his heart couldn't take all the caffeine and nicotine he may have ingested during the day. Most of the slots in his nicotine gum container were empty. Almost half of his nicotine patches for the week were missing. No telling how many cups of coffee and cans of Coke he had consumed all day. An autopsy should confirm it.

More wired than Howdy-Doody, Merl thought.

Taking a moment to locate their new room, Merl peeked in on Mallison and Robbie. Both appeared in the midst of restful naps. So serene. He quietly pulled the door closed. He halted.

Robbie's hand.

He re-entered the room. He examined Robbie's palms. Empty. He scanned the bed and floor for the three pennies. He found none.

He retreated to Robbie's previous room. The coins weren't there either. Merl thought better than to ask Maggie if she had found three pennies in either room. That was not a question he wanted following him the rest of his days.

Merl ambled down the hall to the elevator. He poked the button for the lobby. He never thought Dr. Tyson would be the third. Had no expectations that the doctor would enter the equation. *Did he get caught in the crossfire or did he intervene for Robbie? Did he just have a heart attack?* Merl sensed nicotine didn't kill the doctor. One look confirmed that. When the elevator doors opened, Jack Thompson almost walked straight into Merl. They shared a momentary knowing look.

"Damnedest thing," Merl said. "Tyson dropped dead. Heart attack. Right there in Robbie's room. Apparently, dead before he hit the floor."

"You delivered ... the pennies. ... Right?" Jack said.

"Yep."

"Robbie?"

"Asleep. You don't think we need to keep an eye on him, do you?"

Jack shook his head. They stood in silence for a few moments.

"What was the deal with those pennies, anyway," Merl said.

"Payment ... rendered," Jack said.

"What?"

"Payment rendered."

Merl shook his head. Jack moved toward the window. Merl followed.

"Did Robbie ... still have those ... three ... pennies?" Jack asked.

"No. I couldn't find them."

Merl recalled the doctor's rigid fingers.

"Tyson didn't have them either," he added.

Jack maintained a blank expression.

"More than ... enough cents ... for Robbie," Jack said. "But not ... the doc, apparently."

"So this was about three pennies?" Merl asked.

Jack shrugged. He knew that wasn't an answer.

"I just knew they were important," he finally said.

Merl closed his eyes. *Common cents.* He took a deep breath. He didn't want to solve any more riddles. Not now. Right now, he wanted to relax his mind. Give it a steaming hot bath. Hand it an ice cold beer. When he opened his eyes, he turned. For the first time all day, he took in his friend's entire face. Not just his eyes. Not just his smile. His whole, stubbled face.

"What's with the whiskers, Wolfman," Merl said.

"Thinking about … growing a beard," Jack said, stroking his chin. "Whattya … think?"

"As the local law enforcement, I'd like to advise you of your rights to remain shaven."

Jack's laugh accompanied a quick obscene gesture. Merl ignored it. He stared out the window into the night. Jack joined him. Together, they watched the lights twinkling in the town of Soke.

Merl raised an eyebrow. "So it's done?"

Jack nodded.

"This time," he said.

Chapter 66

The hug felt so real, Robbie wanted it to last forever.
"I'm so proud of you," his dad said.
Robbie scrunched his face to restrain his tears. He knew that the first one to fall dragged out all the others. He was losing this battle. When the massing flood broke, Robbie buried his head in the softness of his dad's flannel shirt. He sobbed. His dad hugged tighter while Robbie's body shook.
"You were amazing," his dad said. *"I knew you could do it. You are the bravest son a father could hope to have. But you've got one more task."*
Robbie looked up at his father. Bobby brushed hair back from his son's forehead. He smiled sadly.
"It's time to leave," his dad said, the voice, soft but commanding. *"You can't stay here anymore."*
"Why not," Robbie said, an exhalation and sniffle cutting short further query.
"You've got to go home."
"I am home."
"No. This isn't where you belong now."
"I want to be with you!" Robbie wailed. He couldn't understand why his dad didn't love him anymore. Why his dad didn't want him anymore. He'd promise to be good forever. To behave. He'd promise anything. *Please don't make me go.*

Robbie felt his dad gently ease him back. Robbie didn't look up, his mind all a jumble. He stared at the wet spot his tears produced on his dad's shirt. *Like an oil stain in the garage.* Robbie wiped his nose on his own sleeve. He thought of all the things he could promise: to keep his room clean, to make up his bed, brush his teeth before bed, keep his new clothes clean. Anything. He peered into familiar eyes he'd never seen so blue before.

"I want to be with you so much it hurts," his dad said. *"But I love you too much to keep you here. It's not right. Not now. Not for a long time. You have to go. Mommy needs you more than you know. You've got to be her man of the house for me. Can you do that? For me?"*

Robbie didn't want to. He wanted nothing more than for things to stay just as they were.

"I promise I'll be here when you get back," his dad said.

"Promise?" Robbie bit his lower lip.

"Bank on it, Bub!"

A surge of pride coursed through Robbie. He felt almost heroic. He always felt like this when he knew he pleased his dad. He would do it.

"This is the hardest thing we'll ever do," his dad said. *"Go back to your mother. Show me you can do it. She's calling you. She needs you so much. Go. And remember how much I love you."*

"I love you too, Dad." Robbie didn't fight the tears this time. He let them race across his cheeks. They tickled his ears. He thought he saw Dad wave.

"Dad!" Robbie cried. "Dad!"

Then he was gone.

Mom's voice answered.

"Robbie!" She sounded so near. She'd be able to stop Dad.

Where was she? She seemed so close he swore he could smell her. He didn't want to open his eyes, afraid if he did, he'd never see Dad again. He wanted to see him again. He heard strange beeping. And whooshing. *What sounded like an engine whining?* Something touched his chest. Something tugged at his head. His face suddenly felt cooler.

"Robbie!" Her voice was soft. "Robbie, wake up, Honey. It's Mommy."

Breakfast filled Robbie's mind. He opened his eyes. Mom, though blurry, stood over him. She wore the most beautiful smile. Her hair unkempt, her eyes bloodshot, Robbie thought she never looked more beautiful. She laughed. Then, she burst into tears. He touched her, testing if she were real. He felt her wet cheek on his as she nuzzled her baby. *Maybe she doesn't know I lost my jacket.* Robbie flexed his sore left hand. It was empty. He wanted to ask for a drink since his throat was dry. Mom smothered him with kisses. When he realized there were other people in the room, he flushed with embarrassment.

"Mommmm!" Robbie stretched out the word with annoyance. His mom would have none of it.

"My baby's back," she said. "Don't you ever leave me again!" Her hug muffled his reply.

She leaned back. "What is it, Baby?"

"May I have a Pop-Tart?"